**Praise for #1 *New York Times*
and #1 *USA TODAY* bestselling author**

ROBYN
CARR

"As usual, Carr delves into the lives of others in town,
laying the groundwork for future books.
This cozy read satisfies."
—*Publishers Weekly* on *The Chance*

"Carr focuses her superior storytelling on one couple
for a can't-put-down read."
—*RT Book Reviews* on *The Chance*

"A touch of danger and suspense make the latest
in Carr's Thunder Point series a powerful read."
—*RT Book Reviews* on *The Hero*

"With her trademark mixture of humor, realistic
conflict, and razor-sharp insights, Carr brings
Thunder Point to vivid life."
—*Library Journal* on *The Newcomer*

"No one can do small-town life like Carr."
—*RT Book Reviews* on *The Wanderer*

"Carr has hit her stride with this captivating series."
—*Library Journal* on the Virgin River series

Look for Robyn Carr's next book
THE WISH
available soon from Harlequin MIRA

#1 *NEW YORK TIMES* BESTSELLING AUTHOR

ROBYN CARR

'TIS THE SEASON

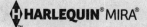

ISBN-13: 978-0-7783-1664-0

'Tis the Season
Copyright © 2014 by Harlequin S.A.

The publisher acknowledges the copyright holder of the individual works as follows:

Under the Christmas Tree
Copyright © 2009 by Robyn Carr

Midnight Confessions
Copyright © 2010 by Robyn Carr

Backward Glance
Copyright © 1991 by Robyn Carr

Recycling programs
for this product may
not exist in your area.

Printed in U.S.A.

CONTENTS

UNDER THE
CHRISTMAS TREE

One

During the Christmas holidays a side trip through Virgin River was a must; the town had recently begun erecting a thirty-foot tree in the center of town, decorated in red, white, blue and gold and topped with a great big powerful star. It dominated the little town, and people came from miles around to see it. The patriotic theme of the decorations set it apart from all other trees. Local bar owner Jack Sheridan joked that he expected to see the three wise men any minute, that star was so bright.

Annie McKenzie didn't pass through Virgin River very often. It was out of her way when driving from Fortuna, where she lived, to her parents' farm near Alder Point. It was a cute little town and she liked it there, especially the bar and grill owned by Jack Sheridan. People there met you once, maybe twice, and from that point on, treated you like an old friend.

She was on her way to her folks' place when, at the last moment, she decided to detour through Virgin River. Since it was the week after Thanksgiving, she hoped they'd started on the tree. It was a calm and sunny Monday afternoon and very cold, but her heart warmed when she pulled into town and saw that the tree was up and decorated. Jack was up on an A-frame ladder straightening out some trimmings, and standing at the foot of the ladder, looking up, was Christopher, the six-year-old son of Jack's cook, Preacher.

Annie got out of her truck and walked over. "Hey, Jack," she yelled up. "Looking good!"

"Annie! Haven't seen you in a while. How are your folks?"

"They're great. And your family?"

"Good." He looked around. "Uh-oh. David?" he called. Then he looked at Christopher as he climbed down the ladder. "Chris, you were going to help keep an eye on him. Where did he go? David?" he called again.

Then Chris called, "David! David!"

They both walked around the tree, checked the bar porch and the backyard, calling his name. Annie stood there, not sure whether to help or just stay out of their way, when the lowest boughs of the great tree moved and a little tyke about three years old crawled out.

"David?" Annie asked. He was holding something furry in his mittened hands and she got down on her knees. "Whatcha got there, buddy?" she asked. And then she yelled, "Found him, Jack!"

The child was holding a baby animal of some kind, and it looked awfully young and listless. Its fur was black-and-white, its eyes were closed, and it hung limply in little David's hands. She just hoped the boy hadn't squeezed the life out of it; boys were not known for gentleness. "Let me have a look, honey," she said, taking the creature out of his hands. She held it up and its little head lolled. Unmistakably a puppy. A brand-new puppy.

Jack came running around the tree. "Where was he?"

"Under the tree. And he came out with this," she said, showing him the animal very briefly before stuffing it under her sweater between her T-shirt and her wool sweater, up against the warmth of her body. Then she pulled her down vest around herself to hold him in place. "Poor little thing might be frozen, or almost frozen."

"Aw, David, where'd you find him?"

David just pointed at Annie. "*My* boppie!" he said.

"Yeah, he's right," Annie said. "It's a boppie…er, puppy. But it's not very old. Not old enough to have gotten out of a house or a yard. This little guy should've been in a box with his mom."

"David, hold Chris's hand," Jack ordered.

And David said something in his language that could be translated into *I want my puppy!* But Jack was on his belly on the cold ground, crawling under the tree. And from under there Annie heard a muffled "Aw, crap!" And then he backed out, pulling a box full of black-and-white puppies.

Annie and Jack just stared at each other for a moment. Then Annie said, "Better get 'em inside by the fire. Puppies this young can die in the cold real fast. This could turn out badly."

Jack hefted the box. "Yeah, it's gonna turn out badly! I'm gonna find out who would do something so awful and take him apart!" Then he turned to the boys and said, "Let's go, guys." He carried the box to the bar porch and Annie rushed past him to hold the door open. "I mean, there are animal shelters, for God's sake!"

The fire was ablaze in the hearth and there were a couple of guys dressed like hunters at the bar, shar-

ing a pitcher of beer and playing cribbage. She patted the place by the hearth and Jack put down the box.
Annie immediately began checking out the puppies.
"I'm gonna need a little help here, Jack. Can you warm
up some towels in the clothes dryer? I could use a couple more warm hands. There's not enough wriggling
around in this box to give me peace of mind." Then
suddenly, she herself began wriggling. She smiled a
big smile. "Mine's coming around," she said, patting
the lump under her sweater.

Annie knelt before the box, and David and Chris
squeezed in right beside her. She took the wriggling
puppy out from under her sweater, put him in the box
and picked up another one. At least there was a blanket under them and they had their shared warmth, she
thought. She put another one under her sweater.

"Whatcha got there?" someone asked.

She looked over her shoulder. The hunters from the
bar had wandered over to the hearth, peering into the
box. "Someone left a box of newborn puppies under the
Christmas tree. They're half-frozen." She picked up two
more, made sure they were moving and handed them
over. "Here, put these two inside your shirt, warm 'em
up, see if they come around." She picked up two more,
checked them and handed them to the other man. The
men did exactly as she told them, and she stuffed one
more under her sweater.

Then she picked up a puppy that went limp in her
palm. "Uh-oh," she muttered. She jostled him a little,
but he didn't move. She covered his tiny mouth and nose
with her mouth and pushed a gentle breath into him. She
massaged his little chest gently. Rubbed his extremities,

breathed into him again and he curled up in her palm. "Better," she murmured, stuffing him under her shirt.

"Did you just resuscitate that puppy?" one of the hunters asked.

"Maybe," she said. "I did that to an orphaned kitten once and it worked, so what the heck, huh? Man, there are eight of these little guys," she said. "Big litter. At least they have fur, but they are so *young.* Couple of weeks, I bet. And puppies are so vulnerable to the cold. They have to be kept warm."

"Boppie!" David cried, trying to get his little hands into the box.

"Yup, you found a box full of boppies, David," Annie said. She picked up the last puppy—the first one she'd warmed—and held it up to the hunters. "Can anyone fit one more in a warm place?"

One of the men took the puppy and put it under his arm. "You a vet or something?"

She laughed. "I'm a farm girl. I grew up not too far from here. Every once in a while we'd have a litter or a foal or a calf the mother couldn't or wouldn't take care of. Rare, but it happens. Usually you better not get between a mother and her babies, but sometimes… Well, the first thing is body temperature, and at least these guys have some good fur. The next thing is food." She stuck her hand into the box and felt the blanket they'd been snuggled on. "Hmm, it's dry. No urine or scat— which is not so good. Besides being really cold, they're probably starving by now. Maybe getting dehydrated. Puppies nurse a lot and they were obviously taken from the mother's whelp box."

Jack reappeared, Preacher close on his heels. Preacher was tall enough that he was looking over

Jack's shoulder into the empty box. "What's up?" Preacher asked.

"Dad! David found a box full of puppies under the tree! They're freezing cold! They could be *dying!*" Christopher informed him desperately.

"We're warming 'em up," Annie said, indicating her and the hunters' lumpy shirts. "About half of them are wriggling and we'll know about the other half in a little bit. Meanwhile, we need to get some fluids and nourishment into them. They shouldn't be off the tit this young. Infant formula and cereal would be ideal, but we can make due with some warm milk and watered-down oatmeal."

"Formula?" Jack asked. "I bet I can manage that. You remember my wife, Mel. She's the midwife. She'll have some infant formula on hand."

"That's perfect. And if she has a little rice cereal or baby oatmeal, better still."

"Do we need bottles?" he asked.

"Nah," Annie said. "A couple of shallow bowls will work. They're young, but I bet they're awful hungry. They'll catch on real quick."

"Whoa," one of the hunters said. "Got me a wiggler!"

"Me, too!" the other one said.

"Keep 'em next to your body for a while," Annie ordered. "At least until we get those warm towels in the box."

Because of a box full of cold, hungry, barely moving puppies, Annie had all but forgotten the reason she'd ended up in Virgin River. It was three weeks till Christmas and her three older brothers, their wives and their kids would descend on her parents' farm for the holiday. Today was one of her two days off a week from the beauty shop. Yesterday, Sunday, she'd baked with her mom all day and today she'd gotten up early to make a couple of big casseroles her mom could freeze for the holiday company. Today, she'd planned to cook with her mom, maybe take one of her two horses out for a ride and say hello to Erasmus, her blue-ribbon bull. Erasmus was very old now and every hello could be the last. Then she'd planned to stay for dinner with her folks, something she did at least once a week. Being the youngest and only unmarried one of the McKenzie kids and also the only one who lived nearby, the task of looking in on Mom and Dad fell to her.

But here she was, hearthside, managing a box of newborn puppies. Jack rustled up the formula and cereal and a couple of warm towels from the dryer. Preacher provided the shallow bowls and mixed up the formula. She and Chris fed a couple of puppies at a time, coaxing them to lap up the food. She requisitioned an eyedropper from the medical clinic across the street for the pups who didn't catch on to lapping up dinner.

Jack put in a call to a fellow he knew who was a veterinarian, and it turned out Annie knew him, too. Old Doc Jensen had put in regular appearances out at the farm since before she was born. Back in her dad's younger days, he'd kept a thriving but small dairy farm. Lots of cows, a few horses, dogs and cats, goats and one ornery old bull. Jensen was a large-animal vet, but he'd be able to at least check out these puppies.

Annie asked Jack to also give her mom a call and explain what was holding her up. Her mom would laugh, knowing her daughter so well. Nothing would pry Annie away from a box of needy newborn puppies.

As the dinner hour approached, she couldn't help but notice that the puppies were drawing a crowd. People stopped by where she sat at the hearth, asked for the story, reached into the box to ruffle the soft fur or even pick up a puppy. Annie wasn't sure so much handling was a good idea, but as long as she could keep the little kids, particularly David, from mishandling them, she felt she'd at least won the battle if not the war.

"This bar has needed mascots for a long time," someone said.

"Eight of 'em. Donner, Prancer, Comet, Vixen, and… whoever."

"Which one is Comet?" Chris asked. "Dad? Can I have Comet?"

"No. We operate an eating-and-drinking establishment," Preacher said.

"Awww, Dad! Dad, come on. *Please,* Dad. I'll do *everything.* I'll sleep with him. I'll make sure he's nice. *Please.*"

"Christopher…"

"*Please.* Please? I never asked for anything before."

"You ask for everything, as a matter of fact," Preacher corrected him. "And get most of it."

"Boy shouldn't grow up without a dog," someone said.

"Teaches responsibility and discipline," was another comment.

"It's not like he'd be in the kitchen all the time."

"I run a ranch. Little hair in the potatoes never put me off." Laughter sounded all around.

Four of the eight pups were doing real well; they were wriggling around with renewed strength and had lapped up some of the formula thickened with cereal. Two were trying to recover from what was certainly hunger and hypothermia; Annie managed to get a little food into them with an eyedropper. Two others were breathing, their hearts beating, but not only were they small, they were weak and listless. She dripped a little food into their tiny mouths and then tucked them under her shirt to keep them warm, hoping they might mistake her for their mother for now, all the time wondering if old Doc Jensen would ever show.

When yet another gust of wind blew in the opened front door, Annie momentarily forgot all about the puppies. Some of the best male eye candy she'd chanced upon in a long while had just walked into Jack's Bar. He looked vaguely familiar, too. She wondered if maybe she'd seen him in a movie or on TV or something. He walked right up to the bar, and Jack greeted him enthusiastically.

"Hey, Nate! How's it going? You get those plane tickets yet?"

"I took care of that a long time ago." He laughed. "I've been looking forward to this forever. Before too long I'm going to be lying on a Nassau beach in the middle of a hundred string bikinis. I dream about it."

"One of those Club Med things?" Jack asked.

"Nah." He laughed again. "A few people from school. I haven't seen most of them in years. We hardly keep in touch, but one of them put this holiday together and, since I was available, it sounded like an excellent idea. The guy who made the arrangements got one of those all-inclusive hotel deals—food, drinks, everything included except activities like deep-sea fishing or scuba diving—for when I'm not just lying on the sand, looking around at beautiful women in tiny bathing suits."

"Good for you," Jack said. "Beer?"

"Don't mind if I do," Nate replied. And then, like the answer to a prayer she didn't even know she'd uttered, he carried his beer right over to where she sat with the box of puppies. "Hello," he said.

She swallowed, looking up. It was hard to tell how tall he was from her sitting position, but certainly over six feet. Annie noticed things like that because she was tall. His hair was dark brown; his eyes were an even darker brown and surrounded with loads of thick black lashes. Her mother called eyes like that "bedroom eyes." He lifted his brows as he looked down at her. Then he smiled and revealed a dimple in one cheek.

"I said hello," he repeated.

She coughed herself out of her stupor. "Hi."

He frowned slightly. "Hey, I think you cut my hair once."

"Possible. That's what I do for a living."

"Yeah, you did," he said. "I remember now."

"What was the problem with the haircut?" she asked.

He shook his head. "Don't know that there was a problem," he replied.

"Then why didn't you come back?"

He chuckled. "Okay, we argued about the stuff you wanted to put in it. I didn't want it, you told me I did. You won and I went out of there looking all spiky. When I touched my head, it was like I had meringue in my hair."

"Product," she explained. "We call it product. It's in style."

"Yeah? I'm not, I guess," he said, sitting down on the raised hearth on the other side of the box. He reached in and picked up a puppy. "I don't like *product* in my hair."

"Your hands clean?" she asked him.

He gave her a startled look. Then his eyes slowly wandered from her face to her chest and he smiled slightly. "Um, I think you're moving," he said. "Or maybe you're just very excited to meet me." And then he grinned playfully.

"Oh, you're funny," Annie replied, reaching under her sweater to pull out a tiny squirming animal. "You make up that line all by your little self?"

He tilted his head and took the puppy out of her hands. "I'd say at least part border collie. Looks like mostly border collie, but they can take on other characteristics as they get older. Cute," he observed. "Plenty of pastoral breeds around here."

"Those two are the weakest of the bunch, so please be careful. I'm waiting for the vet."

He balanced two little puppies in one big hand and pulled a pair of glasses out of the pocket of his suede jacket. "I'm the vet." He slipped on his glasses and, holding both pups upside down, looked at their eyes, mouth, ears and pushed on their bellies with a finger.

She was speechless for a minute. "You're not old Doc Jensen."

"Nathaniel Junior," he said. "Nate. You know my father?" he asked, still concentrating on the puppies. He put them in the box and picked up two more, repeating the process.

"He…ah… My folks have a farm down by Alder Point. Hey! I grew up there! Not all that far from Doc's clinic and stable. Shouldn't I know you?"

He looked over the tops of his glasses. "I don't know. How old are you?"

"Twenty-eight."

"Well, there you go. I'm thirty-two. Got a few years on you. Where'd you go to school?"

"Fortuna. You?"

"Valley." He laughed. "I guess you can call me old Doc Jensen now." And there was that grin again. No way he could have grown up within fifty miles of her farm without her knowing him. He was too delicious-looking.

"I have older brothers," she said. "Beau, Brad and Jim McKenzie. All older than you."

At first he was startled at this news, then he broke into a wide smile. Then he laughed. "Are you that skinny, fuzzy-haired, freckle-faced, tin-mouthed pain in the neck who always followed Beau and Brad around?"

Her eyes narrowed and she glared at him.

"No," he said, laughing. "That must have been some-one else. Your hair isn't pumpkin orange. And you're not all that…" He paused for a second, then said, "Got your braces off, I see." By her frown, he realized he hadn't scored with that comment.

"Where is your father? I want a second opinion!"

"Okay, you're not so skinny anymore, either." He smiled, proud of himself.

"Very, very old joke, sparky," she said.

"Well, you're out of luck, *cupcake*. My mom and dad finally realized a dream come true and moved to Arizona where they could have horses and be warm and pay lower taxes. One of my older sisters lives there with her family. I've got another sister in Southern California and another one in Nevada. I'm the new old Doc Jensen."

Now it was coming back to her—Doc Jensen had kids, all older than she was. Too much older for her to have known them in school. But she did vaguely remember the son who came with him to the farm on rare occasions. One corner of her mouth quirked up in a half grin. "Are you that little, pimply, tin-mouthed runt with the squeaky voice who came out to the farm with your dad sometimes?"

He frowned and made a sound. "I was a late bloomer," he said.

"I'll say." She laughed.

Nate was now checking out his third set of puppies.

"Why don't I remember you better?" she mused aloud.

"I went to Catholic school down in Oakland my junior and senior year. I wasn't going to get into a good college without some serious academic help, and those Jesuits live to get their hands on a challenge like me. They turned me around. And I grew five inches my first year of college." He put down the puppies he'd been holding and picked up the first one. He became serious. She noticed a definite kindness, a softness, in his expression. "Annie, isn't it? Or do you go by Anne now?"

"Annie. McKenzie."

"Well, Annie, this little guy is real weak. I don't know if he'll make it."

A very sad look came into her eyes as she took the puppy from him and tucked him under her sweater again.

Nodding at her, Nate said, "As much incentive as that is to live, I don't know if it'll do. How long were these guys outside before someone found them?"

"No one knows. Probably since before sunrise. Jack was in and out all day, fussing with the tree, and he never saw anyone. His little boy crawled under the tree and came out holding a puppy. That's how we found them."

"And what's the plan now?"

"I don't know," she said, shaking her head.

"Want me to drop them off at a shelter for you? Then you don't have to witness the bad news if one or two don't make it."

"No!" she exclaimed. "I mean, that's probably a bad idea. Some of the shelters over on the Coast are excellent, but you know what it's like this time of year. All those people adopting cute puppies for Christmas presents and then returning them in January. And returning them is the *good* scenario. All too often they're neglected or abused. Wouldn't it be better to take care of them until reliable homes can be found?"

"Who, Annie?" he asked. "Who's going to take care of them?"

She shrugged. "I have a small house in Fortuna and I work all day."

"What about the farm?" he asked.

She was shaking her head before he finished. "I don't think so. My dad's arthritis is bad enough that he slowly sold off the stock and my mom runs around like a crazy woman taking care of all the things that wear him out."

"Your dad's Hank McKenzie, right? He gets around pretty good for someone with bad arthritis."

"Yeah, he's proud. He doesn't let on. But it would fall to my mom and I can't ask her to take on eight puppies. And the whole family is coming home to the farm for Christmas. All thirteen of 'em."

"Well, Annie, I can't think of many options here," he said. "I know a few vets in the towns around here and I don't know one that would take this on. They'd put 'em in a no-kill shelter."

"Can't you help? You and your wife?"

He smiled at her. "No wife, Annie McKenzie. I have a real nice vet tech who's going to keep an eye on the stable while I'm out of town over Christmas, but that's the only help I have out there, and she doesn't have time to add eight puppies to her roster."

"Jack!" Annie called. She stood up. "Can you come here?"

Jack ambled over, wiping his hands on a towel.

"We have a situation, Jack," Annie said. "Dr. Jensen can't take the puppies and get them through this rough patch. He offered to drop them off at a shelter, but really, that's not a great idea." A couple of people had wandered over to listen in to the conversation, eavesdropping and making no bones about it. "I've volunteered at some of those shelters and they're awesome, but they're really, really busy at Christmastime. A lot of animals get adopted for presents, especially the really young, cute ones like these. You have no idea how many people think they want a fluffy pet for little Susie or Billie—until the first time the dog thinks the carpet is grass."

"Yeah?" Jack said, confused. A couple more people had wandered over from the bar to listen in to the conference.

Annie took a breath. "It's bad enough animals get returned. The worst case is they're not taken care of properly, get neglected or abused or get sick and aren't taken to the vet because the vet costs money. Sometimes people are embarrassed to return them and admit it was a mistake. Then they just take them to animal control,

where they're on death row for three days before…"
She stopped. "It can be a bad situation."

"Well, what are you gonna do?" Jack said. "Better
odds than freezing to death under a Christmas tree."

"We could take care of them here, Jack," she said.

"We?" he mimicked, lifting a brow. "I see you about
four times a year, Annie."

"I'll drive up after work every day. They're kind of
labor-intensive right now, but I'll tell you exactly what
to do and you can get—"

"Whoa, Annie, whoa. I can't keep dogs in the bar!"

An old woman put a hand on Jack's arm. "We already
named 'em, Jack," she said. "After Santa's reindeer. At
least the ones we could remember. Little Christopher
already asked Preacher if he could have Comet. 'Course
no one knows who Comet is yet, but—"

"There's no mother to clean up after them," Nate
pointed out. "That means puppy excrement. Times
eight."

"Aw, that's just great," Jack said.

"Don't panic," Annie said. "Here's what you do. Get
a nice, big wooden box or big plastic laundry basket.
You could even put a wooden border around a plastic
pad from an old playpen, then toss an old blanket or a
couple of towels over it. Pull the blanket back to feed
'em the formula and cereal every few hours. Or feed
a couple or three at a time outside the box so you can
wipe up the floor. Trade the dirty towels for clean ones,
wash one set while you use the other, and vice versa.
Oh, and at least two of these little guys need a lot of encouragement to eat—the eyedropper gets 'em going. I
could take the littlest, weakest ones to a vet but, Jack,
they're better off with their litter mates."

"Aw, f'chrissake, Annie," Jack moaned.

"You can just grab someone at the bar and ask them to take a couple of minutes to coax some food into a sick puppy," she said hopefully.

"Sure," the old woman said as she pushed her glasses up on her nose. "I'll commit to a puppy or two a day."

"Annie, I can't wash towels with puppy shit on 'em in the same washer we use for napkins for the bar."

"Well, we did at the farm. My mom sterilized a lot," she said. "Bet you washed shitty baby clothes in the same... Never mind. If you just get the towels, bag 'em up in a big plastic bag, I'll do it. I'll come out after work and spell you a little, take home your dirty laundry, bring back fresh every day."

"I don't know, Annie," he said, shaking his head.

"Are you kidding?" Annie returned. "People will love it, keeping an eye on 'em, watching 'em plump up. By Christmas, all of them will be spoken for, and by people who know what to do with animals. These little guys will probably turn into some outstanding herders around here."

"Nathaniel, did you put her up to this?" Jack asked.

Nate put up his hands and shook his head. He didn't say so, but she did have a point. Adopted by a town, these puppies would get looked after.

"I can't say yes or no without Preacher," Jack said, going off to the kitchen.

Annie smiled crookedly as she listened to the people who had followed Jack to the hearth, muttering to each other that, sure, this plan could work. They wouldn't mind holding a puppy every now and then, maybe donating a blanket, getting a puppy to eat, wiping up the floor here and there.

When Preacher trailed Jack back to the box of puppies, his six-year-old son was close on his heels. Jack tried to speak very softly about what all this would entail, but Christopher didn't miss a syllable. He tugged at Preacher's sleeve and in a very small voice he said, "Please, Dad, please. I'll help every day. I'll feed and hold and clean up and I won't miss anything."

Preacher pulled his heavy black brows together in a fierce scowl. Then, letting out an exasperated sigh, he crouched to get to eye level with the boy. "Chris, there can never be a dog in the kitchen. You hear me, son? And we have to start looking for homes right away, because some may be ready to leave the litter sooner than others. This has to be real temporary. We prepare food here."

"Okay," Chris said. "Except Comet. Comet's going to stay."

"I'm still thinking about that. And I'll have to look up on the computer how you take care of a bunch of orphaned pups like these guys," Preacher added.

Annie let a small laugh escape as she plucked the smallest, weakest puppy from under her sweater and put him back in the box. "Well, my work here is done," she said with humor in her voice. "I'll try to cut my day as short as I can at the shop, Jack. I'll see you tomorrow."

"Annie, they're not your responsibility," Jack said. "You've already been a huge help. I don't really expect you to—"

"I'm not going to turn my back on them now," she said. "You might panic and take them to the pound." She grinned. "I'll see you tomorrow."

Two

The puppies were found on Monday and Nate managed to stay away from the bar on Tuesday, but by Wednesday he was back there right about dinnertime. He told himself he had a vested interest—they might be about a hundredth the size of his usual patients, but he had more or less treated them. At least he'd looked at them and judged the care Annie recommended to be acceptable. In which case he didn't really need to check on them. But Jack's was a decent place to get a beer at the end of the day, and that fire was nice and cozy after a long day of tromping around farms and ranches, rendering treatment for horses, cows, goats, sheep, bulls and whatever other livestock was ailing.

But then there was Annie.

She was no longer a skinny, flat-chested, fuzzy-haired metal-mouth. Something he'd been reminding himself of for more than twenty-four hours. The jury was still out on whether she was a pain in the butt. He suspected she was.

She was tall for a woman—at least five-ten in her stocking feet—with very long legs. That carrot top was no longer bright orange—maybe the miracle of Miss Clairol had done the trick. In any case, her hair was a dark auburn she wore in a simple but elegant cut that framed her face. It was sleek and silky and swayed when her head moved. Her eyes were almost exotic— dark brown irises framed by black lashes and slanting shapely brows. And there was a smattering of youthful freckles sprinkled over her nose and cheeks, just enough to make her cute. But that mouth, that full, pink, soft mouth—that was gonna kill him. He hadn't seen a mouth like that on a woman in a long time. It was spectacular.

She was a little bossy, but he liked that in a woman. He wondered if he should seek therapy for that. But no—he thrived on the challenge of it. Growing up with three older sisters, he'd been fighting for his life against determined females his entire life. Meek and docile women had never appealed to him and he blamed Patricia, Susan and Christina for that.

The very first thing Nate noticed when he walked into the bar on Wednesday was that Annie was not there. He smiled with superiority. Hah! He should have known. She talked Jack and Preacher into keeping eight tiny puppies—a labor-intensive job—promising to help, and was a no-show. He went over to the box and counted them. Seven. Then he went up to the bar.

"Hey, Jack," he said. "Lose one?"

"Huh?" Jack said, giving the counter a wipe. "Oh, no." He laughed and shook his head. "Annie took one back to Preacher's laundry room for a little fluff and buff. He mussed his diaper, if you get my drift. It's the littlest, weakest one."

"Oh," Nate responded, almost embarrassed by his assumption. "He hanging in there?"

"Oh, yeah. And wouldn't you know—Christopher has decided that that one is *his*. Comet. Annie tried to talk him into falling in love with a stronger, heartier pup, but the boy's drawn to the one most likely not to make it."

Nate just laughed. "It was that way for me," he said. "I was older, though. We had the most beautiful Australian Kelpie—chocolate brown, silky coat, sweet face, ran herd on everything. My dad had her bred and promised me a pup. Out of her litter of six, I picked the runt and practically had to hand-feed him for weeks. The other pups kept pushing him off the tit. I was fifteen and, probably not coincidentally, also small for my age. I named him Dingo. He was big and tough by the time I was through with him, and he lived a long life for a hardworking Kelpie. We lost him just a few years ago. He lived to be fifteen. 'Course, he spent his last four years lying by the fire."

"You'd think a boy would pick the strongest in the pack."

"Nah." Nate snorted. "We don't feel that strong, so we empathize. Can I trouble you for a beer?"

"Sorry, Nate—I wasn't thinking. Fact is, I've been sitting on our nest on and off all day. I have a whole new appreciation for what you do."

"Have they been a lot of trouble?"

"Well, not really, just time-consuming," Jack said. "They eat every three hours or so, then their bedding has to be changed, then they nap, then they eat. And so on. Kind of like regular babies. Except there are eight of them and half of them need encouragement to eat.

Plus, every so often, you have to check that they're not too warm or too cold. I don't want to freeze 'em or cook 'em. And the bar's getting lots more company during the day—visitors to the litter. Since they're here, they decide to eat and drink—more serving, cooking and cleanup than usual. Other than that, piece of cake. And if I ever find the SOB that left 'em under the tree, I'm going to string him up by his—"

"Well, hey, Doc Jensen," a female voice sang out.

Nate turned to see Annie come out the back of the bar, Christopher trailing so closely that if she stopped suddenly, he'd have crashed into her. She carried a furry ball of black-and-white that fit perfectly into her palm. Looking at her, he realized he hadn't remembered her quite accurately. Or rather, quite *enough.* Tall, curvaceous, high cheekbones, soft dark auburn hair swinging along her jaw, long delicate fingers… She was beautiful. And her figure in a pair of snug jeans and turquoise hoodie with a deep V-neck just knocked him out. Where the heck had this girl been hiding?

And why was he, a man who could appreciate cleavage and tiny bikinis, suddenly seeing the merits in jeans, boots and *hoodies?*

Then he remembered she'd been hiding in a little hair salon in Fortuna, under a pink smock.

He picked up his beer and wandered over to the hearth. Christopher and Annie sat on opposite sides of the box, which left no place for him, so he stood there in the middle.

Annie passed Chris the puppy. "Hold him for just a minute, then snuggle him back in with his brothers and sisters," she said. "It's good for him to be part of his family. They give him more comfort than we can right now."

"A little maintenance?" Nate asked.

Annie looked up at him and smiled. "This is the part that gets to be a bother—without a mother dog to change their diapers and keep them clean, by the end of the day they're looking a little worse for wear. Some of them actually needed washing up. My dad always used to say a little poop never hurt a puppy, but you let that go long enough and it will. Gets them all ugly and matted and sick."

"You bathed him?"

"Four of them, without dunking them," she said. "Can't let them get cold. Preacher's wife loaned her blow-dryer to the cause. Okay, Chris, he's been away from home long enough now." She reached into the box and pushed some puppies aside to make room, and Chris gently put his puppy into the pile. "They'll be ready to eat again in about an hour. Why don't you get back to your homework, or dinner, or chores, or whatever your folks have in mind."

"Okay, Annie," he said.

And Nate fought a smile as Chris vacated his place on the hearth. But before he sat down he asked Annie, "Can I buy you a beer? Or something else?"

She tilted her head and smiled at him. "I wouldn't mind a beer, thanks." He was back with a cold one for her in just moments and sat down opposite her. "I think they're doing okay here," she said to him.

He wasn't a hard-hearted guy, but he only pretended interest in the pups, picking one up and then another, looking at their little faces. He'd rather be looking at her, but didn't want to seem obvious. "Were you here yesterday?" he asked, studying a puppy, rather than her.

"Uh-huh," she said, sipping her beer. "Ah, that's very nice. Thanks."

"You planning to come every day?" he asked.

"If I can swing it," she said. "I kind of made a deal—if they wouldn't hand them over to some shelter, I'd do my part. These little guys are just too cute and vulnerable. They could turn into impetuous Christmas presents, no matter how carefully the shelter volunteers screen the potential owners. And look at their markings—I'd say Australian-shepherd-and-border-collie mix. Outstanding herders. They should find good homes around here, and they'll be glad to work for a living."

Nate lifted his eyebrows. "Good guess," he said. "You get off work before five?" he found himself asking.

"Not usually. I have a small shop in Fortuna—six chairs. It's a franchise—my franchise. So I'm responsible, plus I have a large client list and it's Christmastime. But I'm moving appointments around the best I can—a few of my clients will take another stylist in a pinch. And I've been training an assistant manager, so she's getting thrown into the deep end of the pool because of these puppies. And I'm doing my puppy laundry and paperwork at midnight."

"What kind of paperwork?" he asked.

"The kind you have with a small business—receipts, receivables, bills, payroll. Jack and Preacher are managing real well during the day when it's sort of quiet around here, but when it gets busy at the dinner hour, they need a hand. And you heard Jack—he's not washing puppy sheets with his napkins." She smiled and sipped her beer. "We should all take comfort in that, I guess."

"I guess." He smiled. "How'd you end up with a beauty shop?"

"Oh, that's not interesting. I'd rather hear about what you do. I grew up around animals and being a vet is my fantasy life. You're living my dream."

"Then why didn't you pursue it?" he asked.

"Well, for starters, I had exactly two years of college and my GPA was above average, but we both know it takes way more than that to get into veterinary college. Isn't it harder to get into veterinary college than medical school?"

"So I hear," he said. "So, after two years of college…?"

She laughed and sipped her beer. "One of my part-time jobs was grooming dogs. I loved it. *Loved* it. The only thing I didn't love was going home a grimy, filthy mess and not exactly getting rich. But I saw the potential and needed to make a living. I couldn't focus on a course of study in college, so I went to beauty school, worked a few years, hit my folks up for a loan to buy a little shop, and there you have it. I do hair on two-legged clients now. And it's working just fine."

"And your love of animals?"

"I stop by this little bar every evening and babysit a bunch of orphaned puppies for a few hours," she said with a laugh. "I still have a couple of horses at the farm. My dad got rid of the livestock years ago except for Erasmus, a very old, very lazy, very ill-tempered bull who my dad says will outlive us all. They're down to two dogs, my mom keeps some chickens and their summer garden is just amazing. But it was once a thriving dairy farm, plus he grew alfalfa and silage for feed."

"Why isn't it still a thriving farm?" he asked.

"No one to run it."

"Your brothers don't want the farm life?"

"Nope," she said. "One's a high-school teacher and coach, one's a physical therapist in sports medicine and one's a CPA. All married with kids and working wives. All moved to bigger towns. And the closest one lives a few hours away."

"What about you?" he asked.

"Me?"

"Yeah, you. You sound like you love the farm. You love animals. You still have a couple of horses at your parents' farm...."

She smiled. "I'd be real happy to take on the farm, but that's not a good idea. Not the best place for me."

"Why not? If you like it."

She cocked her head and smirked. "Single, twenty-eight-year-old woman, living with Mom and Dad on the farm, building up the herd and plowing the fields. Picture it."

"Well, there's always help," he said. "Hired hands for the rough stuff."

She laughed. "Rough stuff doesn't scare me, but I can't think of a better way to guarantee I'll turn into an old maid. My social life is dull enough, thanks."

"There are ways around that," he pointed out. "Trips. Vacations. Visitors. That sort of thing. Something to break up the isolation a little."

"That's right—that's what I heard. Before I knew who you were, I heard Jack ask you if you had your plane tickets yet and you said something about Nassau, a Club Med vacation and lots of string bikinis. Right?"

For some reason he couldn't explain, that embarrassed him slightly. "No, no. I don't know anything about that Club Med stuff. A buddy of mine, Jerry from vet school, set up a get-together over Christmas with our old study group. We've only been in touch by email and haven't been together since graduation. The Nassau part is fact, the string-bikinis part is fantasy. I'm planning to do some scuba diving, snorkeling, some fishing. I haven't been away in a while." He laughed. "Frankly, I haven't been warm in a while."

"You don't get together with your family over the holidays?" she asked.

"Oh, they were gracious enough to invite me to join them all on a cruise. *All* of them," he stressed. "My folks, three sisters and brothers-in-law, four nephews and two nieces. It's going to be hell to give up all that shuffleboard, but I'll manage somehow."

"Do they ever come back here?" she asked. "You know—to the old homestead? Where you all grew up?"

"Frequently. They move in, take over, and I move out to the stable and take up residence in the vet tech's quarters."

"You and the tech must be on very good terms."

He grinned at her. "She's married and lives in Clear River, but we keep quarters for her for those times we have cases that are going to need attention through the night. She was my dad's assistant before he retired. She's like a member of the family." Then he studied her face. Was that relief? "The family was all home for Thanksgiving," he went on to explain. "It was great to see them all, and boy was I glad when they left. It's madness. I have really good brothers-in-law, though. At least my sisters did that much for me."

She sipped her beer. "You must be looking forward to your vacation. When do you leave?"

"The twenty-third. Till the second of January. I plan to come home tanned and rested." And with any luck, he thought, sexually relaxed. Then he instantly felt his face grow hot and thought, *Why the hell did I think that?* He wasn't typically casual about sex. He was actually very serious about it.

Annie peered at him strangely. "Dr. Jensen, are you blushing?"

He cleared his throat. "You don't have to be so formal, Annie. Nate is fine. Is it a little warm by this fire?"

"I hadn't noticed, but—"

"Have you eaten?" he asked.

"No. I hadn't even thought about it."

"Let's grab that table, right there close by, before anyone else gets it. I'm going to tell Jack we want dinner. How about that?"

"Fine," she said. "That sounds fine. By the time we're finished, Chris will be back, ready to feed his puppy."

Through the rest of that first week the puppies seemed to do just fine. Thrived in fact. So did Annie, and she hoped it didn't show all over her face. There was no particular reason for Nate to show up day after day; the pups weren't sick, didn't need medical care and he hadn't made the commitment to help that she had. Yet he returned on Thursday, Friday and Saturday. She'd love to believe he was there to see her, but it seemed such a far-fetched idea. So highly unlikely that she could interest a man like him through this odd doggie-day-care-in-a-bar that she wouldn't allow herself to even think about it.

But he was there by six every day, right about the time she finished her puppy chores. He always bought her a beer, then Jack provided dinner, which they ate together at a table near the hearth. They talked and laughed while catching up on their families and all the locals they knew, getting to know each other in general. Although she knew this friendship would probably fade and disappear by the time the puppies were adopted, and even though traipsing out to that bar every day was wearing her out, she was enjoying his company more than she could admit even to herself.

"Did you always plan to come back here? To take over your father's practice?" Annie asked him one evening.

"Nope," he said. "Wasn't part of my plan at all. First of all, I prefer Thoroughbreds to cows. I wanted to treat them, breed them, show them, race them. I did a couple of years' residency in equine orthopedics, worked in a big practice in Kentucky, then in a real lucrative practice outside Los Angeles. Then my dad wanted to retire. He'd put in his time—he's seventy-five now. Years back, he and my mom bought a horse property in a nice section of Southern Arizona, but they wanted to keep the house and stable, not to mention the vet practice, in the family. You have any idea how hard it is to build a practice with these tough old farmers and ranchers?" He chuckled. "The name Nathaniel Jensen goes a long way around here, even though I am the upstart."

"So here you are…back at the family practice?" she asked. But she was thinking that he'd been rubbing elbows with big-money horse people. Society people, whom she'd seen at a distance at certain competitions and fairs, but knew none of. She'd been riding since she could walk, took lessons and competed in dressage, and so was more than a little familiar with the kind of wealth associated with breeding, racing and showing Thoroughbreds. The well-to-do could send their daughters to Europe for lessons, fly their horses to Churchill Downs in private planes and invest millions in their horse farms. Humboldt County farm girls couldn't compete with that. She swallowed, feeling not a little out of her league.

"I said I'd give it a chance. My plan was to put in a year or two, save some money, maybe break in a new guy with an interest in the stable and practice. But I haven't gotten around to that and it's been two years."

"I see," she said. "You're still planning to leave?"

"I don't have to tell you what's great about this place." He smiled. "And I think I don't have to tell you what's missing. It's kind of a quiet life for a bachelor. Remember that dull social life you mentioned?"

"How could I forget?" she threw back at him.

"You seeing someone?" he asked suddenly, surprising her.

"Hmm? No. No, not at the moment. You?"

"No. Date much?" he asked.

Startled, she just shook her head. "Not much. Now and then." She thought for a moment and then said, "Ah. The vacation. Getting away to see if you can jump-start your social life a little bit?"

He just smiled. "Couldn't hurt. And it'll be nice to catch up with friends. We were real tight in vet school. We got each other through a lot of exams."

"How many of you are going?" she asked.

"Five men, including me, two of them married and bringing wives. Two women vets."

"Women vets? Married?"

"One's still single and one's divorced."

"Gotcha," she said. "I bet one's an old girlfriend."

"Nah," he said.

"Come on—didn't you ever date one?"

"I think I dated both of them. Briefly. We worked out better as study partners than...well, than anything else." He took a drink. "Really, I want to fish."

She took a last bite of her dinner. "Fishing is real good around here," she said.

"I fish the rivers here. A little deep-sea fishing sounded like a good idea. Some sun would be acceptable. I have golf clubs," he said with a laugh. "I used to play a lot of golf in L.A. Yeah," he mused, "a little sunshine won't hurt."

After a moment she reminded him with a smile, "And soon you'll be lying on a beach in the middle of a hundred string bikinis."

"Maybe you're right," he said with a grin. "Maybe I should do more fishing around here if I want to catch the big one."

By the time Sunday rolled around, Annie was back at the farm. She went early in the day so she could drop by the bar later that afternoon. Today, so close to Christmas, she was baking with her mother all day— breads, pastries, cookies to be frozen for the barrage of company—but she would have her dinner at the bar. Because of the puppies, of course.

"You're very quiet, Annie," her mother said. "I think

you're letting this adventure with the puppies wear you out. You've always had such a tender heart."

"I am tired," she admitted, rolling out cookie dough. "I'm getting up extra early, starting at the shop earlier so I can leave earlier, staying up late to finish work. And you know I won't leave my house alone—I'm decorating for Christmas. I've been doing a little here and there, before and after work."

"Then you shouldn't be out here two days a week," Rose McKenzie said. "Really, I appreciate the help, but I'm not too old to do the holiday baking."

"I count on our baking as gifts," Annie said. "So I'm glad to help.

"I didn't realize we had a new and improved Doc Jensen," she went on, changing the subject. "I thought it was still old Doc Jensen who came for the horses and Erasmus when you needed a vet. But when he stopped to look at the puppies, he explained he was Nathaniel Junior. You never mentioned."

"Oh, sure we did, honey. His coming home was good gossip there for a while. He had some woman living with him, but she took off like a scalded cat. I don't think we talked about anything else for months."

"A woman? When was that?"

"A couple years ago. Some fancy young Hollywood girl," Rose said with an indulgent laugh. "We ran into them a few times—at the fair, the farmers' market, here and there." Her mother was kneading dough as she chattered. "You know, you don't run into people that often around here. They could've been here a year before anyone met her, but Nathaniel had her out and about. Probably trying to help her get acquainted. But it didn't work too well, I guess."

"I'm sure I would have remembered, Mom. I don't think you ever mentioned it."

Rose looked skyward briefly, trying to remember. "That might've been about the time you were preoccupied with other things. Like buying the Clip and Curl shop. And then there was Ed, and that ordeal with Ed. You might've had other things on your mind."

Ed. Yes, Ed. She hadn't exactly been engaged, thank God, but they'd been an item for about a year and she'd expected to be engaged. They *had* talked about marriage. She laughed humorlessly. "That could have distracted me a little," Annie agreed.

"The bum," Rose McKenzie muttered, punching dough more aggressively than necessary. "He's a pig and a fool and a liar and a...a bum!"

Loving it, Annie laughed. "He's really not a bum. He works hard and earns a good living, which it turned out he needed for all the women he had on a string. But I concede to pig, liar and fool, and I'm certainly not missing him. The louse," she added. "I can't remember now—why was it we didn't let the boys shoot him in the head?"

"I can't remember exactly, either," Rose said. "I knew all along he wasn't right for you."

"No, you didn't," Annie argued. "You had me trying on your wedding dress about once a month, asking me constantly if we'd talked about a date. You expected him to give me a ring."

"I just thought *if*..."

Ed was in farm-equipment sales and had a very broad territory in Northern California, a job that had him on the road most of the week. Then she learned that for the entire time they'd dated, Ed was involved with another woman in Arcata. About six months ago he'd decided it was time to make a choice, and he chose the other woman.

Ouch.

Annie's pride was hurt, but worse than hurt pride was her embarrassment. How had this been going on without her getting so much as a whiff of it? When she hadn't seen him, she had talked to him every single day. He never betrayed the slightest hint that she was not the only female in his life. And it made her furious to think he'd been with another woman while he was with her. She even drove to Arcata to sneak a look at her, but she couldn't figure out, based on looks, just what it was that won her the great prize that was Ed.

Before she could ponder that for long, that Arcata woman found *her,* looked her up, informed her they weren't the only two. Ed, as it happened, was quite the dabbler. He had at least one other steady girlfriend to spend the nights with.

Her tears had turned to fumes. She threw out everything that reminded her of him. She bought all new bedding and towels. Went to the doctor and got a clean bill of health. But at the end of the day when she grieved, it wasn't so much for Ed as for the *idea* of Ed; she had invested a year in a man she thought would give her the stability of marriage and family, a settled life. The dependence of love. Security. When she thought about Ed, she wanted to dismember him. She wanted her brothers to go after him and beat him senseless. But not only would she never take him back, she'd cross the street to avoid him. So maybe Rose was right—maybe they both really knew all along he just wasn't the one.

But neither was anyone else. She hadn't been out

on five dates since the breakup a little more than six months ago, and the number of boyfriends she'd had before Ed had come along were too few to count. She went out with her girlfriends regularly, but the best part of her life was spending a couple of days on the farm, riding, cooking or baking or putting up preserves with her mom.

The farmhouse had a wide porch that stretched the length of the house, and from that porch you could watch the seasons come and go. The brightness of spring, the lushness of summer, the burnt color of fall, the white of winter. She watched the year pass from that porch, as she had since she was a little girl. But lately it seemed as though the years were passing way too quickly and she wondered if she'd ever find the right partner to sit there with rather than alone.

A Hollywood woman? A fancy Hollywood woman? That would explain things like Caribbean vacations. Nate was drawn to flashy, sexy women. Or maybe the kind of women found in the private boxes at races or horse shows; Annie had seen enough of those televised events to know the type—model gorgeous, decked out in designer clothes, hand-stitched boots, lots of fringe and bling. Or the type seen at the fund-raisers and society events attended by the wives, daughters and sisters of Thoroughbred breeders, the kind of women whose horses were entered in the Preakness. Or perhaps he preferred medically educated women, like another vet who could appreciate his professional interests—the kind of women who also rubbed elbows with the well-to-do because of their profession.

But probably ordinary, sensible-shoes farm girls didn't do anything special for a man like Nate.

Annie's thoughts were broken when her father walked into the kitchen and refilled his coffee cup. He put a hand on the small of his back and stretched, leaning back, rolling his shoulders.

"Are you limping, Dad?"

"Nah," he said. "Got a little hitch in my giddyup is all."

"As soon as I'm through with this puppy project, I'll make it a point to get out here more often to help."

"The doctor says the best thing is for him to keep moving," Rose said. "You do enough to help already."

"You don't remember that fancy Hollywood woman?" Hank asked, going back to the conversation he had overheard. Without waiting for an answer, he added, "Breeze woulda blown her away. Skinny thing. Could see her bones. Not at all right for Nathaniel." He took a sip of coffee and lifted his bushy brows, looking at her over the rim of his mug. "You'da been more his speed, I think. Yeah, better Nathaniel than that son of a so-and-so you got yourself mixed up with."

"I didn't even know Nate Jensen was here until a few days ago, remember?" Annie pointed out. "And before that, I was with the so-and-so, and Nate was taken."

"Yeah, you'da had to kill that skinny thing, but she looked near death, anyhow." Then he grinned at her and left the kitchen.

"Will Nathaniel have his family for Christmas?" Rose asked.

"Actually, he said his parents, sisters and their families are going on a cruise. I gathered, from the way he said it, he'd throw himself off the boat if he were along. He said something sarcastic, like it would be hell to give up all that shuffleboard, but he'd manage."

"Oh, you must invite him to join us for the holiday dinners, Annie. As I recall, he was friendly with one of your brothers when they were kids."

"Mom, he's not hanging around. He's going on some highfalutin Caribbean vacation, meeting up with some old classmates from veterinary college, hoping to get lost in a sea of very tiny bikinis on the beach. Apparently his taste in women hasn't changed much."

"Really?" Rose asked. "Now to me, that sounds dull."

"Not if you're a single guy in your thirties, Mom."

"Oh. Well, then take him some of these cookies."

"I'm sure he couldn't care less about home-baked cookies." *Not if what he prefers is some fancy, skinny, rich girl,* she thought.

"Nonsense. I don't know the man who doesn't like home-baked cookies. Reminds them of their mothers."

"Just the image I'd most like to aspire to," Annie said.

Three

Rose McKenzie insisted that Annie take a plate of Christmas cookies to Dr. Jensen, but it made Annie feel silly, farm girlish, so she left them in the car when she went into Jack's Bar later that afternoon.

She gasped in pleasure when she walked in—the place had been decorated for Christmas. A tree stood in the corner opposite the hearth, garlands were strung along the bar and walls, small evergreen centerpieces sat on the tables, and the buck over the door wore a wreath on his antlers. It was festive and homey, and the fresh pine scent mingled with wood smoke and good cooking from the kitchen to complete the holiday mood.

It took her less than two seconds to see that Nate wasn't there, which made her doubly glad she hadn't trotted in her plate of baked goods. Maybe this was the day he wasn't going to show. It wasn't as though he had any obligation here. In fact, besides giving the puppies a cursory look and asking Annie if there was anything wrong with any of them, he didn't do anything at all.

She gave Jack a wave and went directly to the puppies, which, in the past week, had gotten surprisingly big. Boy, if those weren't all border collies, she was no judge of canines. Out of the eight, two were solid black with maybe a little silver or gray or perhaps a mere touch of white—the only indication another breed might've been involved. But they had grown so much! And they were doing so beautifully—plump and fluffy and adorable. Just like everyone else who passed by that box, she couldn't resist immediately picking a puppy up and cuddling it against her chin.

Jack came over to the hearth and she grinned at him. "The bar looks wonderful, Jack. All ready for Santa."

"Yeah, the women got it ready for their hen party. Cookie exchange tomorrow at noon—you should come."

"Nuts, I'll be at work. But tell them the decorations are beautiful."

"Sure," he said. "Annie, we've got a situation. We're going to have to come up with another plan here."

Instinctively she picked up Comet to judge his size and strength; he wriggled nicely. "Why's that, Jack?" she asked.

He was shaking his head. "This isn't going to work much longer. I can go another day, two at the most, while you figure something out, but the puppies have to find a new home. They're getting bigger, more energetic, and giving off the kind of odor reminiscent of a box full of puppy shit. This is an eating-and-drinking establishment, Annie."

"Are people complaining?" she asked.

"Just the opposite," he said, shaking his head. "We're drawing a nice crowd on account of the big tree and the cute little puppies. But you know puppies, Annie. They're wetting on a lot of laps while they're being held and snuggled. This is going to go from cute and fun to a big problem real soon."

"Oh," she said, helpless. "Oh." Well, it wasn't as though she had trouble understanding. It was different when the litter was in your downstairs bathroom or under the laundry sink in a home, or when there was a mother dog around tending the nursery. You just didn't realize how hard that mother dog worked unless you had to care for the puppies yourself. Even when there were eight of them, as long as they were nursing, good old Mom licked them from head to toe, keeping them clean and dry. The second you started giving them solid food, Mom stopped cleaning up after them and it took no time at all for them to get a little stinky and messy. But under normal circumstances, that came at about six weeks, right about the time they were ready to leave the nursery anyway.

In this case, there'd been no mom, and the formula and cereal that went in one end came out the other. Their bedding couldn't be changed fast enough or their cute little bottoms washed often enough to avoid a smell.

"What am I going to do?" she asked herself.

"We've got homes for some of them figured out," Jack said. "I'm not sure any of them are ready to be out of the box yet, but we've got a few adoptions worked out. There's Christopher, of course. He's not letting Comet get away."

"Comet's not ready to be the responsibility of a six-year-old. He needs a couple more weeks. And good as Chris is with him, he'll have to be supervised," Annie said.

"I know. And I'm sunk," Jack said. "David keeps babbling about his 'boppie.' I've been thinking about getting a dog, anyway, something to clean up the spills around my place. But…"

"And, Jack, you can't turn a puppy this size over to a three-year-old boy any more than you can put him in charge of eggs and ripe tomatoes."

"Yeah, yeah, when it's time, we'll be careful. And Buck Anderson, sheep rancher, says it's about time to get a couple of new herders ready. He's got a little child of his own and seven grandchildren. He can speak for two—his sons can help get 'em grown before they turn them over to the other dogs and the sheep. He'd like them to be Christmas dogs, though. Now, I know you don't trust people looking for puppies as Christmas gifts, but you can count on Buck. He knows the score." Jack took a breath. "I don't like their chances if they won't herd sheep, however."

"Okay, that's four taken care of," she said.

"Couple of other people have been thinking about it, but that's the progress so far. Did you realize everyone in town has named them after the reindeer?"

"Yeah, cute, huh? Jack, I don't have a place for them. I guess I could take them to my house and run home between haircuts to make sure they're fed and watered, but to tell the truth, I don't have that kind of time. At Christmastime, everyone wants to be beautiful. And I try to spend as much time at the farm as I can—the whole family's coming."

"Maybe we need to rethink that shelter idea. Couldn't they just look after them for a couple of weeks? Then we'll take at least a few off their hands…."

Just then Nathaniel blew in with a gust of wind. He pulled off his gloves and slapped them in his palm. He looked around the recently decorated bar and whistled approvingly. "Hey," he said to Annie and Jack. "How's everything?" Silence answered him. "Something wrong?"

Annie stepped toward him. "Jack can't keep the puppies here anymore, Nate. They're starting to smell like dogs. It is a restaurant, after all."

Nate laughed. "I think you've hung in there pretty well, Jack. Lasted longer than I predicted."

"Sorry, Nate. If Annie hadn't been so convincing, these guys would have gone to a shelter right off the bat. Or someplace way worse. At least we've figured out homes for a few—when they're old enough and strong enough to leave the litter."

"Yeah, I understand," Nate said good-naturedly. "Well, if Annie promises not to bail on me, I'll take 'em home. I'm pretty busy most days, but I have a vet tech at the clinic to help. And they don't need quite as much hands-on care as they did a week ago—at least they can all lap up their meals without an eyedropper now. I can put 'em in the laundry room and close the door so they don't keep me up all night."

"Will they be warm enough?" Annie asked. "Are they strong enough?"

"They'll be fine, Annie. Jack—what's for dinner?"

"Chili. Corn bread. Really? You'll take them out of here?"

Nate laughed. "Can we mooch one more meal before we cart them away? I'm a bachelor—there's hardly ever any food in the house." He draped an arm around Annie's shoulders. "This one is spoiled now—she's used to getting fed for her efforts. And two beers."

"Yeah," Jack said, lifting a curious eyebrow. "Coming right up."

"After we eat, you can follow me home," he said to Annie, as if the matter was settled.

Annie knew approximately where the Jensen clinic, stable and house were, but she couldn't remember ever going there. You might take your poodle or spaniel to the small-animal vet, but the large-animal vet came to you, unless you had a big animal in need of surgery or with some condition that required long-term and frequent care. His stable also provided occasional short-term boarding for horses. And he had breeding facilities, but that also was most often done at the farm or ranch by the farmers and ranchers. Some owners of very valuable horses preferred to leave their prefoaling mares with the vet.

Nate transported the puppy box in the covered bed of his truck. They were bundled up with extra blankets and wouldn't get too cold on the short ride. Annie followed in her own truck. They made a left off the main road at the sign that said Jensen Stables, Dr. Nathaniel Jensen, DVM. The road was paved, which was high cotton in this part of the world. It was tree-lined and the snow-covered brush was cut back from the edge. The road had to be at least half a mile long. Then it opened into a well-lit compound. The stable was on the left of a large open area, with a corral surrounding it on the side and back. The clinic itself was attached to the stable. There were Christmas lights twinkling in one of the windows. On the right was a sprawling, modern one-story house with a brick sidewalk that led up to double front doors of dark wood set with beveled-glass windows. Not a single Christmas light or ornament on the house at all. Annie wondered if the vet tech had decorated the clinic.

Between the house and stable were two horse trailers. One could hold six horses, the other two, and both were so fancy they probably came with a bar and cabin attendants.

The garage door at one end of the house opened automatically, and Nate pulled in. Annie parked outside and walked through the garage. She carried the formula and baby cereal while he carried the box, managing to open the door into the house and flick on lights with his elbow as he walked through the kitchen and then disappeared. The kitchen was the kind Annie's mother would have died for—large new appliances, six-burner stove, double oven, work island with a sink. It was gorgeous. It looked newly remodeled.

Annie moved more slowly, peering past a long breakfast bar into a spacious family room with big, comfy-looking furniture and a beautiful fireplace. On each side of the fireplace were floor-to-ceiling bookcases filled with leather-bound volumes.

"Annie? Where are you?"

She stopped gawking and followed the voice. She passed a very long, old oak table in a large breakfast nook inside bay windows that looked out on the back of the property. A sharp left and down a short hall took her past a bathroom, a bedroom and into a laundry room. In addition to cabinets, there was a stainless-steel washer and dryer, along with a deep sink. This was not an old farmhouse, that was for sure.

"I'll use linens from the clinic to line their box," Nate said. "They'll be fine in here. Listen, I know you signed on for this duty, but I don't want you to feel like you have to rearrange your schedule to get out here the first minute you can escape work every day. Virginia, my tech, can help during the day and I get called out sometimes, but this time of year, no one's breeding or birthing, so it's not usually too hectic. But—"

"Okay," she said. "I won't come. I'll leave a number. If you need me."

"Well, could you still come sometimes?" he asked with a laugh. "If you give me a hand feeding and cleaning up, I'll thaw a hunk of meat to throw in the broiler or something. Nothing like Preacher's, but edible. Just let me know when you can be here."

"You have your tech...."

"I don't like to ask Virginia to stay after five unless we have special patients—she wants to get home, have dinner with her husband. I'll fix you up with a key, in case I'm tied up on a case and you beat me home."

"Sure. Tell me exactly what you want," she said.

He put his hands on his hips. "I want to know what's wrong. Why are you frowning like that? You've been frowning since I walked into Jack's."

Mentally, she tried to smooth out her eyebrows, but she could still feel the wrinkle. She'd been trying to picture him with a trophy girl on his arm, that was what. Or with an equestrienne from a high-muck-a-muck ranch who raced or showed horses all over the world. Or maybe a mature and attractive woman his age who was as smart and successful as he was. And he was so damn handsome it wasn't hard to imagine all this. But she said, "You're downright chipper. This is *exactly* what you didn't want, but you're almost thrilled about having the puppies here. What's up with that?"

He laughed. "Nah. I knew it was going to come to this. I'm glad Jack and Preacher handled them for that first week for two reasons—they had to be fed, dried and checked frequently, and I enjoyed stopping by the bar on the way home every day. Don't know when I've eaten so well," he added, rubbing a flat belly. "Now that it's apparent they're all going to make it, they only have to be checked and fed every few hours, something Virginia and I can handle during the day. I agree with you about the shelter. They'd probably be just fine— those folks are devoted, and they interview and screen efficiently before they let a tiny, orphaned animal out of there. But why take chances? If we have to use the shelter, we'll just do so after Christmas."

"That's it? You knew all along you'd get stuck with them?"

He just laughed. "Come on, I'll show you the house I grew up in, we'll put on some coffee, feed the pups and put 'em down for the night. How about that?"

"You don't have to show me the house. I'm not going to be poking around in here."

He grabbed her hand. "I'm not worried about you poking around. Come on," he said again, pulling her back through the kitchen. He took her through a spacious great room, where he said, "Many fights between my sisters happened here. When I grew up, there was old, floral, ratty furniture in here, but once everyone got educated and off Mom and Dad's payroll, new things began to appear around the house. Things got updated and remodeled." He pulled her down the hall, showed her where the master bedroom and three others were located. "I got the bed-and-bath on the other side of the kitchen. Kept me away from the girls." Then he took a right turn off the great room. "Formal living room, used only on family holidays like Christmas, and dining room, used for overflow at big family dinners." And then they were back in the huge kitchen.

"It's enormous," she said breathlessly. "It's very beautiful. What must it have been like to grow up in a house so large?"

"I probably took it for granted, like any kid would," he said with a shrug. "It's still my parents' house, though I doubt they'll ever move back here. Come on, I'll put on coffee."

"You don't have to entertain me, Nate."

"Maybe I'm entertaining myself. I don't have much company out here."

The moment they had the coffee poured Annie remembered. "Damn," she said. "Don't move. I have something for you." She dashed out the garage door to her car, retrieved the cookies and brought them in. In typical country fashion, they were arranged on a clear, plastic plate with plastic wrap covering them. "For you," she said. "They should be warm, but now they're nearly frozen. My mother insisted."

"She baked them for me?" he asked, surprised, as he peeled off the wrap and helped himself.

"Well, kind of."

"Kind of?"

"We baked together today. All day. We do that for the holidays. Stuff for the freezer, gifts for neighbors and for my girls at the shop. We bake on my days off for weeks right up to Christmas."

"You bake?" he asked, looking mesmerized, maybe shocked.

She smirked. "All farm girls bake. I also know how to quilt, garden, put up preserves and chop the head off a chicken. I couldn't butcher a cow by myself, but I know how it's done and I've helped."

"Wow."

She was not flattered by his response. She'd hardly led a glamorous life and she'd much rather have told him she'd gone to boarding school in Switzerland and dressage training in England. "I bet I remind you of your mother, huh?"

He chuckled. "Not exactly. Do you fish? Hunt?"

"I've been fishing and hunting, but I prefer the farm. Well, I shot a mountain lion once, but that was a long time ago and I wasn't hunting. The little bastard was after my mother's chickens, and the boys had already moved away, so I—"

"How old were you?" he asked.

She shrugged. "I don't know—thirteen or fourteen. But I'm not crazy about hunting. I like to ride. I miss the cows. I loved the calving. Ice cream made from fresh cream. Warm eggs, right out from under the chicken. I have more 4-H ribbons than anyone in my family. Erasmus, that mean old bull? He's mine. Blue ribbon—state fair. I was fifteen when he came along— he's an old guy now, and the father of hundreds. I have a green thumb like my mother—I can stick anything in the ground and it grows. I once grew a rock bush." He threw her a shocked expression and she rolled her eyes. He recovered. "Just one of those plain old farm girls. Size-ten boot and taller than all the boys till I was a senior in high school. My dad calls me solid. Steady. Not the kind of girl men are drawn to. I attract…*puppies*. That's what."

He smiled hugely, showing her his bright white teeth and that maddening dimple. "Is that a fact?"

"Not *your* type, certainly. I've never had a string bikini. I wouldn't know what to do with one. Floss your teeth? Is that what you do?"

He laughed. "There are sexier things than string bikinis," he said.

"Really?" she asked. "The minute I heard you describe being lost in the middle of a hundred string bikinis, I got a picture in my mind that I haven't been able to get rid of. It's like having a bad song stuck in your head."

"Oh, Jesus, don't you just have a giant bug up your ass," he said, amused.

"I have no idea what you mean," she said, though she knew *exactly*. She was a terrible liar. "I didn't even know you weren't your father, you know. I had no idea you were the vet until you showed up at Jack's. And today while we were baking, my folks told me that when you came up here to take over the practice, they'd talked about nothing else for months. I guess you brought your girlfriend with you. A beautiful, fancy, Hollywood woman."

Shock widened his mouth and eyes. "Get outta here," he said. Then he erupted into laughter. "Is that what they're saying?"

A little embarrassed, she shrugged. "I don't know that anyone's saying anything anymore, and I don't know who besides my folks saw it that way."

He laughed for a long time, finally getting himself under control. "Okay, look. She was my fiancée, okay? But it was my mistake, bringing her up here, because she was far too young. I must have been out of my mind. She wasn't ready to get married. Thank God. And she wasn't a Hollywood woman, although she really wanted to be. Maybe she is by now, for all I know. Susanna was from Van Nuys. The only thing she knew about horses was that they have four legs and big teeth. She was twenty-four to my twenty-nine, had never lived in a small town and really didn't want to."

"And thin," Annie added. "Very thin."

He put his hands in his pockets, rocked back on his heels, lifted expressive dark brows and with a grin he said, "Well, not all over."

"Oh, that's disgusting," she returned, disapproval sounding loud.

"Well, it's not nice to talk meanly about past girl-friends."

"I bet she looked great in a string bikini," Annie said with a snort.

"Just unbelievable," he said, clearly taunting her. "Now, why would you be so jealous? You don't even know poor, thin Susanna. For all you know, she's a sweet, caring, genuine person and I was horrible to her." And he said all this with a sly smile.

"I am certainly not jealous! Curious, but not jealous!"

"Green as a bullfrog," he accused.

"Oh, bloody hell. Listen, I'm shot. Long day. Gotta go." She grabbed her purse and jacket and whirled out of the kitchen. And got lost. She found herself in the wide hall that led to the bedrooms. She found her way back to the great room, then to the kitchen. "Where the hell is the door?"

He swept an arm wide toward the door that led to the garage, still wearing that superior smile. What an egomaniac, she thought, heading for the door.

When she got to her car, she thought, well, that was perfectly awful. What's more, he saw right through her.

She was attracted to him, and because she knew there had probably been many beautiful women in his past, she'd let it goad her into some grotesque and envious remarks about the only one she knew of, Susanna. The child-woman who obviously had a little butt and nice rack. Why in the world would she do that? What did she care?

It probably had something to do with touring a four-thousand-square-foot custom home, beautifully furnished, across the compound from a spacious stable with a couple of horse trailers her dad would have killed for. Well, what was one to expect from a veterinary practice that served so many, over such a wide area? And not a new practice, either, but a mature one—probably forty years old. Established. Lucrative.

She'd grown up in a three-bedroom, hundred-year-old farmhouse. Her three brothers shared a bedroom and never let her forget it for a second. They *all* shared one very small bathroom. But she loved the way she'd grown up and had never been jealous a day in her life— why would she be now? Could it be that in addition to all that, she'd never gone to special, private schools, never worn custom-tailored riding gear, never could afford the best riding lessons or most prestigious competitions? Also, she had wide hips, big feet and a less-than-memorable bustline. "Oh, for God's sake, Annie," she said to herself. "Since when have you even thought about those things!"

How long had she been sitting here in her car? Long enough to get cold, that was how long. Well, it was time to suck it up. She'd go back in there and just tell him she was cranky, that being one of those "sturdy" farm girls who owns exactly one pair of high heels she can barely walk in, it just rubbed her the wrong way hearing about the kind of woman who could get the attention of one of the county's few bachelors. Not that *she* wanted his attention, but just the same… She'd apologize and promise never to act that way again. She wasn't usually emotional. Or irrational.

She walked back into the still-open garage, up to the back door and gave a short tap. It flew open. He reached out and grabbed her wrist, pulled her roughly into the house, put his arms around her, pressed her up against the kitchen wall just inside the door, and *kissed* her! His mouth came down on hers so fiercely, with such dominance and confidence, her eyes flew open in shock. Then he began to move over her mouth while he held her against the wall with his wide, hard chest, his big hands running up and down her rib cage, over her hips.

She couldn't move. She couldn't raise her arms or let her eyes drift closed or even kiss back. She held her breath. What the hell…?

He finally lifted his lips off hers and said, "You like me. I knew it."

"I don't like you that much. Never do that again," she said.

"You want me," he said, smiling. "And I'm going to let you have me."

"You're conceited. I do not want you."

He kissed her again, and again her eyes flew open. This time she worked her arms free and pushed against his chest.

"Well, hell, just kiss me back and see if I start to grow on you," he said.

"No. Because you think this is funny. I came back

in here to apologize for being crabby. I don't care about that skinny woman. Girl. I'm just a little tired."

"You don't have to apologize, Annie. I think it's kind of cute. But you don't have to be jealous of Susanna. She's long gone and I hardly even missed her. We weren't right for each other. At all."

"That's what my dad said."

"Hank said that?"

She nodded.

"What did he say? Exactly?" Nate wanted to know.

She shouldn't. But she did. "He said I'd be more your type, but I'd have had to kill the skinny blonde first. He said she looked near death, anyway."

Nate thought that was hilarious. He laughed for a long time, but he didn't let go of her. "Good thing she left, then. She couldn't hold her own in any kind of fight. She cried if she broke a nail."

"I bet she was just one of many."

He withdrew a little, but the amusement stayed in his eyes. "You think I'm a player."

"How could you not be? It's not like I don't know about those rich horse people. And you're the *doctor!* Of course you've had a million girlfriends."

The smile finally vanished. "No," he said. "I'm not that guy, Annie. Just 'cause I've been around those folks doesn't mean I'm that kind of guy."

"Well, there are the girl vets you're going to the islands with," she reminded him.

"Tina and Cindy," he said with a laugh. "Shew. I hate to brag, but I'm thirty-two, Annie, and there have been a couple of women in my past. But I bet there are a couple of guys in yours, too. Tina and Cindy are just friends of mine."

"Uh-huh. I'm sure. Old friends and a hundred string bikinis."

"Come back in and finish your coffee," he said with a tolerant chuckle.

"I have to go. I have to get home to Ahab."

"Who's that?" Nate asked.

"My cat. Ahab. Tripod. He has a lot of names. He's three-legged."

"What happened?" Nate asked.

"I don't know. I adopted him from the shelter when it was clear no one else would ever take him. He's got a bad attitude, but he loves me. He's very independent, but he does like to eat. I have to go."

"Are you coming back tomorrow after work?"

"Are you going to be a gentleman?" she asked.

He lifted one of those handsome brows. "You want me to?"

No. "Absolutely. Or I'm leaving the puppies all to you without helping."

"Just come tomorrow after work. Swing by home and feed your cat first so you don't have to be in a hurry to leave." He gave her a very polite kiss on the cheek that just oozed with suggestiveness. "I'll see you then."

Four

Christmastime in a beauty shop was always frantic and the Clip and Curl was no exception. There were less than two weeks till Christmas and Annie's clientele, the clientele of the whole shop, wanted to look their best for parties, open houses, family visits, neighborhood gatherings. Appointments were one after the other. There was a lot of gossip, a lot of excited chatter. Annie was pretty quiet the next day, but there was plenty of talk in the place to cover the void.

Pam, who was older than Annie by a few years and had been married for ten, was training to be the assistant manager. While Annie was applying foil to strips of hair for highlighting, Pam approached with the appointment book in her hands. "We have three choices. We can turn away some of our best regular customers, stay open till nine a couple of nights or open up the next two Mondays to fit them in."

"Why don't people schedule ahead of time?" Annie asked.

"As you taught me, they expect to be accommodated and we can either do that or lose them to another shop."

"Staying late is hard for me and you have a family. I don't want to stick you with that duty," Annie said. Then after thinking about it, she said, "Maybe I should work nights. That would settle that."

"Settle what?" Pam asked, holding the large appointment book in her crossed arms, against her chest.

"Oh, that guy. The vet. You know."

"Know what?"

"The guy at the bar, Jack, he said they couldn't keep the litter of puppies there anymore. The dogs are doing very well, growing, which means they'll soon be up to their eyeballs in puppy poop. Not a real appetizing prospect for a restaurant. So Jack said that's it, they have to go. Dr. Jensen took them to his house, which is part of the whole stable-and-vet-clinic operation. And since I made a commitment to help...he's counting on me coming over after work."

"To his house?"

"Yeah. He said if I'd help, he'd thaw something for us to eat. We've been having a beer and dinner at that bar."

"Listen, it's up to you, Annie. It's your shop. My husband's on board to get the kids from school and take care of their dinner and homework. You know I need whatever hours..."

"Then *you* make the decision," Annie said.

Pam lowered the appointment book and held it against her thigh. "Annie, I don't need you to stay if the shop is open till nine or open Mondays for a couple of weeks. Two of the girls are willing to work a little extra to help pay for Christmas. But you have to feel comfortable about leaving me in charge. And I don't want to push you to do that before you're ready. You've run a pretty tight, one-woman show here."

"Have I?"

Pam nodded. "But I don't blame you, Annie. This is your shop, your investment, your responsibility. Whenever you think I'm ready, I'm glad to help."

"Thing is, he kissed me."

It became very quiet in the shop. Pam's mouth dropped open.

"Nuts," Annie said. There were no ears gifted with supersonic hearing like those found in a beauty shop, despite the noise of dryers and running water. She looked around the small shop. It was tiny—three chairs on each side of the room. Two dryers and two deep sinks in back. Behind that was their break room and Annie's little office.

In the salon now were women in various stages of beautifying, rods, rollers, foils or back-combed tresses blooming from their heads. Beauticians with blow-dryers, curling irons, combs and brushes in their hands, poised over those heads. All silent. All waiting. "Talk among yourselves," Annie instructed.

"Lotsa luck," Pam said. "Is this guy, this vet, in any way appealing?"

Annie's cheeks got a little rosy.

"Is he cute?" Pam asked.

Annie leaned toward Pam and whispered, "You'd wet yourself."

And Pam's cheeks got a little pink. "Whew."

"Well, tell us about him," someone said.

"Yeah, what kind of guy is he?"

"Should you call the police or wear something with a real low neckline?"

"How old is he? How many times has he been married? Because that's key. Believe me!"

"Listen, I can't talk about this," Annie said. "I've known the man barely a week! And only because of these puppies! Honestly, if it weren't for these puppies, we wouldn't even know *about* each other. He's a large-animal vet. He was just doing the bartender, Jack, a favor by looking at the orphaned litter."

"Um, Annie, don't *you* have large animals? Who's your vet?"

"Well, *he* is, but I didn't *know* that. I mean, my folks keep an eye on the horses and Erasmus. My bull," she clarified for those confused stares in the room. "When they said they called Doc Jensen to the farm, I thanked them and paid the bill. I mean, it hardly ever happens that the horses or the bull needs something. I thought he was the same Doc Jensen who'd been looking after our animals since I was in diapers. But it turned out to be his son. Doc Jensen Junior." She cleared her throat. "He's thirty-two. And never been married."

"Whoa," someone said. Another woman whistled.

"He's had girlfriends," Annie said. "Not from around here. But when he came up here to take over his dad's practice a couple of years ago, he brought a young buxom blonde fiancée with him and it didn't work out, but—"

"Low neckline," someone advised.

"Tight jeans. Snug, anyway. I mean this in the nicest way, but if you could think about a little extra makeup, like eyeliner and lip liner," someone said.

"You don't need that," Pam said quietly.

"I was thinking that maybe being unavailable would be a good—"

"No!" three women said at once.

"Why would you do that?" Pam asked.

"He's just too damn sure of himself," Annie answered.

"Well, how about this," Pam said. "Maybe you could try being sure of *your*self?"

Annie thought about that for a second. "See, that's the hard part."

Usually Annie was very confident. She knew she was intelligent; she was a small-business owner and it was going well. She was independent and doubted that would ever change, even once she partnered up. And as for her modest upbringing, she had not yet met the person she'd trade places with. Life on the farm was rich in many ways. She might've had a moment of shallow jealousy over the skinny, fancy, city girl who could attract not only Nathaniel's attention, but acquire a big engagement rock, as well, but all that had passed pretty quickly.

There was one area in her life where her confidence was a little shaky, however. She'd barely recovered from Ed. She'd put a lot of faith and trust in a man who'd clearly been using her. If this new guy, the big-shot vet, was really interested in her, he'd have some proving to do. She wasn't going to be played for a fool. And she certainly wasn't going to be the only available two-legged female he'd run across lately.

Later that day after work, she fed Ahab, dug around in her refrigerator and fluffed up a nice green salad, fixed a plate of frosted brownies and headed for Nate's place.

When she pulled up to his house, a woman was just leaving the clinic, locking the door behind her. She was a tiny thing with salt-and-pepper hair cut supershort, and when she might have headed for the only car parked outside the clinic, she stopped and waited for Annie with a smile on her lips.

Annie approached her. "You must be Virginia," she said.

"And you would be Annie McKenzie," the older woman said. "Nice to meet you. I met your parents some years ago, but I think all you kids were either at school or had maybe already left home. Nate's not home yet, but you have a key, right?"

"I do," she said. "Thanks for helping with those puppies. These are for you," she added on a whim, passing Virginia the plate of brownies.

"You shouldn't have, but I'm glad you did. Annie, tell Nathaniel to give you both the clinic and my home phone numbers and to leave your phone number for me. If we run into a situation when he's stuck out at a farm or ranch, we can work together to cover for him. I live in Clear River and he tells me you're in Fortuna. It's about the same distance for both of us to get here."

"Sure. And I'll tell him to call me first. I don't have a husband to irritate by running off somewhere to take care of puppies."

Virginia tilted her head, regarding her. "He doesn't talk about women, you know," she said.

"Your husband?" Annie answered, confused.

Virginia laughed. "Nathaniel. Can't get a word out of him about his love life. And I've known him since he was this high," she said, her hand measuring about midthigh.

"Maybe it's not much of a—"

"But he's talked about you for a week now. Annie this, and Annie that."

Annie's eyes grew round and maybe a little panicked. "This and that *what?*" she asked.

"I think he finds you delightful. Maybe amazing. You knew exactly what to do with the puppies because, raised by Hank and Rose, you were trained to know. And you're tall. For years he's been asking me if I've always been this short. I think he likes tall women. When you were little, he said, you had a big batch of curly, carrot-orange hair, but you obviously outgrew it. You shot a mountain lion, butchered a cow, raised a blue-ribbon bull. Oh, and you're beautiful. But a little crabby, which he finds humorous." Virginia shook her head. "Nathaniel likes to try to find his way around a difficult woman," she said with a grin. "Being the youngest of four with three bossy older sisters, he can't help it, so don't let down your guard."

Annie laughed. No problem there—her guard was up.

"It's nice that you two have renewed your friendship," Virginia added.

"But, Virginia, we were never friends," Annie said. "We barely recall each other from childhood. He knew my older brothers, but not that well. We all went to different schools and might've run into each other at fairs, 4-H stuff, that sort of thing. Really—a long time ago. A couple of decades ago."

But the woman only flashed her friendly grin. "Isn't it great when you renew an acquaintance with someone you have that kind of history with?"

That kind of history? Annie wondered. That wasn't much history. "But we don't know each other as adults. Not at all."

Virginia laughed. "Bet that'll be the fun part. Now,

you call me if you need me," she said, moving toward her car. "And thanks for the brownies! My husband will be as thrilled as I am!"

"Sure," Annie said. "Of course."

Virginia paused at her car door. "Annie, if you need anything other than puppy care, don't hesitate to call on me."

"Thanks," she said.

It wasn't long after Annie had spoken to Virginia and let herself into Nate's house that he came home. She heard his truck enter the garage, and when he walked in the door to the kitchen, his face lit up. "Hey," he said. "I thought I'd beat you here."

"Just got here," she said. "And something smells good."

"I just hope it also tastes good. I admit, Virginia gave me a hand."

"No shame in that, Nate." Then she smiled at him. Standing in the kitchen like that, waiting as he walked in the door after work, felt very nice. And then she told herself not to fantasize. Just one day at a time.

They fed the puppies and while a roast simmered in the Crock-Pot, complete with potatoes, carrots, onions and whole mushrooms, they let the puppies loose in the family room. They sat on the floor with them, a roll of paper towels handy, and laughed themselves stupid trying to keep track of the little animals, which escaped under the sofa, down the hall, behind furniture. They kept grabbing the puppies, counting, losing count, temporarily misplacing one. Nate estimated they were just over four weeks old because they were starting to bark, and every time one did, he or she fell over. It was better than television for entertainment.

After the puppies were put away again, dinner eaten, dishes cleaned up, Annie made noises about leaving, and Nate talked her into sitting down in the family room. "It's early," he said. "Let's just turn on the TV for a while."

She plopped onto the couch. "Oh, God," she said weakly. "Don't let me get comfortable. I really have to go home. You have no idea how early I start my day."

"Oh, really?" he asked. "Do you have eight whiny, hungry puppies in your laundry room? I start pretty early myself. Besides, I want you comfortable. This is such a great make-out couch."

"How do you know that?" she asked.

He shrugged like it was a stupid question. "I've made out on it."

"You said you'd be a gentleman!"

"Annie, you just have to try me out—I'm going to be very gentlemanly about it. Come on, don't make me beg."

She grinned at him. "Beg," she said. "I think that's what it's going to take."

He got an evil look in his eye and said, "Come here." He snaked his fingers under her belt and tugged, pulling her down into the soft sofa cushions. "Let's put a little flush on your cheeks."

The next night Annie took eight lengths of ribbon in eight different colors to Nate's house. They tied the ribbons around the puppies' necks, so they could be identifiable. They weighed them, made a chart, had dinner—and Nathaniel was more than happy to put a flush on her cheeks again.

Night after night, she fed Ahab right after work so she'd be free to—ahem—help with the puppies. And talk and play and kiss. The kissing quickly became her favorite part. Greedy for that, she trusted Pam to hold the shop open two nights a week and a half day on Monday. In exchange for that, Annie insisted Pam take a little comp time to get her own Christmas baking and shopping done; she came in late a few days to compensate.

There was more contributing to that flush of happiness on Annie's cheeks than just the kissing. Minor though it might seem, getting to know him when he had his shirt pulled out of his jeans and his boots off seemed so much more than casual. Of course her boots were off, also, and while they necked, their feet intertwined and they wiggled their toes. They wiggled against each other, too. It was delicious.

When they were feeding or cleaning up after puppies, preparing a meal together, they were also getting to know each other. Annie had never really thought about it before, but that was what courtship was all about— figuring out if you had enough in common after the spark of desire to sustain a real relationship.

Nathaniel had wanted to work with Thoroughbreds since he was a kid. He owned a couple of retired racehorses, good for riding. "One good stud can set you up for a great side business," he said. The initial investment, however, could be major. "In the next year or two, I'm going to invest. See what I can do."

"Why not show horses?" she asked.

"That's good, too, but I like the races."

"I love horses," she said. "You knew that. But did you know this? I've competed in dressage events all over the state. When I was younger, of course. Eventually it became too expensive for me. The best training was never in my neighborhood and the biggest competitions, including for the Olympics, were out of my reach. But if I could ever do anything, I would teach beginner dressage. Maybe even intermediate."

She told him she had thought about inviting him out to the farm to meet her parents and horses, but realized he already knew them. He knew them before he knew her, in fact. So she invited him to see her little Fortuna house and she made him dinner there. "I don't have a great make-out couch, however," she warned him.

"Doesn't matter anymore," he said. "I needed that couch to get you going, but now that you're all warmed up, we can do it anywhere. The floor, the chair, against the wall, the car…"

"I was so right about you. You're just arrogant."

He was also sentimental. Nathaniel was charmed by her two-bedroom house with a detached garage. The decorating was not prissy like a little dollhouse, but dominated by strong colors and leather furniture. The best part was, she had it completely decorated for Christmas, a garland over the hearth, lights up on the outside eaves. She had drizzled glitter on her huge poinsettia, had a Christmas cactus as big as a hydrangea bush, lots of what his mother had always called gewgaws. Ribbons, candles, potpourris, a Santa collection and, of course, a tree. A real tree, decorated to match the house—in burgundy, green, cream and gold. "And you're not even spending Christmas at home," he said.

"But I live here," she reminded him.

"It just doesn't make sense for me to put up decorations," he said. "Mother left a ton of them in the garage cabinets, but I'm leaving before Christmas. And I didn't think anyone would be around to see them."

"I do it for myself," she said. "I'm having holidays, too. I'll spend nights here since it gets so crowded at the farm. In years past, I've been known to loan the house to one of the brothers and sisters-in-law and kids and just take the couch. Brad brings an RV, which the teenage boys pretty much commandeer. During summer visits, the kids stake out the barn and front porch."

"Sounds like fun. I think I would have liked that, growing up," he said. "When they all get here, will you let me meet them? Or re-meet them? I haven't seen the boys since junior high."

"Sure, but you have to be prepared."

"For what?"

"They're going to treat you like you're my boyfriend."

He smiled and pulled her against him. "What makes you think I'd have a problem with that?"

"I don't think we're in that place," she informed him. "I think we just eat, talk, take care of puppies and kiss."

"Annie," he said as if disappointed. "What do you think a boyfriend is?"

"Um, I never really…"

"Tomorrow is Sunday, your day at the farm with your folks," he said. "Get done with whatever it is you do by early afternoon. Come for a ride with me. Let me show you my spread—it's so peaceful in the snow. Bring a change of clothes so you can freshen up before we have dinner."

"I can do that," she said. "I'd like that."

* * *

Annie had seen herself as plain and sturdy, until she'd been under the lips and hands of Nathaniel Jensen, because he was so much more than she'd ever reckoned with. Handsome, smart, funny, compassionate, independent, strong, sexy—the list was endless. And he made her feel like so much more than a solid, dependable farm girl. When he kissed her, dared to touch her a bit more intimately than she invited, pulled his hands back when she said *not yet,* she felt sexy and pretty and adored. This was a man she looked forward to exploring, and she was taking him in slowly, with such pleasure.

So she told Rose she had a date to go riding with the vet and was, of course, excitedly excused from Sunday baking and dinner at the farm. "Please don't get all worked up," Annie told her mother. "This isn't anything special. We've become friends on account of those puppies."

"Right," Rose said. "Still, could you wear a little color to bring out your hair and eyes?"

"I said, take it easy," Annie stressed. "And don't mention it to anyone. I don't want to be the talk of the county the way that skinny Hollywood woman was."

But Annie wasn't taking it lightly—she was almost sizzling with pleasure. And she tried dressing up a little more. For riding, she wore her best jeans, newest boots and oldest denim jacket over a red turtleneck sweater. She added a black scarf. She brought along attractive slacks and high-heeled boots with a silk blouse and her best suede blazer to wear for dinner afterward. They talked about horses while they rode two of Nate's favorite mounts, a couple of valuable, albeit retired, Thoroughbreds, disciplined and with just the right amount of spirit. The conversation about breeding, training, racing and showing horses was so stimulating she could almost forget for a while that she was trying not to fall in love with him.

"I'm not around horse people enough anymore," she said. "When I was riding in competition as a girl, that was enough to keep me occupied twenty-four hours a day. No wonder I didn't have fun in college—I wasn't riding."

"You're good on a horse," he said. "You should ride every day. So should I—it's the best part of what I do."

They rode into the foothills behind Nate's stables along a trail that, although covered by a layer of snow, had been well used. The trees rose high above them and the sun was lowering in the afternoon sky. They talked about growing up as the youngest in their families, and the only one of their gender. While Annie's brothers treated her like a football, Nathaniel's older sisters played with him as if he were a baby doll they could dress up at will. "It's amazing I'm not weirder than I am," he said. "The next oldest is Patricia, who's thirty-seven. Then Susan, and the oldest is Christina— one every two years. My parents had decided to quit while they were ahead and then, bingo." He grinned. "Me. I upset the balance in a big way."

"I think a similar thing happened at the farm," she said. "The boys are thirty-three, thirty-four and thirty-seven. Then I came along and upset the bedroom situation. My parents decided I had to have my own, which left one for the boys. And then I raised a bull—did I mention he won a blue ribbon?"

"Several times, I believe."

"We actually needed him. We had a couple of old

bulls who just couldn't step up to the plate anymore, y'know? But Erasmus was Ready Freddy. I'm real proud of that old bull." She smiled. "My brothers had their shot at raising animals and they did all right, but Erasmus was the blue-ribbon baby. I blew my brothers out of the 4-H water with that guy." She sighed wistfully. "I think having a daughter was harder on my dad and brothers than being the only girl was on me. And being the only girl wasn't easy. They were ruthless."

"Yet protective?" he asked.

"It's an uncomfortable place sometimes, to be tossed around like a beanbag and hovered over like a china doll."

"Did they make it hard on your boyfriends?" he asked.

"There weren't very many boyfriends," she said.

"I don't believe you," he replied with a grin. "You're lying to make me feel better."

So she told him about Ed. She hadn't planned to, but this was a perfect segue to explaining that she might have an issue or two with trust. Not only had the man in the only really serious relationship of her adult life cheated on her, horribly, but she had never had a clue. That bothered her. After it was over, it was so obvious, but while it was going on, she was oblivious. Not good.

They were headed back toward the stables when she told him. She expected him to be sympathetic and sweet. Instead, he was fascinated. "Are you *serious?* He had about three women going at once? Scattered around? Telling each one he was in love with only her? Really?"

"Really," she said, annoyed.

"How in the world did he manage that?" Nate asked.

"Well, a lot of phone calls while he was working. He talked to each one of us every day, sometimes several times a day. But with very few exceptions, we were assigned certain nights. We thought those were the days he didn't have to leave town. I should have known where I stood in the line. I was getting Mondays and Tuesdays. The woman he decided was the real one in his life was getting the weekends—Saturdays and Sundays. She dumped him, of course, when she discovered Ms. Wednesdays, Thursdays and Fridays. Three days a week must be the trump, huh?"

"Holy cow," Nate said. "He didn't even need a house or apartment! He had all his nights covered!"

"You know, I'm not impressed by his ability to pull it off."

"Of course you're not," Nate said. "But if you just think about it, he had quite a scam going. Did he take you lots of places? Buy you nice things?"

"He couldn't do either," she explained. "First of all, he couldn't risk being seen out and about with a woman, since one of the other women or their friends might run into him. So he said he was so tired, and after a week of being on the road and eating in restaurants, he enjoyed staying home."

"Where you could cook for him," Nate stated.

She pursed her lips, narrowed her eyes and nodded. "He did buy me a hot-water heater when mine went out," she admitted. "He might've needed that hot shower," she muttered.

"The man's a genius," Nate said. Then upon studying her face, he said, "Oh, he's a bastard, but you have to give him some credit for all the planning and subterfuge that—"

"I give him no credit," she said harshly.

He grabbed her hand then, pulled her closer and said, "Of course not. No credit. He should be killed. But I'm glad he didn't choose you. What if he'd chosen you? Can you imagine? We'd never meet and fall in love!"

She was so stunned that she pulled back on the reins and stopped her horse. "Are we in love?" she asked.

"I don't know about you, but I'm just getting started here—there's lots of potential. And he doesn't deserve you. I, however, deserve you. And will take you anywhere you want. And I'm going to hold your hand the whole time. I'll feed you cookies and kiss your neck in public."

"People will think I'm your girlfriend."

"That's what I want people to think. I'm going to start right away. We're going to go out. We'll drive into town to look at Christmas decorations, go to Virgin River to check out the tree and have some of Preacher's dinner, and then I'm going to take you to a nice restaurant on the weekend. And anything else you feel like doing."

"Why?" she asked.

"I want everyone to know you're with me. I want everyone to know you're not Sundays and Mondays—you're every day."

Again she pulled back on the reins and stopped her horse. "What's sexier than a string bikini, Nathaniel?"

"Are you kidding me?" He reined in beside her. His voice grew quiet and serious. He rubbed a knuckle down her cheek, over her jaw, gazing into her dark eyes. "Denim turns me on. Long legs in jeans and boots astride a big horse, making him dance to subtle commands. A rough work shirt under a down vest, feeding a newborn foal with a bottle because the mare isn't responding." He threaded his fingers into her hair and said, "Silk, instead of cotton candy. A fire on a cold, snowy night. A woman in my arms, soft and content, happy with the same things that make me happy. Help making homemade pizza—that turns me on. A woman who knows how to deliver a calf when there's trouble—that blows my horn. A woman who can muck out a stall and then fall into the fresh hay and let me fall right on top of her. I'd like to try that real soon."

Her eyes clouded a bit. "Are you just leading me on? Because when Ed pulled his trick, my brothers wanted to kill him, but I wouldn't let them. You? If you're lying, I'm going to let them. You'll suffer before you die."

"I'm not lying, Annie. And you know it."

"Well, okay, then answer this—if you like me, why haven't you liked someone before me? Because these hills are full of girls just like me—sturdy farm girls who have pulled their share of foals from the dams, fed them and kept them warm and—"

"No, there aren't," he said. "I've been looking. Just like you, I haven't had a whole lot of dates because there really wasn't anyone like you. You're one of a kind, Annie McKenzie. I'm sorry you don't seem to know that. But now that I've found you, we need to date… and a whole lot more."

"Be warned," she said. "I'm not casual about this stuff."

"Me, neither," he said.

After they put up the horses' tack and brushed them down, when it was time to change for dinner, he suggested they share a shower.

"I don't think so, Nate. Not yet," she said. "Does my door lock?" And he laughed at her.

On the way to Arcata they enjoyed the multicolored Christmas lights all along the coastal towns and up into the mountains. The Arcata square was decorated with lights, lit-up trees and a life-size nativity scene. Many of the shop windows were also decorated and filled with Christmas ornaments, gaily dressed mannequins and animated toys. Just as he'd promised, he held her hand everywhere they went. He had chosen an Italian restaurant on the square, and as it happened, it was one of her favorites. It boasted homemade pasta, robust red wine and excellent tiramisu.

"When are your brothers and their families arriving?" he asked over dinner.

"Tomorrow," she said. "By the way, you're invited to dinner. Please be cool around my brothers and don't give anything away. They haven't grown up at all since you knew them, despite the fact they have sons of their own."

"I'll be cool, all right," he promised. "Don't you worry." And then he grinned.

Five

It was a successful date, proved by the way they were in each other's arms, kissing deeply, before they were even in his house. It was still early enough to get in a good, long session of kissing on that soft, deep, inviting couch, and they fell on it together, taking turns helping each other out of boots and jackets without hardly breaking the kiss. Within moments they were in their favorite position on that great sofa, lined up against each other, exploring the inner softness of their mouths. Her body grew predictably supple and soft while his grew more urgent and hard.

Nathaniel whispered, "Annie. Come to my bed."

And she said, "No."

"No?" he answered weakly. "Annie, you don't mean that."

"I do mean it. No."

"But you kiss me like you're ready. Why not?"

She pushed herself up on the couch just slightly so she could look at his eyes. "We've only known each other three weeks, for starters."

"I've kind of known you my whole life, even if I

haven't known you since you got your braces off. But I've known you *intensely* for three weeks."

"We knew each other superficially for one week and intensely for the next two weeks. I might require a little more than that."

"Why?"

"Because I just broke up with Ed. Six months ago. It isn't that long."

"It's forever," he said. "I should have made you forget he ever existed by now."

"I think in another couple of weeks, I will have forgotten. And I'd kind of like to know how you feel after you've had your chance to lie on the beach surrounded by beautiful bodies in very small bathing suits."

"Oh, that. Listen, that's not even part of the equation," he said. "Really. That trip has nothing to do with how I feel."

"It has to do with how *I* feel," she said.

"Annie, if I hadn't made arrangements for this vacation long before I met you, I sure wouldn't plan it now. And it was a lot more than wanting to be lost in bikinis, believe me. It was a very convenient, very convincing plan, so I wouldn't find myself held hostage on a cruise ship with all my sisters and their kids. I explained—my brothers-in-law are great, but when their wives are around…"

"They have to act like husbands and fathers?"

"As opposed to regular guys," he clarified with a nod. "We've been on a couple of fishing trips together and I'm telling you, these guys are the best. They *are* my brothers. But when my sisters and the kids are around…"

"Husbands and fathers," she said helpfully again.

"But I'm not," he said. "I'm bored out of my mind. The only reprieve I get is a brandy and cigar with my dad and a conversation about veterinary medicine. Come on, don't you feel sorry for me? It's murder."

"So, you're not looking forward to seeing all your old buds?" she asked.

"That? Sure, that'll be great. We used to study together several nights a week. And then after graduation, we went off in all directions. This was a great idea Jerry had, but I can think of things I'd rather do." He lifted one eyebrow and grinned lasciviously.

She laughed at him. "Still, I'm not ready. Not till after your Club Med vacation."

"It's not Club Med, I told you. Are you waiting for me to say I love you, because if you're waiting for that, I—"

She put a finger to his lips and shushed him. "Don't go out on a limb here, Nathaniel."

"I'll call the travel agent in the morning and get you a ticket," he said. "Come with me."

She laughed, actually pleased by the offer. "My goodness, you'll go to a lot of trouble and expense for sex."

"For *you*," he clarified. "Not just for sex, for *you*."

"I am kind of impressed, but no thank you."

"Why not?"

"Ordinarily, if it were another time of year, I would, but not this time. Plus, I don't get to be with the whole family that often. The boys have it worked out that they do either Thanksgiving or Christmas with our side, the other holiday with their wives' side. So it's been a couple of years since we've all done Christmas together and I love that. My mom and I knock ourselves out to make it great."

He kissed her deeply. He pressed her down into the sofa with his body and held her hands at her sides, entwining his fingers with hers. "How about if I decide not to go on that vacation?"

"That you've paid for? To see your old best friends from school? Don't be ridiculous."

"Then come with me."

"No."

"Then I won't go," he said.

"You have to go. This is important, Nathaniel. You should get away, broaden your horizons. You've probably forgotten how much you miss your friends, how much you'd like to see a hundred tiny bikinis on perfect women. You have to go. I'm kind of interested in what you'll be like when you come back."

He thought about this for a few seconds. "Okay, then," he whispered. "A compromise."

"Hmm?"

"I'll go to the stupid beach without you, my virtuous girlfriend, you'll have Christmas with your family, and tonight you come to my bed."

She laughed. "No. Not till you've passed your time with the bikinis. And the women vets you used to date. Are they pretty?"

"Tina and Cindy? Oh, yeah, very pretty, but like I said, we were better as study partners. Honey, I've completely lost interest in bikinis. Unless you want to put one on for me just for fun."

"I don't know that that will ever happen."

"Annie, I'm not interested in bikinis. Not now. I'm only interested in you. Hey! This doesn't have anything to do with skinny Susanna, does it? Because I'm not all weirded out by Ed, who's really much stranger than Susanna."

She shook her head. "The only thing about Susanna that I still have to get over is that she was beautiful, feminine, small—except for her apparently exceptional boobs—and fancy, while I'm flat-footed and can cut the head off a chicken. But I'm working on that."

"They weren't real," he said. "She bought herself a pair for her twenty-first birthday. I'd much rather touch smaller real ones."

She kissed him, a short one on the lips. "Well, Nathaniel, if this works out, I like your chances." Then she grinned at him.

He was quiet for a moment and his eyes were serious, burning into hers. "You know, if I hadn't already paid for the whole damn thing, I'd cancel that trip. It's not what I want right now."

"Hey, I want you to go, and you'll have a good time. I'm not really worried about the bikinis. Not that much."

He pressed himself against her, proof that he was still all turned on. "It turns out three weeks is enough time for me," he said. "I'd rather just not go."

She put a hand against his cheek and smiled at him. "Even a grand gesture like that wouldn't get you lucky tonight."

He shook his head. "I don't want to be away from you for ten days. I barely found you. What if stupid Ed comes around and somehow proves to you that he's worth another chance?"

"Can't happen," she said. "I hardly remember what he looks like. I'll be right here when you get back."

"What if I get so lonely and distraught I make love

to some big-breasted nymphomaniac while I'm down there and come back to you all innocent, lying about it, just to teach you a terrible lesson?"

"I'd know."

"You didn't know with Ed," he reminded her.

"I know. I've been thinking about that a lot because it's been a real issue with me, that somehow I didn't know. I think Ed wasn't that important to me, or I would have been upset we had so little time together, and I wasn't. Wouldn't I have known something was *off* if he'd meant more to me? I don't think I cared as much as I wanted to. Lord, I think I would have married him even knowing he'd only spend two nights a week with me." She took a breath. "Maybe I would've married him *because* he'd only spend two nights a week with me." She ran her fingernails through the hair at Nate's temple. "But much as I fight it, Nathaniel, it's different with you." Then she smiled.

"In only three weeks?" he asked softly.

She was shaking her head. "It didn't take three whole weeks."

He took a breath, then groaned deeply just before he covered her mouth in a deep, hot, wet kiss that went on and on and on. When he finally lifted his lips from hers, he said, "Okay. We'll do this your way. We'll wait until you're ready. And when it's over and we're together forever, don't think you can boss me around like this."

"You've got a deal," she said, laughing.

Nathaniel called Annie twice before noon on Monday. First he wanted to know if there was anything he could bring to the farm. "I think we're throwing a couple of big pans of lasagna in the oven for dinner, and

Mom is busy making bread. How about bringing some good red wine?"

The next time he called, he said, "I know you work on Tuesday. I'm leaving Tuesday afternoon. So tonight, if I pass the brother test, will you come home with me for just a little while?"

"For just a little while. And don't try that 'I'm going into battle and you have to show your love before I leave' trick. Okay?"

And he laughed.

That was the best part about Annie—her sense of humor. No, he thought—it was her beauty. Her dark red hair, her creamy, freckled complexion, her deep brown eyes. But then a smile came to his lips as he recalled how good she was on a horse. An accomplished equestrienne. And while she would not find the term *sturdy* at all complimentary, he admired that about her. Fortitude had always appealed to him. Sometimes when he was holding her, he felt like he was clinging to her as if she anchored him to the ground. She had no idea how unattractive flighty, timid, weak women were to him. Did such women make some men feel strong and capable? Because for Nathaniel, to be chosen by a woman of strength and confidence met needs he didn't even know he had.

He had calls to make, ranches to visit, patients to see, inoculations to administer, a couple of cows who had a fungus to look in on, breeding animals who would deliver early in the year to check. He phoned the vet from Eureka who would cover for him while he was away, paid a visit to a local winery to select a few bottles of good red and finally made his way to the McKenzie farm.

When he pulled in, the place almost resembled a fair in progress. Not one but two RVs were parked near the back of the house, which probably eliminated the need to borrow Annie's house for the family. There were also trucks and snowmobiles on trailers. A bunch of cross-country skis leaned up against the back porch. The McKenzies were here to play. Kids ran around while several sat on the top rail of the corral. Inside the corral, Annie had a couple of young children mounted on her horses. She held the reins and led them around the corral while they held the saddle pommels. Four men— her brothers and father—leaned on the rail, watching.

Nate wandered up to the fence and leaned his forearms on the top rail with the rest of them. "So," he said. "I'm here for the inspection."

The man next to him turned and his mouth split into a huge grin. "Hey, man," Beau McKenzie said. "I heard a rumor you were dating my sister. Good to see you, buddy." He stuck out his hand. "This true? You and Annie? Because I can tell you things that will give you ultimate control over her!"

"Nathaniel Jensen," the next man said. Brad McKenzie stuck out his hand. "I don't think I've seen you in twenty years! You finally made it over five foot six, good for you."

"Yeah, and beat the acne." Nate laughed. "How you doing, pal?"

"Jim, any chance you remember this clown?" Beau asked his oldest brother.

"I just remember this squirt from football," Jim McKenzie said, sticking out a hand. "Couldn't tackle worth shit, but you sure could run."

"I had to run," Nate said. "If anyone had caught me, I'd be dead. I was the smallest kid on the team."

"You take steroids or something? You caught up."

"Nah, I just got old like the rest of you," he said. "Thanks for letting me invade the family party. Annie's been looking forward to it so much."

"This is true, then?" Beau asked, Brad and Jim and even Hank looking on with rather intense gazes.

What had she said? That he'd have to be cool? Maybe she expected him to joke around the way they did? One side of his mouth tilted up in a sly smile. He supposed it wasn't cool, but could they beat him up for being honest? "She knocks me out," he said. "Where have you been hiding her? I didn't even know she was here! I bumped into her in a bar!"

"That's our Annie," Beau said. "Out tying one on."

Nate laughed again. "Actually, she rescued eight orphaned puppies. Mostly border collie, we think. Cute as the devil. How many you want?"

Beau put a hand on his shoulder. "Pass on the puppies, my friend. But we got beer, Nathaniel. And seriously, we can give you stuff on her that will give you years worth of control. Power. Mastery. Don't we, guys?"

"We do," said Brad.

"Indeedy," said Jim.

It was an amazing day for Nathaniel, though not exactly a brand-new experience. The venue was a little smaller and more crowded than his family gatherings, but the family interaction was pretty much the same as in his family. The men got a little too loud, the kids ran wild and had to be rounded up several times, the women had a little tiff about kitchen things like whether the bread should have garlic butter or not and whether the salad should be dressed or not. There was a lot of furniture moving to accommodate a dinner for seventeen. They needed the dining-room table extended, and two card tables. The youngest child present at dinner was three and the oldest fourteen, and they sat at the kid table, as it was known in both the Jensen and McKenzie households. Nathaniel felt at once a special guest and right at home.

The McKenzie boys had married well; their wives were attractive, fun, energetic, and there was a lot of family rapport—which always helped. The kids were mostly well behaved, just a couple of small problems that the mothers foisted off on the fathers. Mrs. McKenzie fussed over Nate in a welcoming fashion, maybe a hopeful fashion, showing her approval. Mr. McKenzie, whom Nate had only known as Hank for the couple of years he'd been practicing here, handed Nate his jacket and took him out to the front porch during the after-dinner cleanup. Hank gave him a cigar. None of the brothers joined them, so Nate knew this was the father-and-man-in-his-daughter's-life talk.

Hank lit Nate's cigar. "I don't have a whole lot to say about this. Always got along with you just fine, so I don't have any basic complaint," Hank said.

"That's good," Nate said, puffing. Coughing. He smoked about a cigar a year and never remembered to take it easy.

"Just a couple of things I want to say."

"I'm ready."

"I like Annie," her father said. "She's good people." He puffed. "Now that might not seem like much of a recommendation, but in my book, it's the best there is. She's just plain good. She'd never in a million years hurt a soul. But don't get lazy on her, because she's nice but she's tough. She can hold her own if there's some injustice, and she's not afraid of a fight. And smart? She could've run this dairy farm single-handed, she's that smart. That strong-willed. I offered it to her, too. Boys didn't want it, so I said, 'Annie, you could do it just fine, even if I dropped dead tomorrow,' and she said, 'Dad, if I stick myself out here with the cows, I'll never leave and never do anything else and I think maybe there's got to be more to my life. At least more people in my life.' That's what she said. So that's how it was. She bought that beauty shop and I sold off the Holsteins. You better be nice to her."

"Yes, sir," he said.

"Don't even think about hurting her, Nathaniel. I can handle about anything but seeing my girl, who I admire and respect, hurt."

"I promise," Nate said.

"Because if you do…"

"You'll shoot me?" Nate asked.

"Aw, hell, why would I do that? I'm not a violent man. I'll just spread the word that as a vet, you're not worth a crap."

Nate couldn't help it, he burst out laughing.

"The boys, though," Hank went on, "they're a tad violent. When it comes to Annie. So be nice."

Nate hadn't had a lot of dates in the past couple of years, but in the past ten he'd had quite a few. When he was tending Thoroughbreds in Kentucky and then in Los Angeles County, plenty of women were attracted to him. Socialites, daughters of rich breeders, women he'd met at parties, on ranches, at races. He'd never been talked to by a father, however. Not even Susanna's, not even when he'd given her a rock and carted her up to Humboldt County with the misguided notion of marrying her.

As father talks went, Hank's hadn't been stunning. But Nate liked it. It made him feel like a man with a job to do.

"It's probably way too early to talk about intentions," Hank said.

"No, sir, it's not," Nate replied. "I like Annie even more than you do. It's my intention to treat her very well while we're dating, and I think it might be a good match for both of us. I also think we might have a future, me and Annie. But you know what? She's a smart, stubborn girl—it's going to be up to her."

"Yeah, I reckon," Hank said.

"So. Could you at least wish me luck?" Nathaniel asked.

"You bet," Hank said, sticking out his hand. "Best of luck there, Nathaniel. Try not to screw this up."

"You bet, sir. Nice cigar, by the way."

"Yeah, not bad, huh? Have no idea where I got 'em. One of the boys, probably."

Nate wasn't sure, but he didn't think his own father had ever had one of these talks with his brothers-in-law or he would've heard about it. But right there, right then, he decided that if he ever had a daughter, he was going to do that. It was a good idea—take the young man aside, expound on the girl's wonderful qualities, threaten his life a little. It had merit.

A few minutes later Beau joined them, clipping off the tip of a cigar. Then Brad, then Jim. Nate leaned close to Beau's ear. "How'd you know he was done with me?" Nate asked.

"If he wasn't done, you weren't going to work out," Beau said with a shrug.

"Just out of curiosity," Nate asked, "has he had many of these talks?"

"I think you're the first."

"What about that loser, Ed?"

"Ah, Ed. I don't think Annie brought him around all that much. From what we heard, he was very busy. I met him once, I think, and not on a holiday. He did sell a couple of things to my dad, though. Farm things. Before he and Annie hooked up. Dad? We didn't like Ed much, did we?"

Hank just snorted and said something derisive under his breath.

"Just out of curiosity, why didn't you like him?" Nate asked.

"He swindled me on a hay baler," Hank said. "Said he had the best price in the county. Took me about a month to find all kinds of better deals."

"So, it didn't have anything to do with how he treated her?" Nate asked.

"Son, you really think if a man will swindle you on a hay baler, you can trust him with your kin?"

"I hadn't ever thought about it that way."

"I can't imagine another way to think about it," Hank said.

"Wow," Nate said, feeling more than a little privileged. *Yeah,* he thought. *I'm picking out my daughter's guy and giving him a talking-to.*

When the cigars were finished, the men wandered back inside where the women were sitting in the kitchen with coffee. Nate paused in the doorway and signaled Annie. "Got a second?" he asked her. When she stood before him, he said, "I'm going to get a head start. Spend as much time as you want with the family. I'll go home and make sure the puppies are fed and watered and their bedding is dry."

"I can come now."

"No, stay. I'll get the puppy chores done and when you get there, I'll have more time with you. By the way, are we all set on their care while I'm gone? We talked about it a little…."

"Not to worry, Nate. Virginia and I worked out the details. We're going to share the load and they'll be looked after. And if it's okay with you, I'll make sure the adopted ones are delivered on Christmas Eve. I think Pam from the shop is going to take one, which brings us down to three left to place. I'll make sure they're okay."

"Tell anyone you take a pup to that if they bring 'em by in a couple of weeks, I'll check them over and give them shots, free of charge."

"That's nice, Nathaniel."

"Then I'll see you in a little while," he said, giving her a platonic peck on the cheek. "Thank you, Mrs. McKenzie," he said to Rose. "Nice meeting you all."

"Have a great trip, Nate," someone said.

"Good meeting you."

"Travel safe."

He shook the men's hands and was on his way.

Two thoughts occupied him as he drove home. He couldn't wait to get his arms around Annie. And he didn't want to be away from her for ten days. He didn't think a beach full of naked women could make him more inclined to leave right now. But he had packed his bags earlier, not leaving it to the last minute, and he would get this over with. Then, as far as he was concerned, it was full steam ahead with her. And she'd better not give him the slip, either. He was thirty-two and had had plenty of girlfriends, but he couldn't remember ever wanting a woman like he wanted this one. Heck, he wanted her whole family. He wanted to bring her into his. He wanted them to merge and grow.

He'd even been engaged without wanting all that. It was eerie.

He was barely home, the puppies slopping up their dinner, when the pager on his belt vibrated. He recognized the phone number of a horse breeder whose animals he took care of. His favorite patients, Thoroughbreds. This family was not nearby—they were over the county line in Mendocino.

He answered the call. One of their valuable broodmares was miscarrying, and she was all freaked out, kicking at the stable walls.

He disconnected the line, but he held the phone. He took a deep, disappointed breath before he dialed the McKenzie farm and asked for Annie.

"Nate? What's up?" she asked when she came on the line.

"You don't know how much I hate to do this. I have to go out on an emergency. There's a mare miscarrying, and the stable is in the next county. It could be complicated. It could be late."

"Don't worry about the time, Nate. See about the horse," she said.

"Honey, you shouldn't wait here for me. I might be tied up until very late. There's a chance I'll be out all night with just enough time to come home, clean up, get ready to leave. But, Annie, I won't leave without seeing you—worst case, I'll stop by your shop on my way out of town tomorrow."

"You don't have to do that, Nate. If you find yourself pressed for time, just give me a call."

"But I *do* have to," he said softly. "I can't leave without holding you, without kissing you goodbye."

"That's so sweet. But if it doesn't work out that way, I understand. Drive carefully. I hope everything is all right with the mare."

Despite Nate's warning that he might not make it home until very late, she went to his house anyway. She could hear in his voice his desire to spend a little time with her, and what did she have to keep her away? If he wasn't back by early morning, she'd feed the puppies and go home to shower and get ready for work.

She was inexplicably drawn to the master bedroom, though she had no real reason to go there. It was the sight of a couple of suitcases open on the floor, filled with clothing, that saddened her so deeply she felt a small ache in her heart. Oh, she was going to miss him so much! Disappointment filled her—she had looked forward to an hour or two of cuddling before she had to give him up for his ten-day adventure. Now it was probably not to be.

Suck it up, Annie, she said to herself. And with that, she shucked her jacket and went to make sure the puppies were taken care of. "Well, my little loves," she said to the box of squirming, jumping, yelping, vibrating puppies. "Ew," she said, taking a sniff. "Time for a refresh, I see." And she set about the task of giving her little charges clean fur and dry bedding. "Yeah, you're ready for new homes. You have to be about six weeks by now. Close enough, as far as I'm concerned."

Her puppy chores didn't take long. She wandered into the family room and sat on that comfy sofa. That lonely sofa. She hated to leave prematurely; she wanted to give him time to get home, to catch up with her. As she looked around the family room, it seemed so barren. At least compared to the farmhouse, which was full to the brim with food, decorations, people, laughter and happiness.

She turned on the fire to make it more welcoming for him, and then on a whim she went to the garage and looked through the storage cabinets that lined the walls of the three-port garage. She smiled to herself. Nathaniel's mother had certainly made it easy. One entire cabinet held boxes that were neatly labeled. She skipped the one that said "ornaments" but opened another. And another. And another.

She really only meant to bring a touch of Christmas into the house for Nate, even if it was only for one night, or just an early morning. First was a centerpiece for that long, oak kitchen table, then a couple of fat, glittery candles on a bed of artificial holly, which she put on the coffee table. She thought if she were decorating this house for real, there would be lots of fresh stuff and the smell of pine. And the aroma of hot chocolate and cookies.

She put her jacket on to go back into the garage and soon she had a garland for the mantel, stockings and brass stocking holders, and three-foot-tall nutcracker characters for a grouping in the corner. She found a large basket of red ceramic apples mixed with huge pinecones, a poinsettia with little twinkling lights. That gave her another idea, and she found some tiny tree lights in a box, which she brought in and used to adorn the house plants—a couple of tall ficus trees and a couple of lush philodendron and ivy. She tied thick, red velvet bows to the backs of the kitchen chairs.

A box labeled "Christmas dishes" was just too much to resist. Inside were some festive plates and cups. So she turned on the oven and poked around in the pantry, laughing to herself. Hadn't she said she wouldn't poke around? Well, Nathaniel obviously didn't do a lot of baking, and who knew how long that canister of flour had been there? And the brown sugar was like a brick. But he did have butter, sugar and M&M's. It took only thirty minutes to produce a plate of pseudo chocolate-chip cookies. She found chocolate-milk mix and fixed up a couple of cups with spoons in them, ready for filling. It was probably in her DNA—she covered the festive plate of cookies with plastic wrap.

"Christmas for a day," she said to herself, pleased.

She made sure all the boxes were stowed in the garage. Then she looked at the clock. Almost eleven, and she had to get up early for work. But it didn't take her a second to make her decision—a girl doesn't find a quality boyfriend every day. She turned down some lights in the house, took off her boots, reclined on the sofa in front of the fire with the throw over her legs and promptly fell asleep.

Six

Nate was physically tired and emotionally drained. By the time he reached the Bledsoe stables, the mare had miscarried a five-month foal and she was skittish. Frantic might be a better word. Indication was that the horse was sick, the cause of the miscarriage, though Nate had checked her over before she was bred and she'd been in good shape. Because he wasn't going to be around to follow up, he had called Dr. Conner, the Eureka vet. He tranquilized the mare to calm her, administered antibiotics, made sure the placenta was whole, and then transported the products of conception to Eureka so that Dr. Conner could follow up with a postmortem to try to determine the cause. Conner would probably choose to do an endometrial biopsy. Other horses in the stable would have to be examined immediately; Bledsoe had six breeding at the moment.

But that was not the hardest part. Not only was the mare valuable and the stud a champion, the owners' teenage daughter had raised this horse from a filly and it was her first foal. The girl was as distraught as the horse, and terrified her mare was going to die.

She wasn't going to die, but the jury was still out on whether she was a good broodmare. Some mystery problem or illness had taken its toll and caused her to drop the foal and suffer a considerable amount of bleeding. Time and follow-up would tell the story. But when Nate left the family, quite late at night, it looked as though the teenage girl was going to sleep in the stable with her horse.

Now that was something he could see Annie doing.

And to speak of the devil herself, when he pulled up to his house, it was dimly lit from inside and her truck was parked out front. The clock on the car console said two-fifteen. Lord, what was she doing? Half of him was so grateful he could burst, the other half wanted to spank her for staying up so late—he knew she had a long day in the shop ahead of her so that she could be closed the afternoon of the twenty-fourth and all day the twenty-fifth.

Annie, he had learned, was not afraid of hard work.

He entered the dimly lit house quietly. His first reaction was surprise, but pleasure quickly followed. On the breakfast bar a thick red candle flickered beside a plate of cookies and a couple of cups. There was chocolate powder in the cups, ready for hot milk to be added. Bows on the chairs, garlands strung around, table decorations, twinkling lights everywhere, and his girl, asleep in front of a fire. He chuckled to himself. Well, hadn't *she* been busy.

It was like really coming home. Holidays meant a lot to her. Her sense of love and family spilled over to everyone around her, and he felt so…embraced inside, like it was his first Christmas. He smiled to himself. In an important way, it was.

He took off his boots, belt and jacket in the kitchen. He blew out candles, turned off all but the twinkling tree lights and fireplace, and knelt down by the sofa, softly kissing her beautiful lips.

"Mmm," she murmured, half waking. "You're home. I must've fallen asleep."

"You were probably exhausted, digging through the storage," he said with humor in his voice.

"I'll put it all away before you get back," she whispered. "I should go, now you're home...."

"Are you crazy?" he asked. He slipped one arm under her knees, the other behind her back and stood with her in his arms. "We're going to get some sleep. It's almost morning, anyway. And this couch isn't going to do it. I want to hold you. I want to fall asleep with you in my arms. Now close your eyes and your mouth."

She hummed and snuggled closer to him. "Everything all right? With the mare?" she asked.

"It'll get sorted out. I'll tell you about it in the morning." He carried her to his bedroom and laid her gently on the bed. "Do you need the alarm?" he asked her. "I can set it for you."

"Nah. I haven't slept past seven in my life."

"Good," he said. He pulled back the comforter and crawled in, jeans and all, and she did the same. "Come close," he said. "All I want in life is to feel you against me. Mmm, just like that. Aaah, Annie, my Annie..."

Suddenly he knew that even as exhausted as he was, he wasn't going to sleep. He had a stunning thought— *this is what it feels like when you actually fall in love.* He'd thought that whole falling-in-love thing was some girl story that guys didn't experience. He was familiar with being attracted. Oh-ho, was he familiar with that!

And of course he had known desire in all sizes, from warm to boiling. Wanting a woman, yes, that was a fairly regular occurrence. But this was all those things mixed together and yet something completely different at the same time.

He wanted to be only with Annie; if he were allowed one friend for the rest of his life, he would choose her. He wanted to come home to the kind of warmth she could bring to a room. He wanted to crawl in beside her and feel the comfort of her body, which fit so perfectly against his. He didn't want to be away from her; he wanted her for life.

He began unbuttoning her blouse. In spite of the fact that she seemed to be asleep, he was undressing her, knowing he shouldn't. But then he felt her fingers working away at *his* shirt buttons and he sprang to life, hard and ready. His hands went to the snap on her jeans while hers worked at his. Like choreography, they were slipping each other's jeans down and off and he pulled her hard against him, his shorts to her dainties. "God," he said. "God, God, God."

She pulled away just enough to shrug out of her shirt and remove her socks. She left the panties for Nate to handle, which he did immediately. "Let me have these," he said, clutching them in his fist. "Let me keep these for the rest of my life. Can I?"

She laughed at him and tugged down his boxers. "Sure," she whispered against his lips. "And you can keep your underwear."

He moaned as if in pain, his hand finding a breast. "Why are you wearing a bra?" he asked.

"Because you've been undressing me for five seconds and haven't gotten to that yet?" she returned. She unsnapped the clasp and it fell apart, just in time for his lips on her breast. He rolled on top of her, probing. "Condom," she whispered. "Condom, Nate."

"Right," he said. "Got it." And he leaped out of bed, raced unceremoniously to the master bath, running back to the king-size bed with a packet in his hand, ripping it open as he went. He flopped on the bed and pulled her close. Then he froze. All motion stopped. Their thighs were pressed together, their lips straining toward each other, their hands pulling their bodies closer, and he said, "Annie? Are you ready for this?"

She didn't say anything and he couldn't see her face in the darkness of the room. She took his hand and captured the foil packet. She pulled his hand down between her legs where his fingers could answer his question.

He moved his hand up her inner thigh, opened her legs a bit, caressed her wonderfully wet folds. "Aaah," he said once more against her lips.

"Ready," she whispered. "Ready." And then she applied the protection.

"You know what, Annie?" he said. "Coming home to you, making love to you, it feels like the one thing I've always been ready for."

"Then let's not waste any more time," she said.

He fell asleep while still inside her, holding her close. Sometime in the night, they roused just enough to make love again. When he awoke in the morning, he was alone. There was a little puppy, whimpering, faint and distant.

He found her note in the kitchen:

Nate—you were so tired, you slept through puppy breakfast, which was noisy. I decided you should sleep. I want you to have the most wonderful time of your life on your trip. I'll take care of everything while you're gone and I'll put away the decorations. And thank you for last night. It was perfect. Love, Annie

He picked up the note and read it again and again. "It's awful hard to leave you, Annie," he whispered. "Especially at Christmas."

Nathaniel booked his flights to coordinate with the rest of the group—they were all meeting for breakfast in Miami. From there they would fly together to Nassau. He had to take a commuter from Santa Rosa to San Francisco. That meant a two-hour drive south to pick up the first leg of his trip. From San Francisco he would take a nonstop red-eye to Miami. He would be there in early morning. He'd have breakfast in the airport with his old gang. It brought to mind the breakfasts they'd had together after all-night study sessions, right before a big exam. Then they'd get to the Bahamas early in the day to begin their ten-day vacation.

He didn't mind driving, which was a good thing, since his practice had him running around the mountains and valleys of three counties looking after livestock. The drive from Humboldt County to Santa Rosa was beautiful and calm. But rather than enjoy the rolling hills and snow-covered pines and mountains, all he thought about was Annie.

Before he left Humboldt County, he had called her at her shop. "I'll be leaving in a couple of hours. Sure you want to let me go without you?" he had asked.

"This is your trip, Nate. Not mine," she said. "You

planned it, you've looked forward to it, you paid for it—now go and enjoy it. I have family things to do. And puppy things. When you get back all the decorations will be put away, the puppies will be distributed to their new homes and you'll be tanned and rested. And it will be a whole new year."

"I hear cell reception is terrible there, but I'll try to call you while I'm gone," he said. "I want to see if you have any regrets about turning down an all-expense-paid vacation. And there's a note for you on the kitchen counter—my hotel info. Call me if you need anything. Anything at all."

When he said that, he had been thinking, *Me. Call if you need me. Call me if you miss me.*

But Annie had laughed cheerfully. "Now, Nate, what are you going to do if I need something? Catch a flight home? You'll be on the other side of the country! And you'll be with your friends—a reunion, Nate. Now stop worrying about stuff you can't do anything about. Just have fun. Besides, I can manage just about anything."

A few weeks earlier Nathaniel had been looking forward to this vacation with such enthusiasm. He'd built a few fantasies about girls in bikinis and low-cut sundresses. He saw himself inviting a beautiful woman out to dinner; maybe he'd be taking some lovely young thing sailing. He envisioned staying up late with his buddies, laughing, drinking and smoking cigars. He figured he'd be needed to rub suntan lotion on a bare female back.

None of those mental images were working for him now. Now all he could think about was how long the next ten days were likely to be. He hoped he'd at least catch an impressive fish or two. That's what he'd like to take home to her—a big, mounted sailfish. Maybe they'd hang it over the bed and remember their first Christmas. And their last one apart.

Annie had laughed brightly while on the phone with Nate, but melancholy stole her laughter away the moment she hung up. She supposed it was a combination of being a little bit tired and sad that he'd be away. She'd been up late decorating his house and baking him those awful-tasting cookies; he just didn't have the right ingredients on hand, and what he had was far from fresh. Of course she hadn't slept much in his bed; he'd kept her busy. And so satisfied. He was such a wonderful lover, but instead of leaving her sated, it left her wanting more of him.

And then she had to get up very early—she had to go home, shower and dress for work and arrange the Christmas gift baskets for the girls in the shop.

She wondered if he had felt her lips press softly against his before she'd left him. Had he heard her say, "Goodbye, Nate. Be safe. Hurry home"? He hadn't stirred at all.

She had been happy to hold him close, warm him and put him to sleep. She wouldn't mind doing that every day for the rest of her life.

She knew her mood had plummeted and she didn't want anyone in the shop noticing, so she grabbed up the appointment book and walked to her small office at the back of the little shop. But sure enough, Pam followed her. Pam stood in the doorway, looking at her.

"Don't worry, Annie. He'll be thrilled to get home to you," Pam said.

"Sure. Of course. I didn't say anything otherwise, did I?"

"You didn't have to," Pam said. "You laughed and joked with him on the phone, but the second you hung up, you got real sober. Serious. Maybe a little worried."

"Do you think it was a mistake to let him go?" Annie asked.

"The time will fly by," Pam said. "It's nice to see you like this. You love him."

"I love him," she admitted. Because he was sensitive but also very confident and strong, she thought. He was a sucker for a bunch of puppies even though they were such a pain to take care of. He didn't even have to think twice about whether to be out till two in the morning because someone had a problem with an animal. The way Annie had been raised, she'd come to accept that people who cared for animals had a special kind of soul, a precious gift. You weren't likely to get much back from animals except a lick on the hand or maybe a good performance in a competition. And in her family's case—the animals provided milk and meat, their roof, their very beds and clothes, their land and legacy. She had been raised with deep respect for animals and the physicians who cared for them. Those gifted doctors were men and women who knew the meaning of unconditional love.

"I love him because he's tender and strong and smart," Annie said. She smiled sentimentally. "And he's so cute he makes my knees wobble. But, Pam, I didn't tell him. I tried to show him, but I didn't tell him."

Pam chuckled. "You'll have your chance very soon." Pam stepped really close to Annie and made her voice a whisper. "Sweetheart, you're beautiful and smart. And I bet you make his knees wobble, too."

She smiled at her friend. "Thank you, Pam. That's sweet. The sweetest part is it wasn't just a compliment—I know you meant it. Did I tell you he asked me to go with him?"

"Ah, no. You might've failed to mention that. And you weren't tempted?"

"Sure I was tempted. But it's his trip and I have family things going on. But after this, if he feels for me what I feel for him, it's the last time I'm letting him get that far away from me without him knowing how I feel."

Pam gave her a fake punch in the arm. "Good plan. I've worked with you for five years, Annie, since before you bought the franchise on this little shop. Have you ever been in love before?"

Annie let go a huff of laughter. "Don't be ridiculous—I'm twenty-eight. I've been in love plenty of times, starting with Dickie Saunders in the second grade."

But never like this, she thought. Nothing even close to this. She wanted to massage his temples when he was stressed or worried, wanted to curl into him and bring him comfort, wanted to trust him with every emotion she had. She'd go into battle for him if he needed that from her, or better still, laugh with him until they both cried. It would feel so good to stand at his side and help him with his work. Or argue with him for a while before making up—she would have to promise never to have PMS again and he would have to pledge not to be such a know-it-all. *Green as a bullfrog,* he'd called her. She'd never had a man in her life who could see right through her so fast, who could read her mind, feel her feelings.

Realizing she'd been off in kind of a daze, she refocused and looked at her friend. She shrugged.

"That's what I thought," Pam said with a smile.

Nathaniel was pressed up against the cold window of a packed 747 all the way from San Francisco to Miami. Over five hours of nighttime flying. Three or four times he got up and walked around the dimmed cabin. Normally he could sleep on long flights, but not on this one. When he arrived at his destination at 7:00 a.m. on the morning of Christmas Eve, he had almost an hour before meeting his friends for breakfast in a preselected restaurant in the international terminal.

By the time he got to the restaurant, Jerry, Ron, Cindy and Tina were there, surrounded by enough luggage to sink a cruise ship. Missing were Bob and Tom and their wives. Jerry spotted Nate first and called, "Hey, look who just dragged himself off the red-eye. You look like hell, man," he said, grinning, sticking out a hand. "Get this man a Bloody Mary!"

Nate shook hands, hugged, accepted the drink, complete with lemon wedge and celery stalk, and raised his glass. "Great to see you guys," he said. "We can't keep meeting like this."

"Beats not meeting at all." Jerry looked at his watch. "We have an hour and a half." He looked around and frowned. "Nathaniel, did you manage to get your luggage checked through?"

"Nah, I left it with a skycap."

There was some head shaking. "Always has been one jump ahead of us," Tina said.

"Thing is—I can't make it. Sorry, guys."

Confused stares answered him. "Um, don't look now,

buddy—but you're in Miami. Almost at Bahama Mama heaven."

Nate chuckled and took a sip of his Bloody Mary. "This was a good idea," he said of the drink. "I left my luggage at the airline counter with the skycap. They're working on a flight for me, but it looks bleak. Who would travel on Christmas Eve on purpose? Why are they booked solid? I'd never travel on Christmas Eve if I didn't have to, but I told them I'd take anything. I might end up eating my turkey dinner right here."

"What the hell…?"

"It's a woman," Nate said. He was shaking his head and laughing at himself. "I gotta get back to a woman."

Jerry clamped a hand on his shoulder. "Okay, let me guess, you got drunk on the plane…"

"Why didn't you just bring her?" Cindy asked.

"She couldn't come," Nate said. "She had all kinds of family stuff going on and she couldn't miss it. She's real close to her family—great family, too. So I said I'd stay home, but she said no to that. She said I should have my vacation. She insisted. And I let her."

"All right, bud, keep your head here. Give her a call, tell her you're miserable without her and you'll be home soon. Hell, get a flight out in two or three days if you still feel the same way."

"I have to go," Nate said. "I don't want to be sitting in a bar with you losers if they find a flight for me." He took another swallow of his drink. He stared at it. "Really, this was a good idea. So was the trip. Anyone game to try this next year? I shouldn't have any complications next year—that I can think of."

"Nathaniel, if she's the right one, she's not going anyplace," Jerry attempted.

He grinned. "That's the best part. She's not going anyplace. But you have no idea how much Christmas means to Annie. She's like the Christmas fairy." He chuckled. "Listen, I don't expect you to get this, but as much as I was looking forward to spending a few days with you guys, it hit me on the plane—I'm going to feel alone without her. I'm going to be with the best friends I've ever had, and I'm not going to have much fun, because she's not with me." He shook his head. "I know where I'm supposed to be right now, and I better get there."

"Nathaniel, this will pass," Ron said. "How long have you known this woman?"

"Oh, jeez—about three weeks. About three of the best weeks of my life. When you find the right one, you don't fly away and leave her wondering how you feel. See, Jerry, in case you ever find some brain-damaged female willing to throw her lot in with you, you'll want to remember this—you better not let her out of your sight and you better not leave her without telling her you love her. Got that?"

Jerry looked confused. "Isn't that why they invented florists? Don't you just dial up a big, expensive batch of flowers and—"

"Nathaniel, that is *so* sweet," Tina said. "I had no idea you were so sweet. Didn't we date once? Were you ever that sweet to me?"

With a laugh, Nate put down his drink, grabbed her, hugged her and gave her a kiss on the cheek. He gave his old pal Cindy a hug. He punched Jerry in the arm and gave Ron's hand a quick shake. "I'll be in touch. Have a good time on the beach. Thanks for the drink. Tell

Bob and Tom I'm sorry I missed them. Merry Christmas." And he turned and strode away.

After closing the shop on the twenty-third, Annie had gotten right out to Nate's house to take care of the puppies. She'd gone back after dinner at the farm to make sure they were fixed for the night and then she'd stayed a while, enjoying her stab at Christmas decorations. Virginia had been good enough to check on the puppies on the morning of the twenty-fourth, as she had to look after the horses anyway.

Annie had purchased five decorated hat boxes at the craft store, and on Christmas Eve she took one little pup—a female, Vixen—to work with her for Pam. Pam's mom would keep the puppy safe and warm until Christmas morning. They closed the shop at noon and Annie headed back to Nate's before going to the farm.

There was a long-standing tradition on Christmas Eve at the farm—Hank covered a hay wagon with fresh hay, hooked up Annie's horses and took the kids for a hayride while the women finished dinner. The winter sun was setting early, so they would have their hayride before dinner. The snow had begun to fall, so the wagon would have to stick to the farm roads. Seven kids, their dads and grandpa set out, singing and laughing.

And in the kitchen, the traditional prime rib was being prepared. In years past, it was their own beef, but now they had to buy it. From the kitchen window, Annie watched the hay wagon pull away from the house. Telling herself not to be moody, she briefly fantasized about sending Nate out with the kids and her dad and brothers. Well, there were years ahead for that.

Rose came up behind her and slipped her arms

around Annie's waist. "You can go with them if you want to," she murmured. "There is *more* than enough help in the kitchen. Too much, if you ask me!"

Annie laughed at her mom. "I'm staying in," she said. "After dinner I have puppies to deliver on behalf of Santa. We're down to three boys. I think after Christmas, when things are quieter at work, I'll advertise. And I'll call the shelters to see if anyone they consider good potential parents are looking for a puppy."

Rose used a finger to run Annie's hair behind her ear. "Are you a little down this year?" she asked quietly.

"I'm fine," she said, shaking her head.

"It's okay to miss him, especially over the holidays," Rose said. "I like Nathaniel. He seems like a good boy."

Boy, Annie thought, amused. She couldn't tell her mother that he was all man. More man than she'd experienced in her adult life. And she hoped he pestered her as much when he came home as before he left. "Let's get everything on the table, Mom. They'll be back and freezing before we know it."

Of course the kids didn't want the hayride to end until they were blue with cold. Hank pulled right up to the back of the house to let the kids off so their mothers could fuss over them, warming them. Then with the help of his sons they unhooked the horses, took them to the barn and brushed and fed them. By the time everyone was inside, the house was bursting with noise and the smells of food, along with the scent of hay and horses. Stories from the ride, punctuated by laughter, filled the house while the meat was carved and dish after dish of delicious food was carried to the tables, then passed around.

The hayride wasn't meant for pure enjoyment; it was

calculated to wear out the kids who might otherwise stay up half the night. After the main course and dessert, the women headed to the kitchen for cleanup and coffee, while Grandpa, Annie's brothers and the kids got out a variety of board games. That was when Annie took her leave. She had to go back to Nate's house, gather up her Christmas puppies and make some deliveries.

Bundled up and on the way to her truck, she wandered around the house to the back. The moon was so high and bright it lit up the farm. The weathered barn in rusty red stood quiet. She remembered when it was teeming with life—cows, horses, goats, chickens, not to mention people. Every single one of the McKenzie kids had had big parties at the farm. Her dad would dig a hole and fill it with hot coals to cook corn; hot dogs would be turned on the grill, and Rose would put out a huge bowl of potato salad and deviled eggs to die for. The kids who came to the farm from town would run wild through the pastures, barn and woods. They'd swing from the rafters of the barn on a rope and fall into a pile of hay, ride the horses, chase the goats. She could remember it like it was yesterday as she looked over the rolling hills and pastureland.

Someday, she thought, my own children and their friends will play here.

She climbed up on the hay wagon and lay down in the sweet hay, looking up at the sky. It was clear, black, speckled with stars. At the moment the house was throbbing with noise, but ordinarily it was so quiet in the country you could hear a leaf rustle a hundred yards away.

The sound of a car approaching caused her to sit up,

and she recognized the Dicksons' truck, their nearest neighbors. Another country custom—people dropped in on each other, bringing homemade treats and staying for at least a cup of coffee. Of course the McKenzies didn't go visiting when the family was home—there were too many of them. A second truck trundled along behind the Dicksons'—looked like the whole fam-damn-ly was coming over. She plopped back down on the hay, hoping to be invisible. Once they all got inside, she'd take off. She wasn't feeling sociable.

There was only one person she wanted to be with right now. She hugged herself and tried to pretend his arms were—

"Annie? You out here?" Beau called from the back porch.

Don't answer, she told herself.

"Annie!"

But her truck was parked out front. "I'm looking at the stars, but I'm leaving in a second. What?"

"I just wanted to know where you are!" he yelled back.

"Well, go away and leave me alone! You're scaring the stars!" And then more quietly she muttered, "Pest."

Seconds later she felt the wagon move, heard it squeak and a large body flopped down next to her in the hay.

"Aw, Beau, you jerk!" she nearly yelled. She sat straight up, plucked straw out of her hair with a gloved hand and looked at the body next to her. Not Beau. Nathaniel lay facedown in the hay beside her. "What are you doing here?" she asked in confusion.

He turned his head to one side. "I came back to sweep you off your feet, but I've been either flying or driving or hanging around airports so long that I'm too tired to roll over, much less sweep you anywhere. And I didn't get much sleep the night before I left, either." He grinned. "Thank you very much."

"You didn't go?" she asked.

"I went. I made it all the way to Miami."

"And came *back?*"

He yawned hugely. "I realized halfway there that I couldn't go to the Bahamas without you, but they wouldn't turn the plane around."

She was quiet for a second. "You've lost your mind."

"Tell me about it," he said. "What have you done to me?"

"Like this is *my* fault? That you're a lunatic?"

He yawned again. "I was normal until three weeks ago," he said. "It's amazing how many people fly on Christmas Eve. I couldn't get a nonstop. I was up and down all day. I had to go from Miami to Lansing to Seattle to San Francisco. The last leg—I had to ride in the bathroom."

"You did not," she said with a laugh. She lay down in the hay beside him.

"Then I had to rent a car and drive to Santa Rosa to get my truck. Then drive home."

"Hey!" Beau called from the back porch. "You guys want the horses hitched up?"

Annie sat up again. "No, thank you," she yelled back. "Can you please go away?"

"You guys making out in the hay?"

"Go away!" they both yelled.

"Jeez." The back door slammed.

Annie lay back down. "Now, what do you have in mind?" she asked him.

"I had a plan," he said. "I was going to tell you I love you, then seduce you, put a really nice flush on your cheeks, but I'm not sure I have the strength. I do love you, however. And a little sleep tonight might give me a second wind, so brace yourself."

She giggled. "I have puppies to deliver," she informed him.

"Aw, you haven't done that already? I was so hoping we could just go home and go to bed…."

"Why don't I take you home to your house, then you can sleep and I'll deliver the puppies. I don't think you should be driving if you can't roll over."

"I'll be fine," he said, facedown in the hay. "You'll see. Any second now I'll perk right up."

"You love me?" she asked. "What makes you think so?"

He couldn't roll over, but he looped an arm over her waist and pulled her closer. "You are so under my skin, Annie McKenzie, I'll never be a free man again. Pretty soon now you'll probably want to say you love me, too. Hurry up, will you? I'd like to be conscious for it."

She laughed at him.

"Say it, damn it," he ordered.

"I love you, too," she said. "I can't believe you came back in the same day. Why didn't you just call? Or come back and tell me you had a miserable time? You could have had your vacation and then told me."

"Because, Annie—I realized if I stayed away from you, I'd be lonely. No matter how many people were around, I'd feel alone if I wasn't with you." He pulled her closer. "I wanted you to know how important it was to me, to be with you. I wanted you to know you were worth a lot of trouble. You aren't something I can put off till later. You're not the kind of woman I can send flowers to with a note to say how I feel—you have to be in my arms. I'm not looking for the easy way with you, Annie. I want the forever way. And I don't think that's going to ever change. Now can we please deliver the puppies and get some sleep?"

"Sure," she said, running her fingers through the short hair over his ear. "Merry Christmas, Nathaniel."

"Merry Christmas, baby. I brought you something. A diamond."

"You brought me a diamond?" she asked, stunned.

He dug in his pocket and pulled out a plastic diamond about the size of a lime, attached to a key chain. "Our first Christmas Eve together, and I shopped for your present in an airport gift shop. By the way, when I get the real diamond, I don't think it's going to be this big."

She laughed and kissed him. "You will never know how much I like this one."

"Wanna show me?" he asked, hugging her tight.

"I will," she promised. "For the next fifty years."

"Works for me, Annie. I love you like mad."

"You make my knees wobble," she said. "Let me take you home so you can start wobbling them some more."

"My pleasure." He kissed her with surprising passion for a man dead on his feet. "Let's go home."

* * * * *

MIDNIGHT
CONFESSIONS

One

Sunny Archer was seriously considering a legal name change.

"Come on, Sunny," her uncle Nathaniel said. "Let's go out on the town and see if we can't put a little of that legendary sunshine back into your disposition!"

Out on the town? she thought. In *Virgin River?* A town of about six hundred? "Ah, I think I'll pass…"

"C'mon, sunshine, you gotta be more flexible! Optimistic! You can't lick this wound forever."

Maybe it was cute when she was four or even fourteen to say things like "Sunny isn't too sunny today!"

But this was December 31 and she had come to Virgin River to spend a few quiet days with her uncle Nate and his fiancée Annie, to try to escape the reality of a heart that wouldn't heal. And if the hurt wasn't bad enough, her heart had gone cold and hard, too. She looked at her watch—4:00 p.m. Exactly one year ago at this time she was having her hair and makeup done right before slipping into a Vera Wang wedding gown, excited, blushing and oblivious to the fact that her fiancé, Glen, was getting blitzed and ready to run for his life.

"I'm not really in the mood for a New Year's Eve bash, Uncle Nate," she said.

"Aw, sweetheart, I can't bear to think of you home alone, brooding, feeling sad," Nathaniel said.

And feeling like a big loser who was left at the altar on her wedding day? she wondered. But that's what had happened. How was she supposed to feel?

"Nate," Annie said under her breath, "this might be a bad night to push the party idea...."

"Ya think?" Sunny said sarcastically, noting to herself that she hadn't been so irritable and sarcastic before becoming an abandoned bride. "Listen, you guys, please go. Party like rock stars. I actually have plans."

"You do?" they both asked hopefully.

"I do. I'm planning a ceremonial burning of last year's calendar. I should probably burn three years' worth of them—that's how much time and energy I invested in the scumbucket."

Nate and Annie were speechless for a moment; they exchanged dubious looks. When Nate recovered he said, "Well all righty, then! We'll stay home and help with the ceremonial burning. Then we'll make some popcorn, play some monopoly, make some positive resolutions or something and ring in a much better new year than the last."

And that was how Sunny, who wasn't feeling at all accommodating, ended up going to the big Virgin River blast at Jack's Bar on New Year's Eve—because she just couldn't let her uncle Nate and sweet, funny Annie stay home to watch her sulk and whimper.

There had been a long history in Sunny's family of returning to the Jensen stables for a little rest and rejuvenation. Sunny and her cousins had spent countless vacations around the barn and pastures and trails, riding, playing, inhaling the fresh clean air and getting a regular new lease on life. It had been Sunny's mother's idea that she come to Virgin River for a post-Christmas revival. Sunny's mom was one of Nate's three older sisters, and Sunny's grandpa had been the original owner and veterinarian of Jensen's Clinic and Stable. Now Uncle Nate was the vet and Grandpa was retired and living in Arizona.

Sunny was her mama's only child, age twenty-five; she had one female cousin, Mary—who it just so happened had managed to get *her* groom to the church. Since Uncle Nate was only ten years older than Sunny at thirty-five, she and her cousin had had tragic crushes on him. Nate, on the other hand, who had grown up with three older sisters, thought he was cursed with females.

Until he was thirty, anyway. Then he became a little more avuncular, patient and even protective. Nathaniel had been sitting in the church on New Year's Eve a year ago. Waiting, like everyone else, for the groom to show, for the wedding to begin.

The past year had passed in an angry, unhappy blur for Sunny. Her rather new and growing photography business had taken off—a combination of her kick-ass website and word of mouth—and rather than take a break after her personal disaster, she went right back to work. She had scheduled shoots, after all. The catastrophic twist was that she specialized in engagement, wedding, anniversary, belly and baby shots—five phases of a couple's life worth capturing for posterity. Her work, as well as her emotional well-being, was suffering. Although she couldn't focus, and she was either unable to sleep or hardly able to pull herself out of bed, she pressed on the best she could. The only major change she'd made in her life was to move out of the town house she had shared with Glen and back into her mom and dad's house until she could afford something of her own. She had her workroom in the basement of her parents' place anyway, so it was just a minor shift in geography.

During the past year at her parents', Sunny had a revelation. The driving reason behind most young women her age wanting their own space, their independence and privacy, was their being involved in a serious relationship. Since she was determined not to repeat past mistakes by allowing another man into her life, there was no need to leave the comfort, security and economy of her parents' house.

She was trying her hand at photographing sunrises, sunsets, landscapes, seascapes and pets. It wasn't working—her images were flat and uninteresting. If it wasn't bad enough that her heart was broken, so was her spirit. It was as if her gift was lost. She'd been brilliant with couples, inspired by weddings—stills, slide shows, videos. She saw the promise in their eyes, the potential for their lives. She'd brought romance to the fat bellies of pregnant women and was a veritable Anne Geddes with babies! But now that she was a mere observer who would never experience any of those things firsthand, everything had changed. Not only had it changed, it pierced her heart each time she did a shoot.

When she confessed this to Annie, Annie had said, "Oh, darling, but you're so young! Only twenty-five! The possibilities ahead are endless if you're open to them!"

And Sunny had said, "I'm not upset because I didn't make the cheerleading squad, Annie. My fiancé dumped me on our wedding day—and my age doesn't matter a damn."

The town was carpeted in a fresh blanket of pretty white snow, the thirty-foot tree was lit and sparkling as gentle flakes continued to fall, and the porch at Jack's Bar, strung with lights and garlands, was welcoming. There was a friendly curl of smoke rising from the chimney and light shone from the windows.

Nate, Annie and Sunny walked into the bar at 8:00 p.m. and found the place packed with locals. Jack, the owner, and Preacher, the cook, were behind the bar. There was a festive table set up along one whole wall of the room, covered with food, to which Annie added a big plate of her special deviled eggs and a dill-speckled salmon loaf surrounded by crackers.

"Hey, looks like the whole town is here," Nate said.

"A good plenty," Jack said. "But I hope you don't see anyone here you want to kiss at midnight. Most of these folks won't make it that long. We have a strong skeleton crew that will stay late, however. They're busy getting all the kids settled back at Preacher's house with a sitter—it's going to be a dormitory. Vanessa and Paul's two are bunking in with Preacher's little Dana, my kids are sleeping in Preacher's room, Cameron's twins are in the guest room, Brie and Mike's little one is borrowing Christopher's room because he's planning on sitting up until midnight with the sitter. Oh, and to be very clear, the sitter is there for all the *little* kids—not for Chris," Jack added with a smile. "He's eight now. All man."

"Jack, Preach, meet my niece Sunny. Sunny, this is Jack and Preacher, the guys who run this place."

She gave them a weak smile, a nod and a mumbled nice to meet you.

"Hop up here, you three. As soon as you contribute your New Year's resolution, you get service," Jack said. "The price of admission is a food item and a resolution."

Sunny jumped up on a bar stool, hanging the strap of her large bag on the backrest. Jack leaned over the bar and eyed the big, leather shoulder bag. He peered at her with one brow lifted. "Going on a long trip right after the party?"

She laughed a little. "Camera equipment. I never leave it behind. Never know when I might need it."

"Well, by all means, the first annual New Year's Eve party is your canvas," Jack said. He slid a piece of paper and pen toward her.

Sunny hovered over it as if giving it careful thought. She knew if she said her resolution was to get this over with as soon as possible, it would open up the conversation as to why she now and would forever more find New Year's Eve the most reprehensible of holidays.

"Make it a good one, Sunny," Jack said. "Keep it generic and don't sign it—it's anonymous. There's a surprise coming right after midnight."

Sunny glanced at her watch. God, she thought. *At least four hours of this? I'll never make it!* She wrote on her slip of paper. "Give up men."

Drew Foley was a second-year orthopedic resident at UCLA Medical and had somehow scored ten days off over Christmas, which he'd spent in Chico with his two sisters, Marcie and Erin, their guys Ian and Aiden and his new nephew. The three previous Christmases he'd spent with his family, and also his former fiancée, Penny. That somehow seemed so long ago.

When surgical residents got days off, they weren't *real* days off. They're merely days on which you're not required in surgery, clinic, class, writing reports or being verbally beaten to death by senior residents and attending physicians. But there was still plenty of studying to do. He'd been hitting the books straight through Christmas even with the distraction of family all around, including Marcie's new baby who was really starting to assert himself. With only a few days left before he had to head back to Southern California, he borrowed the family's isolated cabin on the ridge near Virgin River so he could study without distraction. He'd managed to focus completely for a couple of days and had impressed himself with the amount of academic ground he'd covered. As he saw it, that bought him a New Year's Eve beer or two and a few hours of satellite football on New Year's Day. On January 2 he'd head back to Erin's house in Chico, spend one more evening with the family, then throw himself back into the lion's den at UCLA Medical.

He grabbed his jacket. It was New Year's Eve and he'd spent enough time alone. He'd swing through town on his way to Fortuna to collect his beer, just to see what was going on. He'd be surprised if the only bar and grill in town was open, since Jack's Bar wasn't usually open late on holidays. In fact, the routine in Virgin River on regular days was that Jack's shut down before nine, open till ten at the latest, and that was only if there were hunters or fishermen in the area. This was a town of mostly farmers, ranchers, laborers and small-business owners; they didn't stay out late because farm chores and animals didn't sleep in.

But to his surprise, once in town he found that the little bar was hopping. It made him smile—this was going to save him some serious mountain driving and he'd get to have a beer among people. When he walked into the packed bar he heard his name shouted. "Ho! Doc Foley! When did you hit town?"

This was the best part about this place. He'd only been up here maybe a half dozen times in the past couple of years, but Jack never forgot anyone. For that matter, most of Jack's friends and family never did either.

He reached a hand across the bar in greeting to Jack. "How's it going, Jack?"

"I had no idea you were up here!" Jack said. "You bring the family along?"

"Nah, I was with the family over Christmas and came up to get a little studying done before I have to get back to residency. I thought I'd better escape the girls and especially the baby if I intend to concentrate at all."

"How is that baby?" Jack asked.

Drew grinned. "Red-headed and loud. I'm afraid he could be a little rip-off of Marcie. Ian should be afraid. Very, very afraid."

Jack chuckled. "You remember my wife, Mel."

"Sure," he said, turning toward the town's renowned midwife and accepting a kiss on the cheek. "How are you?"

"Never better. I wish we'd known you were up here, Drew—I'd have made it a point to call you, invite you."

Drew looked around. "Who knew you folks ripped up the town on New Year's Eve. Is everyone here?"

"Pretty good number," Jack said. "But expect this

to change fairly quick—most of these folks will leave by nine. They start early. But I'm hanging in there till midnight," he assured Drew. "I bet I can count on one hand the number of Virgin River residents willing to stay up for a kiss at midnight."

And that's when he spotted her. Right when Jack said *kiss at midnight* he saw a young woman he'd be more than willing to accommodate when the clock struck twelve. She was tucked back in a corner by the hearth, swirling a glass of white wine, her golden hair falling onto her shoulders. She seemed just slightly apart from the table of three women who sat chatting near her. He watched as one of those women leaned toward her to speak, to try to include her, but she merely nodded, sipped, smiled politely and remained aloof. Someone's wife? Someone's girl? Whoever she was, she looked a little unhappy. He'd love to make her happier.

"Drew," Jack said. "Meet Nate Jensen, local vet."

Drew put out his hand, but didn't want to take his eyes off the girl. He said, "Nice to meet you," but what he was thinking was how long it had been since just looking at a beautiful woman had zinged him in the chest and head with almost instant attraction. Too long! Whoa, she was a stunner. He'd barely let go of Nate's hand, didn't even catch the guy's response because his ears were ringing, when he asked Jack, "Who is that blonde?"

"That's my niece," his new acquaintance said. "Sunny."

"Married? Engaged? Accompanied? Nun? Anything?"

Nate chuckled. "She's totally single. But—"

"Be right back," Drew said. "Guard my beer with your life!" And he took off for the corner by the hearth.

"But…" Nate attempted.

Drew kept moving. He was on automatic. Once he was standing right in front of her and she lifted her eyes to his, he was not surprised to find that she had the most beautiful blue eyes he could have ever imagined. He put out his hand. "Hi. I'm Drew. I just met your uncle." She said nothing, didn't even shake his hand. "And you're Sunny. Sunny Jensen?" he asked.

Her mouth fixed and her eyes narrowed. "Archer," she corrected.

Drew gave up on the shake and withdrew his hand. "Well, Sunny Archer, can I join you?"

"Are you trying to pick me up?" she asked directly.

He grinned. "I'm a very optimistic guy," he said pleasantly.

"Then let me save you some time. I'm not available."

He was struck silent for a moment. It wasn't that Drew enjoyed such great success with women—he was admittedly out of practice. But this one had drawn on him like a magnet and he was unaccountably surprised to be shot down before he'd even had a chance to screw up his approach. "Sorry," he said lamely. "Your uncle said you were single."

"Single and unavailable." She lifted her glass and gave him a weak smile. "Happy New Year."

He just looked at her for a moment, then beat a retreat back to the bar.

Jack and Nate were watching, waiting for him. Jack pushed the beer toward him. "How'd that work out for you?"

Drew took a pull on his beer. "I must be way out

of practice," he said. "I probably should'a thought that through a little better...."

"What? Residency doesn't leave time for girls?" Jack asked with a twist of the lip.

"A breakup," Drew explained. "Which led to a break from women for a while."

Nate leaned an elbow on the bar. "That a fact? Bad breakup?"

"You ever been around a good one?" Drew asked. Then he chuckled, lifted an eyebrow and said, "Nah, it wasn't that it was so bad. In fact, she probably saved my life. We were engaged, but shouldn't have been. She finally told me what I should've known all along—*if we got married, it would be a disaster.*"

"Bad fit?"

"Yeah, bad fit. I should have seen it coming, but I was too busy putting titanium rods in femurs to pay attention to details like that, so my bad. But what's up with Sunny Archer?"

"Well," Nate said. "I guess you probably have a lot in common."

"Uh-oh. Bad breakup?"

"Let's just say, you ever been around a good one?"

"I should've known. She didn't give me a chance. And here I thought I'd bungled it."

"Gonna go for round two?" Jack asked him.

Drew thought about that a minute. "I don't know," he said with a shrug. "Maybe I should wait until she gets a little more wine in her."

Nate slapped a heavy hand on Drew's shoulder. "That's my niece, bud. I'll be watching."

"Sorry, bad joke. I'd never take advantage of her, don't worry about that," Drew protested. "But if she shoots me down twice, I could get a serious complex!"

Two

Drew nursed his beer slowly and joked around with Jack and Nate over a plate of wings, but the subject of breakups had him thinking a bit about Penny. There were times he missed her, or at least he missed the idea of what he thought they would be.

He had met her while he was in med school. She was a fellow med student's cousin and it had been a fix up. The first date had gone smoothly; the next seven dates in as many weeks went even better and before he knew it, he was dating Penny exclusively. They had so much in common, they grew on each other. She was an RN and he was studying medicine. She was pretty, had a good sense of humor, understood his work as he understood hers and in no time at all they had settled into a comfort zone that accommodated them both. And it didn't hurt that the sex was satisfying. Everything seemed compatible.

Penny had been in charge of the relationship from the start and Drew didn't have to think about it much, which suited him perfectly. He was a busy guy; he didn't have a lot of time for flirtation or pursuit. Penny was very well-equipped to fill him in on their agenda and he was perfectly happy to go along. "Valentine's Day is coming up," she would say. "I guess we'll be doing something special?"

Ding, ding, ding—he could figure that out easy. "Absolutely," he would say. Then he'd get a reservation, buy a gift. Penny thought he was brilliant and sensitive and all was right with his world.

It had been working out effortlessly until he asked her to go to Southern California with him, to live with him. His residency in orthopedic surgery was beginning, he'd dated Penny exclusively for a couple of years and it seemed like the natural progression of things. "Not without an engagement ring," she'd said. So he provided one. It had seemed reasonable enough.

But the move from Chico changed everything. It hadn't gone well for Penny. She'd been out of her element, away from her job, friends and family, and Drew had been far too stressed and overworked to help her make the transition. She was lonely, needed attention, time, reassurance. And he had wanted to give it to her, but it was like squeezing water out of a rock. It wasn't long before their only communication was in the form of arguing—make that fighting. Fights followed by days of not speaking or nights in which she cried into her pillow and wouldn't take comfort from him, if he could stay awake long enough to give it.

Drew shook off the memory and finally said to Nate, "So, tell me about Sunny, who, if you don't mind me saying, might be better named Stormy...."

"Well, for starters, jokes about her name don't seem to be working just now," Nate replied.

"Ahh," he said. Drew was distracted by a sudden

flash and saw that it was none other than Stormy Sunny herself with the camera, getting a shot of a couple in a toast. "What's with the camera?"

"She's a photographer, as a matter of fact. A good one," Nate said. "She started out studying business in college but dropped out before she was twenty-one to start her own business. My sister Susan, her mother, almost had a heart attack over that. But it turned out she knew exactly what she was doing. There's a waiting list for her work."

"Is that a fact?" he said, intrigued. "She seems kind of young…"

"Very young, but she's been taking great pictures since she was in high school. Maybe earlier."

"Where?"

"She lives in L.A. Long Beach, actually."

Long Beach, Drew thought. Like next door! Of course, that didn't matter if she wouldn't even talk to him. But he wasn't giving anything away. "Is she a little artsy-fartsy?" Drew asked.

Nate laughed. "Not at all—she's very practical. But lately she's been trying some new stuff, shooting the horses, mountains, valleys, roads and buildings. Sunrises, sunsets, clouds, et cetera." Nate looked over at Sunny as she busily snapped pictures of a happy couple. "It's kind of nice to see her taking pictures of people again."

Drew watched Sunny focus, direct the pair with one hand while holding her camera with the other. Her face seriously lit up; her smile was alive and whatever it was she was saying caused her subjects to laugh, which was followed by several flashes. She was so animated as she took five or six more shots, then pulled a business card out of the pocket of her jeans and handed it to the couple. She was positively gorgeous when she wasn't giving him the brush. Then she retreated to her spot by the hearth and put her camera down. He noticed that the second she gave up the camera, her face returned to its seriousness. The sight of her was immediately obscured by partiers.

He wanted one of those business cards.

"Hey, buddy, you didn't make out your resolution," Jack said, passing him a slip of paper and pen. "That's the price of admission."

"I don't usually do resolutions," Drew said. "Well, except every morning when I resolve to fly under the radar of the senior residents."

"Because?" Jack asked.

Sometimes Drew forgot that few people knew what the life of a junior resident was like. "Because they're sociopaths with a mean streak."

"Ah," Jack said as if he bought that. "Maybe that's your resolution—to avoid sociopaths? When you've written one, it goes in the pot here."

"And then?" Drew asked.

"When you're getting ready to leave, you can draw one—maybe you'll get a better one than you wrote. Give you something new to strive for."

Drew laughed. "I dunno. This is such a crazy idea," he said. "What if the one I draw is to bike across the U.S.?"

Jack looked around. "Nah," he said. "No danger of that around here. You could draw one that says to remember your annual mammogram, however. Now get on it," he said, tapping the paper on the bar.

Chuckling, Drew wrote. Then he scratched it out.

Thinking about the grumpy but beautiful woman in the corner he wrote "Start the new year by giving a new guy a chance." Then he folded it in half and shoved it in his pocket; he asked for a new piece of paper. On his second try he wrote "Don't let past hurts ruin future possibilities."

Then he took a bolstering swallow of his beer and said, "Excuse me a second." And off he went to the other side of the room.

He stood in front of Sunny, smiled his handsomest smile and said, "So. You're a photographer."

She looked up at him, her expression deadpan. "Yes," she said.

"You like being a photographer?" he asked.

Again there was that pregnant pause before she said, "Yes."

"What do you like best about it?"

She thought for a moment. Then she said, "The quiet."

He had to ask himself why in the world he was interested. She was beautiful, but Drew had never been drawn by beauty alone. He'd known lots of gorgeous women who fell short in other areas, thus killing his interest instantly. For a woman to really intrigue him she had to be fun, smart, good-natured, energetic, driven by something besides her looks and above all, *positive.* So far this one, this Sunny, had only looks going for her and it was not enough. Still, for unknown reasons, he lingered. "The quiet," he repeated. "Anything else?"

"Yes. It doesn't require any other people. I can do it alone."

"Just out of curiosity, are you always this unapproachable, or is it just at New Year's Eve parties?"

She shrugged. "Pretty much always."

"Gotcha. One last question. Will you take my picture?"

"For what occasion?" she asked.

Nothing came to mind. "Passport photo?" he attempted.

"Sorry. I don't do passport photos."

He smiled at her. "Well, Sunny—you're in luck. Because that's all I got. You are, as you obviously wish to be, on your own."

Oh, I'm such a bitch, she thought as she watched Drew's back weave through the people to return to the bar. When he sat up on the stool beside her uncle, she cringed in embarrassment. She adored her uncle Nate and knew how much he cared about her, how it had hurt him to see her in pain on what was supposed to have been her wedding day, how it killed him to see her struggle with it for so long afterward. But while she knew Nate had nothing but sympathy for her, she realized he was running short on patience with her bitterness and what could only be described as attitude a full year later.

He wasn't the only one. Friends had tried to encourage her to let go of the heartache and move on. If she didn't want to date again, fine, but being pissed off all the time was not only wearing on friendships, it was hurting business. And she was hearing a lot about the fact that she was only twenty-five! She wasn't sure if twenty-five was so young it excused her for making such a mistake on Glen or if that meant she had decades left to find the right guy!

Then, right after she arrived in Virgin River, Annie

had taken her aside, sat her down and said, "This rage isn't going to help you get on with your life in a positive way, Sunny. You're not the only one who's been dumped. I found out the man I was supposed to marry had three full-time girlfriends he lived with—each of us part-time, of course."

"How'd he manage that?" Sunny had asked, intrigued and astonished.

"He obviously kept a very careful calendar. He was in sales and traveled. When I thought he was selling farm equipment, he was actually with one of the other girlfriends."

"Oh, my God! You must have wanted to *kill* him!"

"Sure. I was kind of hoping my dad or one of my brothers would do it for me, but when they didn't I got past it. I realize I wasn't left at the altar with a very expensive, nonrefundable wedding to pay for, like you were. I can't imagine the pain and humiliation of that, but even so, I was very angry. And now I'm so grateful that I found a way to get beyond that because if I hadn't, I would never have given Nate a chance. And your uncle Nate is the best thing that ever happened to me."

What Sunny wanted to tell Annie was that the pain and humiliation wasn't the worst part—it was that her friends and family *pitied* her for being left. What was wrong with her, that he would do that?

She knew what was wrong, when she thought about it. Her nose was too long, her forehead too high, her chest small and feet big, her hips too wide, she hadn't finished college and she took pictures for a living. That they were good pictures didn't seem to matter— it wasn't all that impressive. She sometimes veered into that territory of "if I had been a supermodel with a great

body, he'd never have left me." Intellectually she knew
that was nonsense, but emotionally she felt lacking in
too many ways.

Instead she said to Annie, "Did you know? Did you
ever have a hint that something was wrong?"

She shook her head. "Only when it was over, when
I looked back and realized he never spent a weekend
with me, and I was too trusting to wonder why he hadn't
ever asked me to join him on a business trip to one of
the other towns where he stayed overnight on business. Oh, after it was all over, I had lots of questions.
But at the time?" She shook her head. "I didn't know
anything was wrong."

"Me either," Sunny said.

"I probably didn't want to know anything was
wrong," Annie added. "I don't like conflict."

Sunny didn't say anything. She was pretty well acquainted with her own denial and that hurt just about
as much as the hard truth.

"Well, there was one thing," Annie corrected. "After
it was all over I wondered if I shouldn't have been more
desperate to spend every moment with *him,* if I loved
him so much. You know—Nate gets called out in the
middle of the night pretty often, and I never make a
fuss about it. But we both complain if we haven't had
enough time together. We need each other a lot. That
never happened with Ed. I was perfectly fine when he
wasn't around. Should have tipped me off, I guess."

No help there, Sunny thought. Glen had complained
constantly of her Fridays through Sundays always being
booked with shoots. There were times she worked a
sixteen-hour day on the weekends, covering three weddings and receptions and a baptism. Slip in some en-

gagement slide shows, photos of babies, whatever had to be done for people who worked Monday through Friday and who only had weekends available. Then from Monday through Thursday she'd work like a dog editing and setting up proofs.

Glen was a California Highway Patrolman who worked swing shifts to have weekends off and she was always unavailable then.

She revisited that old argument—wait a minute! Here was a clue she hadn't figured out at the time. Glen had a few years seniority with CHP, so why would he work swings just to have those weekends off when he knew she would be tied up with her clients the entire time? She'd been rather proud of the fact that it hadn't taken her long to develop a strong clientele, to make incredibly good money for a woman her age—weddings were especially profitable. But she'd had to sacrifice her weekends to get and keep that success.

So why? It would have been easy for him to get a schedule with a Tuesday through Thursday, her lightest days, off. In fact, if he had been willing to take those days off, and work the day shift regularly, they could have gone to bed together every night. He said at the time that it suited his body clock, that he wasn't a morning person. And he *liked* to go out on the weekends. He went out with "the boys." The *boys?* Not bloody likely.…

After being left at the church a couple of his groomsmen had admitted he'd been having his doubts about the big, legal, forever commitment. Apparently he'd worried aloud to them, but all he ever did was argue with her about it. *We don't need all that! We could fly to Aruba, get married there, take a week of sailing, scuba diving...* He hadn't said the commitment was an issue, just the wedding—something Sunny and her mom were having a real party putting together. So she had said, "Try not to worry so much, Glen—you'll get your week in Aruba on the honeymoon. Just be at the church on time, say your lines and we'll be diving and sunning and sailing before you know it."

Sunny shook her head in frustration. What was the point in figuring it out now? She grabbed her coat, her camera and headed out the door. The snow was still gently falling and she backed away from the town Christmas tree, snapping photos as she went. She zoomed in on some of the military unit patches used as decorations, caught snowflakes glistening against gold balls and white lights, captured angles of the tree until, finally, far enough away, she got the whole tree. If these came out the way she hoped, she might use them for something next Christmas—ads or cards or something.

Then she turned and caught a couple of good shots of the bar porch, the snow drifting on the rails and steps and roof. Then of the street with all the houses lit for holiday cheer. Then the bar porch with a man leaning against the rail, arms crossed over his chest—a very handsome man.

She lowered the camera and walked toward Drew. There was no getting around the fact that he was handsome—tall and built, light brown hair, twinkling brown eyes, and if she remembered right, a very sexy smile. He stood on the porch and she looked up at him.

"Okay, look, I apologize," she said. "It's not like me to be so rude, so 'unapproachable' as you call it. I got dumped, okay? I'm still licking my wounds, as my uncle Nathaniel puts it. Not a good time for me to respond to a come-on from a guy. I'm scared to death to meet a guy and end up actually liking him, so I avoid all males. That's it in a nutshell," she added with a shrug. "I used to be very friendly and outgoing—now I'm on guard a lot."

"Apology accepted. And I had a bad breakup, too, but it was a while ago. Water under the bridge, as they say."

"You got dumped?"

He gave a nod. "And I understand how you feel. So let's start over. What do you say? I'm Drew Foley," he said.

She took another step toward the porch, looking up at him. "Sunny Archer. But when? I mean, how long ago did you get dumped?"

"About nine months, I guess."

"About?" she asked. It must not have impacted him in quite the same way if he couldn't remember the date. "I mean—was it traumatic?"

"Sort of," he said. "We were engaged, lived together, but we were arguing all the time. She finally told me she wasn't willing to have a life like that and we had to go our separate ways. It wasn't my idea to break up." He shrugged. "I thought we could fix it and wanted to try, but she didn't."

"Did you know?" she asked. "Were you expecting it?"

He shook his head. "I should have expected it, but it broadsided me."

"How can that be? If you should have expected it, how could it possibly have taken you by surprise?"

He took a deep breath, looked skyward into the softly falling flakes, then back at her. "We were pretty mis-

erable, but before we lived together we did great. I'm
a medical resident and my hours were…still are hid-
eous. Sometimes I'm on for thirty-six hours and just
get enough time off to sleep. She needed more from me
than that. She…" He looked down. "I don't like calling her *she* or *her*. Penny had a hard time changing her
life in order to move in with me. She had to get a new
job, make new friends, and I was never there for her. I
should have seen it coming but I didn't. It was all my
fault but I couldn't have done anything to change it."

"Where are you from?" she asked him.

"Chico. About four hours south of here."

"Wow," she said. "We actually do have some things
in common."

"Do we?" he asked.

"But you're over it. How'd you get over it?"

He put his hands in his front pants pockets. "She invited me to her engagement party three months ago. To
another surgical resident. Last time I looked, he was on
the same treadmill I was on. Guess he manages better
with no sleep."

"No way," she said, backing away from the bar's
porch a little bit.

"Way."

"You don't suppose…?"

"That she was doing him when she was supposed to
be doing me?" he asked for her. "It crossed my mind.
But I'm not going there. I don't even want to know. All
that aside, she obviously wasn't the one. I know that
now. Which means it really *was* my fault. I was hooking up with someone out of inertia, not because I was
insanely in love with her. Bottom line, Sunny, me and

Penny? We both dodged a bullet. We were not meant to be."

She was speechless. Her mouth formed a perfect O. Her eyes were round. She wished she'd been able to take her own situation in such stride. "Holy crap," she finally said. Then she shook her head. "I guess you have to be confident to be in medicine and all."

"Aw, come on, don't give the study all the credit. I might actually have some common sense." He took a step down from the bar porch to approach her, his heel slid on the step and he went airborne. While he was in the air, there were rapid flashes from her camera. Then he landed, flat on his back, and there were more flashes.

Sunny stood over him, camera in hand. She looked down at him. "Are you all right?"

He narrowed his eyes at her. It took him a moment to catch his breath. "I could be paralyzed, you know. I hope I was hallucinating, but were you actually taking my picture as I fell?"

"Well, I couldn't catch you," she said. Then she smiled.

"You are sick and twisted."

"Maybe you should lie still. I could go in the bar and get the pediatrician and the midwife to have a look at you. I met them earlier, before you got here."

He looked up at her; she was still smiling. Apparently it didn't take much to cheer her up—the near death of a man seemed to put her in a better mood. "Maybe you could just show them the pictures.…"

She fell onto her knees beside him and laughed, her camera still in hand. It was a bright and happy sound and those beautiful blue eyes glittered. "Seriously, you're the doctor—do you think you're all right?"

"I don't know," he said. "I haven't moved yet. One wrong move and I could be paralyzed from the neck down."

"Are you playing me?"

"Might be," he admitted with a shrug of his shoulders.

"Hah! You moved! You're fine. Get up."

"Are you going to have a drink with me?" he asked.

"Why should I? Seriously, we're a couple of wounded birds—we probably shouldn't drink, and we certainly shouldn't drink together!"

"Get over it," he said, rising a bit, holding himself up on his elbows. "We have nothing to lose. It's a New Year's Eve party. We'll have a couple of drinks, toast the New Year, move on. But give it a try not so pissed off. See if you can have some fun." He smiled. "Just for the heck of it?"

She sat back on her heels and eyed him warily. "Is this just more inertia?"

His grin widened. "No, Sunny. This is part chivalry and part animal attraction."

"Oh, God.… I just got dumped by an animal. So not looking for another one."

He gave her a gentle punch in the arm. "Buck up. Be a big girl. I bet you haven't let an interested guy buy you a drink in a long time. Take a chance. Practice on me. I'm harmless."

She lifted one light brown brow. "How do I know you're harmless?"

"I'm going back to sacrifice myself to the gods of residency in two days. They'll chew me up and spit me out. Those chief residents are ruthless and they want revenge for what was done to them when they were the little guys. There won't even be a body left. No one will ever know you succumbed to having a beer with me." And then he smiled with all his teeth.

She tsked and rolled her eyes at him.

He sat up. "See how much you like me? You're putty in my hands."

"You're a dork!"

He got to his feet and held out a hand to her, helping her up. "I've heard that, but I'm not buying it yet. I think if you dig deep enough, I might be cool."

She brushed off the knees of her jeans. "I'm not sure I have that kind of time."

Three

Once Drew got up and moved, he limped. He claimed a wounded hip and leaned on Sunny. Since she couldn't be sure if he was faking, she allowed this. But just as they neared the steps, the doors to the bar flew open and people began to spill out, laughing, shouting, waving goodbye.

"Careful there," he yelled, straightening up. "I just slipped on the steps. They're iced over. I'll get Jack to throw some salt on them, but take it slow and easy."

"Sure," someone said. "Thanks, Drew."

"Be careful driving back to Chico," someone else said.

"Say hello to your sisters," a woman said. "Tell them to come up before too long, we miss them."

"Pinch that cute baby!"

"Will do," Drew said in response, and he pulled Sunny to the side to make way for the grand exodus. The laughing, joking, talking people, some carrying their plates and pots from the buffet table, headed for their cars.

"What the heck," Sunny said. "It's not even nine o'clock!"

Drew laughed and put his arm back over her shoulder to lean on her. "This is a little town, Sunny. These folks have farms, ranches, orchards, vineyards, small businesses and stuff like that. The ones who don't have to get up early for work—even on holidays—might stay later. And some of the folks who are staying are on call—the midwife, the cop, the doctor." He grinned. "Probably the bartender. If anyone has a flat on the way home, five gets you ten either Jack or Preacher will help out."

"Do you know all these people?"

"A lot of them, yeah. I'll give you the short version of the story—my sister Marcie was married to a marine who was disabled in action and then later died. She came up here to find his best friend and sergeant—Ian Buchanan. She found him in a run-down old cabin up on the ridge, just over the county line, but the nearest town was Virgin River. So—she married him and they have a baby now. My oldest sister, Erin, wanted a retreat up here, but she couldn't handle a cabin with no indoor bathroom or where you'd have to boil your bath water and chop your wood for heat, so she got a local builder to renovate one into something up to her standards with electricity, indoor plumbing and a whirlpool tub." He laughed. "Really, Marcie's pretty tough, but if Erin risked breaking a nail, that would make her very cranky." He looked at Sunny and smiled. "It used to be a lean-to, now it should be in *Architectural Digest*. Anyway, I've been up here several times in the past couple of years, and Jack's is the only game in town. You don't have to drop into Jack's very many times before you know half the town. I'm hiding out in the cabin for a few days to get some studying done, away from my sisters and the baby. I have to go back on the second. I just swung through town for a beer—I had no idea there was a party."

They just stood there, in front of the porch, his arm draped across her shoulder. It was kind of silly—she was only five foot four and he was easily six feet, plus muscular. He didn't lean on her too heavily.

"Is it very hard, what you do? Residency?"

"It doesn't have to be. It could be a learning experience, but the senior residents pile as much on you as they can. It's like a dare—who can take it all and keep standing. That's the part that makes it hard." Then he sobered for a second. "And kids. I love working with the kids, making them laugh, helping them get better, but it's so tough to see them broken. Being the surgeon who puts a kid back together again—it's like the best and worst part of what I do. Know what I mean?"

She couldn't help but imagine him taking a little soccer player into surgery, or wrapping casting material around the arm of a young violinist. "Your sister was married to a soldier who was killed...?"

"She was married to a marine. Bobby was permanently disabled by a bomb in Iraq. He was in a nursing home for a few years before he died, but he never really came back, you know? No conscious recognition—the light was on but no one was home. They were very young."

"Were you close to him?"

"Yeah, sure. He was two years older and we all went to high school together. Bobby went in right after graduation. Ian was a little older, so I didn't know him until

Marcie brought him home." He laughed sentimentally. "She's something, Marcie. She came up here to find Ian, make sure he was all right after the war and to give him Bobby's baseball card collection. She brought him home on Christmas Eve and said, 'This is Ian and I'm going to marry him as soon as he can get used to the idea.'"

"This is why," she said softly. "This is why you can move on after getting dumped by your fiancée. You've seen some rough stuff and you know how to count your blessings. I bet that's it."

He turned Sunny so she faced him. Of course he couldn't lean on her then, but he got close. "Sunny, my family's been through some stuff... Mostly my sisters, really—they had it toughest. But the thing that keeps me looking up instead of down—it's what I see at work everyday. I'm called on to treat people with problems lots bigger than mine—people who will never walk again, never use their arms or hands, and sometimes worse. Orthopedic pain can be terrible, rehab can be extended and dreary.... Tell you what, sunshine—I'm upright, walking around, healthy, have a brain to think with and the option to enjoy my life. Well, I'm not going to take that for granted." He lifted a brow, tilted his head, smiled. "Maybe you should spend a little time in my trauma center, see if it fixes up all those things you think you should worry about?"

"What about your chief residents?" she asked, showing him her smile.

"Oh, them. Well, I pretty much wish them dead. No remorse, either. God, they're mean. Mean and spiteful and impossible to please."

"Will you be a chief resident someday?"

His smile took on an evil slant. "Yes. But not soon

enough. Watch yourself on these stairs, honey." Before opening the door for Sunny, he stopped her. "So— want to find a cozy spot by the fire and tell me about the breakup that left you so sad and unapproachable?"

She didn't even have to think about it. "No," she said, shaking her head. "I'd rather not talk about it."

"Fair enough. Want to tell me how you got into photography?"

She smiled at him. "I could do that."

"Good. I'll have Jack pour you a glass of wine and while he's doing that I'll scatter some salt on those icy steps." He touched her pink nose. "Your mission is to find us a spot in that bar where we can talk. If I'm not mistaken, we're the only two singles at this party."

Sunny went back to the place near the fire where she had left her camera bag and put her camera away. She glanced over at Drew. He stood at the bar talking with Jack; Jack handed him a large canister of salt.

And suddenly it was someone else standing at the bar, and it wasn't this bar. Her mind drifted and took her back in time. It was Glen and it was the bar at their rehearsal dinner. Glen was leaning on the bar, staring morosely into his drink, one foot lifted up on the rail. His best man, Russ, had a hand on his back, leaning close and talking in Glen's ear. Glen wasn't responding.

Why hadn't she been more worried? she asked herself in retrospect. Maybe because everyone around her had been so reassuring? Or was it because she *refused* to be concerned?

Sunny wasn't very old-fashioned, but there were a few traditional wedding customs she had wanted to uphold—one was not seeing her groom the day of her wedding. So she and her cousin Mary, who was also her matron of honor, would spend the night at Sunny's parents' house after the rehearsal dinner. Even still, she remembered thinking it was a little early when Glen kissed her good-night that evening.

"I'm going out with the boys for a nightcap, then home," he said.

"Is everything all right?" she asked.

"Sure. Fine." His smile was flat, she knew things were not fine.

"You're not driving, are you?"

"Russ has the keys. It's fine."

"I guess I'll see you tomorrow." She remembered so vividly that she laid her palm against his handsome cheek. "I can't wait for tomorrow."

He didn't move his head, but his eyes had darted briefly away. "Me, too."

When Russ came over to her to say good-night, she had asked, "What's bothering Glen?"

"Oh, he'll be fine."

"But what is it?"

Russ had laughed a bit uncomfortably. "Y'know, even though you two have been together a long time, lived together and everything, it's still a pretty big step for a guy. For both of you, I realize. But guys... I don't know what it is about us—I was a little jittery the day before my wedding. And it was absolutely what I wanted, no doubt, but I was still nervous. I don't know if it's the responsibility, the lifestyle change..."

"What changes?" she asked. "Besides that we're going to take a nice trip and write a lot of thank-you notes?"

"I'm just saying... I've been in a bunch of weddings,

including my own, and every groom I've ever known gets a little jumpy right before. Don't worry about it. I'll buy him a drink on the way home, make sure he gets all tucked in. You'll be on your way to Aruba before you know it." Then he had smiled reassuringly.

"Will you ask him to call me to say good-night?" she asked.

"Sure. But if he's slurring by then, don't hold it against me!"

She'd been up late talking to Mary; they'd opened another bottle of wine. By the time they fell asleep it was the wee hours and they'd slept soundly. In the morning when she checked her cell phone, she found a text from Glen that had come in at three in the morning. Going to bed. Talk to you tomorrow.

She wanted to talk to him, but she thought it would probably be better if he slept till noon, especially if there was anything to sleep off, so he'd be in good shape for the ceremony. All she wanted was for the wedding to be perfect! She had many bridely things to do and was kept busy from brunch getting a manicure and pedicure, surrounded by the women in her family and her girlfriends.

The New Year's Eve wedding had been Sunny's idea. It had been born of a conversation with the girls about how they'd never had a memorable New Year's Eve—even when they had steady guys, were engaged or even married. Oh, there'd been a few parties, but they hadn't been special in any way. Sunny thought it would be fantastic—a classy party to accompany her wedding, something for everyone to remember. An unforgettable event.

Little did she know.

She'd been so busy all day, she hadn't worried that she never heard from Glen. She assumed he was as occupied with his guys as she was with her girls. In fact, it hadn't really bothered her until about five, still a couple of hours till the wedding. She called him and when he didn't pick up, she left him a voice mail that she loved him, that she was so happy, that soon they would be married and off on a wonderful honeymoon.

It was very hard for a photographer to choose a photographer; almost no one was going to measure up to Sunny's expectations. But the very well-known Lin Hui was trying her best, and started snapping shots as soon as the girls showed up at the church with hairdressers and professional makeup artists in tow. Her camera flashed at almost every phase of preparation and in addition captured special memories—shiny, strappy heels against flowers, female hands clutching white satin, mothers of the bride and groom embracing and dabbing each other's eyes. But the poor thing seemed very nervous. Sunny assumed it was because of the challenge of shooting another professional. She had no idea it was because Lin couldn't find the groom for a photo shoot of the men in the wedding party.

It happened at six forty-five, fifteen minutes before the ceremony was to start. Sunny's father came into the wedding prep room with Russ. Both of them looked as if someone had died and she immediately gasped and ran to her father. "Is Glen all right?"

"He's fine, honey." Then he sent everyone out of the room including Sunny's mom and the mother of the groom. He turned to Russ and said, "Tell her."

Russ hung his head. He shook it. "Don't ask me what's got into him, I really can't explain. There's no good reason for this. He said he's sorry, he just isn't ready for this. He froze up, can't go through with it."

She had never before realized how fast denial can set in or how long it can last. "Impossible. The wedding is in fifteen minutes," she said.

"I know. I'm sorry—I spent all day trying to get through this with him. I even suggested he just show up, do it, and if he still feels the same way in a few months, he can get a divorce. Honest to God, it made more sense to me than this."

She shook her head and then, inexplicably, laughed. "Aw, you guys. This is not funny. You got me, okay? But this isn't funny!"

"It's not a joke, baby," her father said. "I've tried calling him—he won't pick up."

"He'll pick up for me," she said. "He always picks up for me!"

But he didn't. Her call was sent to voice mail. Her message was, "Please call me and tell me I'm just dreaming this! Please! You can't really be ditching me at the church fifteen minutes before the wedding! Not you! You're better than this!"

Russ grabbed her wrist. "Sunny—he left his tux in my car to return. He's not coming."

Sunny looked at her father. "What am I supposed to do?" she asked in a whisper.

Her father's face was dark with anger, stony with fury. "We'll give him till seven-fifteen to call or do something honorable, then we make an announcement to the guests, invite them to go to the party and eat the food that will otherwise be given away or thrown out, and we'll return the gifts with apologies. And then I'm going to kill him."

"He said he'll pay back the cost of the reception if it takes his whole life. But there's no way he can pay me back for what he asked me to do today," Russ said. "Sunny, I'm so sorry."

"But *why?*"

"Like I said, he doesn't have a logical reason. He can't, he said." Russ shook his head. "I don't understand, so I know you can't possibly."

Sunny grabbed Russ's arm. "Go tell his mother to call him! Give her your cell phone so he'll think it's you and pick up!"

But Glen didn't pick up and his mother was left to growl angrily into the phone's voice mail right before she fell apart and cried.

Before they got even close to seven-fifteen everyone nearby was firing questions at Sunny like it was her fault. *Why? Did he talk to you about this? Was he upset, troubled? Did you suspect this was coming? You must have noticed something! How can you not have known? Suspected? Were you having problems? Arguing about something? Fighting? Was his behavior off? Strange? Was there another woman?* It didn't take long for her to erupt. "You'll have to ask *him!* And he's not even here to ask! Not only did he not show up, he left me to try to answer for him!"

At seven-ten, right before her father made an announcement to the wedding guests, Sunny quietly got into the bridal limo. She took her bouquet—her beautiful bouquet filled with roses and orchids and calla lilies—made a stop at her parents' house for her purse and honeymoon luggage and had the driver take her home.

Home. The town house she shared with Glen. Her parents were frantic, her girlfriends were worried, her wedding guests wondered what went wrong. She wasn't sure why she went home, maybe to see if he'd moved out while she was having a manicure and pedicure. But no—everything was just as she'd left it. And typical of Glen, the bed wasn't made and there were dirty dishes in the sink.

She sat on the edge of their king-size bed in her wedding gown, her bouquet in her lap and her cell phone in her hand in case he should call and say it was all a bad joke and rather than pulling out of the wedding he was in the hospital or in jail. The only calls she got were from friends and family, all worried about her. She fended off most of them without saying where she was, others were forced to leave messages. For some reason she couldn't explain to this day, she didn't cry. She let herself fall back on the bed, stared at the ceiling and asked herself over and over what she didn't know about this man she had been willing to commit a lifetime to. She was vaguely aware of that special midnight hour passing. The new year didn't come in with a kiss, but with a scandalous breakup.

Sunny hadn't had a plan when she went home, but when she heard a key in the lock she realized that because she'd taken the bridal limo and left her car at her parents', Glen didn't know she was there. She sat up.

He walked through the bedroom door, grabbing his wallet, keys and change out of his pockets to drop onto the dresser when he saw her. Everything scattered as he made a sound of surprise and he automatically reached for his ankle where he always kept a small, backup gun. Breathing hard, he left it there and straightened. Cops, she thought. They like always having *something,* in

case they happen to run into someone they put away…
or a pissed-off bride.

"Go ahead," she said. "Shoot me. It might be easier."

"Sunny," he said, breathless. "What are you *doing*
here?"

"I *live* here," she said. She looked down at the bouquet she still held. Why had she clung to that? Because
it was sentimental or because it cost 175 dollars and she
couldn't return it? "You can't have done this to me," she
said almost weakly. "You can't have. You must have a
brain tumor or something."

He walked into the room. "I'm sorry," he said, shaking his head. "I kept thinking that by the time we got
to the actual date, the wedding date, I'd be ready. I really thought that."

"Ready for what?" she asked, nonplussed.

"Ready for that life, that commitment forever, that
next stage, the house, the children, the fidelity, the—"

She shook her head, frowning in confusion. "Wait
a minute, we haven't found a house we like and can afford, we agreed we're not ready for children yet and
I thought we already had commitment…" His chin
dropped. "Fidelity?" she asked in a whisper.

He lifted his eyes and locked with hers. "See, I
haven't really done anything wrong, not really. I kept
thinking, I'm not married yet! And I thought by the
time—"

"Did you sleep with other women?" she asked, rising to her feet.

"No! No! I swear!"

She didn't believe him for a second! "Then what
did you do?"

"Nothing much. I partied a little. Had drinks, you

know. Danced. Just went out and sometimes I met girls, but it didn't get serious or anything."

"But it did get to meeting, dancing, buying drinks. Talking on the phone? Texting little messages? Maybe having dinner?"

"Maybe some of that. A couple of times."

"Maybe kissing?"

"Only, maybe, twice. At the most, twice."

"My God, have I been brain damaged? To not know?"

"When were we together?" he asked. "We had different nights off, we were like roommates!"

"You could have fixed that easy! You could have changed your nights off! I couldn't! People don't get married or have fiftieth anniversary parties on Tuesday nights!"

"And they also don't go out for fun on Tuesday nights! I guess I'm just a bad boy, but I enjoy a ball game or a run on a bar or club on a weekend when people are out! And you were never available on a weekend! We talked about it, we *fought* about it! You said it would never change, not while you took pictures."

"This isn't happening," she said. "You stood up two hundred wedding guests and a trip to Aruba because I work weekends?"

"Not exactly, but… Well… Look," he said, shaking his head. "I'm twenty-six. I thought you were probably the best thing for me, the best woman I could ever hook up with for the long haul except for one thing—I'm not ready to stop having fun! And you are—you're all business. Even that wedding—Jesus, it was like a runaway train! Planning that astronomical wedding was like a second job for you and I never wanted anything that big, that out of control! Sunny, you're way too young to be so old."

That was one way to deliver what she could only describe as a punch to the gut. Of all the things she thought she knew about him, she hadn't given enough credence to the fact that even at twenty-six, he was younger than she. More immature. He wanted to have *fun*. "And you couldn't tell me this last month? Or last week? Or *yesterday?*" She stared at him, waiting.

"Like I said, I thought I'd work it out in my head, be ready in time."

Talk about shock and awe. "You're an infant. How did I not realize what a liability that could be?"

"Excuse me, but I lay my life on the line every day! I go to work in a bulletproof vest! And you're calling me an *infant?*"

"Oh, I'm so sorry, Glen. You're an infant with a dick. With a little, tiny brain in it." She took a breath. "Pack a bag. Take some things and see if you can find a friend who will take you in for a few days. I'll move home to my mom and dad's as soon as I can. I hope you can make the rent alone. If I recall, I was making more money with my boring old weekend job than you were with your bulletproof vest."

Sunny sat back on the bed, then she lay down. Still gowned in a very big wedding dress, holding her valuable bouquet at her waist, Sunny closed her eyes. She heard Glen rustling around, finding clothes, his shaving kit, the essentials. Her mind was completely occupied with thoughts like, *will the airline refund the money for the first-class tickets because the groom didn't show?* How much nonrefundable money had her parents wasted on a wedding that never happened?

Would the homeless of L.A. be eating thousands of dollars worth of exquisite food discarded by the caterer? And since her name was also on the lease to this town house, would fun-man Glen stiff her there, too? Hurt her credit rating *and* her business?

"Sunny?" Glen said to her. He was standing over her. "Wake up. You look so… I don't know… *Funereal* or something. Like a dead body, all laid out." He winced. "In a wedding dress…"

She opened her eyes, then narrowed them at him. "Go. Away."

Sunny gave her head a little shake to clear her mind and looked up to see Drew standing in front of her. He held a glass of wine toward her. "I salted the steps, got you a wine and me a beer. Now," he said, sitting down opposite her. "About this photography of yours…"

"It happened a year ago," she said.

"Huh? The picture taking happened a year ago?" he asked.

"The wedding that never was. Big wedding—big party. We'd been together three years, engaged and living together for one, and all of a sudden he didn't show. I was all dressed up in a Vera Wang, two hundred guests were waiting, little sausages simmering and stuffed mushrooms warming, champagne corks popping…and no groom."

Total shock was etched into his features. "Get out!" he said in a shocked breath.

"God's truth. His best man told me he couldn't do it. He wasn't ready."

Suddenly Drew laughed, but not unkindly, not of

humor but disbelief. He ran his hand through his hair. "Did he ever say *why?*"

She had never told anyone what he'd said, it was too embarrassing. But for some reason she couldn't explain, she spit it right out to Drew. "Yeah. He wasn't done having fun."

Silence reigned for a moment. "You're not serious," Drew finally said.

"Deadly. It was all so stunning, there was even a small newspaper article about it."

"And this happened when?" he asked.

"One year ago. Today."

Drew sat back in his chair. "Whoa," was all he could say. "Well, no wonder you're in a mood. Fun?" he asked. "He wasn't done having *fun?*"

"Fun," she affirmed. "That's the best explanation he could come up with. He liked to party, go to clubs, flirt, dance, whatever… He's a Saturday-night kind of guy and just wasn't ready to stop doing that and guess what? Photographers work weekends—weddings, baptisms, et cetera. Apparently I'm a real drag."

Drew rubbed the back of his neck. "I must be really backward then. I always thought having the right person there for you, listening to your voice mails and texting you to pick up her dry cleaning or saying she'd pick up yours, someone who argued with you over what sushi to bring home or what went on the pizza, someone who would come to bed naked on a regular basis—I always thought *those things* were fun. Sexy and fun."

She grinned at him. "You find dry cleaning sexy?"

"I do," he said. "I really do." And then they both laughed.

Four

Sunny sat forward, elbows on her knees, a smile on her face and said, "I can't wait to hear more about this— the things you find sexy. I mean pizza toppings and dry cleaning? Do go on."

He took a sip of his beer. "There is a long list, Miss Sunshine, but let's be clear—I am a boy. Naked tops the list."

"Yes, there are some things all you *boys* seem to have in common. But if I've learned anything it's that showing up naked regularly apparently isn't quite enough."

"Pah—for men with no imagination maybe. Or men who don't have to push a month's worth of work into a day."

"Well, then…?" she asked. "What?"

"I like working out a budget you'll never stick to. There's something about planning that together, it's cool. Not the checkbook, that's not a two-person job— it's dicey. No two people add and subtract the same, did you know that? And the chore list, that turns me on like you wouldn't believe. Picking movies—there's a real skill to that. If you can find a girl who likes action, then you can negotiate three action movies to every chick flick, and you can eventually work up to trading chick flicks for back rubs." He leaned close to whisper. "I don't want this to get out, but I actually like some of the chick flicks. I'm picky, but I do like some."

"Shopping?" she asked.

"I have to draw the line there," he said firmly. "That just doesn't do it for me. If I need clothes or shoes I take care of it as fast as I can. I don't like to screw around with that. It's boring and I have no skills. But I get that you have to look at least half decent to get a girl to like you." He smiled. "A pretty girl like you," he added.

"Then how do you manage that? Because tonight, you weren't even aware there was a party and you don't look that terrible."

"Why, thank you," he said, straightening proudly. "I either ask my oldest sister, Erin, to dress me—the one who made the lean-to into a showplace—or failing that I just look for a gay guy working in clothing."

She burst out laughing, not realizing that Nate, Annie, Jack and a few others turned to look. "That's awful, shame on you!"

"Gimme a break—I have gay friends. You can say anything you want about them but the common denominator is—they have fashion sense. At least the guys I know do."

"Then why not ask a gay friend to go shopping with you?"

"I don't want to mislead anyone," he said with a shrug.

"Sure you're not just a little self-conscious about your...um...somewhat *flexible* status?"

He leaned so close she could inhale the Michelob

on his breath. His eyes locked on hers. "Not flexible about that. Ab. So. Lutely. Not." Then he smiled. "I only swing one way."

She couldn't help it, she laughed loudly. Happily.

"You gotta stop that, my sunshine. You're supposed to be miserable. You were left at the altar by a juvenile idiot a year ago tonight. We're grieving here."

"I know, I know," she said, fanning her face. "I'm going to get back into depression mode in a sec. Right now, tell me another thing you find impossibly sexy, and keep in mind we've already covered that naked thing."

"Okay," he said. He rolled his eyes skyward, looking for the answer. "Ah!" he said. "Her lingerie in the bathroom! It's impossible. Hanging everywhere. A guy can't even pee much less brush his teeth or get a shower. I hate that!" And there was that wicked grin again. "Very sexy."

"Okay, I'm a little confused here. You hate it? And it's very sexy?"

"Well, you have to be a guy to get this. A guy goes into the bathroom—which is small like the rest of your house or apartment until you're at least an evil senior resident—and you put your face into all the satin and lace hanging all over the place. You rub it between your palms, wear a thong on your head for a minute, have a couple of reality-based fantasies, and then you yell, 'Penny! Get your underwear out of here so I can get a shower! I'm late.'"

 · She put her hands over her face and laughed into them.

His eyes glowed as he looked at her. "Be careful, Sunny. You're enjoying yourself."

She reached across the short space that separated

them and gave him a playful slug. "So are you! And your breakup was more recent."

"Yeah, but—"

He was about to say *but not more traumatic.* At least he wasn't left in a Vera Wang gown hiding from two hundred wedding guests. But the door to the bar opened and in came the local Riordans—Luke, Shelby and little Brett, their new baby. Luke was holding Brett against his chest, tucked under his jacket. Drew jumped to his feet. "Hey! Son of a gun!" Then he grabbed Sunny's hand and pulled her along. He turned to her and said, "Kind of family. I'll explain."

Leaving Sunny behind him a bit, he grabbed Shelby in a big hug and kissed her cheek. He grabbed Luke, careful of the baby and Luke scowled at him and said, "Do *not* kiss me!"

"All right, but gee, I'll have to really hold myself back," Drew said with a laugh. He winked at Sunny before he pulled her forward. "Meet Sunny, here visiting her uncle. Sunny, remember I told you about the sister who turned the shack into a showplace? That's Erin—and while she was up here finding herself, she also found Luke's brother Aiden. They're engaged. That makes me almost related to these guys and little Brett."

Shelby reached out to shake Sunny's hand. "I heard you'd be visiting, Sunny. We know Nate and Annie. I sometimes ride with Annie."

"Hey, I thought you said you weren't coming out tonight," Jack said from behind the bar. "Baby sleeping and all that."

"We should'a thought that through a little better," Luke said. "Brett prefers to sleep during the day and is a regular party animal at night."

Mel moved closer and said, "Aww, let me have him a minute." She pulled the little guy from Luke and indeed, his eyes were as big as saucers—he was wide-awake at nine-thirty. Mel laughed at him. "Well, aren't you something!"

Shelby said to Sunny, "Mel delivered him. She gets really invested in her babies."

"Let's have your resolutions," Jack said. "Then I'll set you up a drink and you can graze the buffet table."

"What resolutions?" Luke wanted to know.

Jack patted the fishbowl full of slips of paper on the bar. "Everyone has contributed their number one, generic resolution. You know the kind—quit smoking, lose ten pounds, work out everyday. We're going to do something fun with them at midnight. A kind of game."

"I don't do games," Luke said.

"Lighten up, it's not like charades or anything. It's more like cracking open a fortune cookie."

"I don't do resolutions," Luke said.

"I'll do his," Shelby said, sitting up at the bar. "I have some ideas."

"Easy, baby," Luke said. "You know you don't like me too perfect. Rough around the edges caught you in the first place."

Shelby glanced over her shoulder and smiled at him. Nate, who was sitting beside her, leaned in and pretended to read her resolution. "No more boys' nights out or dancing girls?" he said. "Shelby, isn't that a little strict for our boy Luke?"

Luke just laughed. So did Shelby.

Sunny took it all in. She had always liked to be around couples who were making that whole couple thing work—understanding each other, give and take, good humor, physical attraction. She'd done a lot of weddings. They weren't all easy and pleasant. A lot of the couples she photographed she wouldn't give a year.

Drew whispered in her ear. "Shelby is a full-time nursing student. She and Luke run a bunch of riverside cabin rentals and while Shelby goes to school and studies, Luke not only takes care of the cabins and house, but Brett, too. I think dancing girls are way in the past for Luke."

"Hmm," she said. She went for her camera and started taking pictures again, and while she did so she listened. Sunny could see things through the lens that were harder to see with the naked eye. For her, anyway.

She learned that Vanessa and Paul Haggerty were more conventional. She was home with the children while he was a general contractor who did most of the building and renovating around Virgin River, including the reconstruction of that old cabin for Drew's sister, the cabin Drew was staying in. Abby Michaels, the local doctor's wife, had a set of toddler twins and was overseeing the building of a house while her husband, Cam, was at the clinic or on call 24/7. The situation was a bit different for Mel and Jack Sheridan. The local midwife was always on call and Jack had a business that was open about sixteen hours a day—they had to shore each other up. They did a lot of juggling of kids and chores—Jack did all the cooking and Mel all the cleaning. If all the jokes could be believed, apparently Mel could burn water. Preacher and Paige worked together to raise their kids, run the kitchen and keep the accounting books at the bar. Brie and Mike Valenzuela had a child and two full-time jobs—she was an attorney, he was the town cop. And Sunny already knew that Uncle Nate and Annie were partners in running the Jensen's Clinic and Stable. Their wedding was scheduled for May.

Lots of interesting and individual methods of managing the realities of work, family, relationships. She wondered about a couple who would split up because one of them wasn't available to party on Saturday nights. She already knew that wasn't an issue among these folks.

While she observed and listened, she snapped pictures. She instructed Mel to hold the Riordan baby over her head and lower him slowly to kiss his nose. She got a great shot of Jack leaning on the bar, braced on strong arms spread wide, wearing a half smile as he watched his wife with a baby she had delivered, a proud glow in his eyes. Preacher was caught with his huge arms wrapped around his little wife, his lips against her head. Paul Haggerty put a quarter in the jukebox and danced his wife around the bar. Cameron Michaels was clinking glasses with Abby Michaels and couldn't resist nuzzling her neck—Sunny caught that. In fact, she caught many interesting postures, loving poses. Not only was there a lot of affection in the room, but plenty of humor and happiness. God, she never used to be the type that got dragged down.

When Sunny was focusing the camera, she didn't miss much. Maybe she should have been looking at Glen through the lens because clearly she missed a lot about him. Or had she just ignored it all?

She wondered if this was all about it being New Year's Eve, being among friends and the promise of a brand-new start, a first day of a new year. That's what she'd had in mind for her wedding—a new beginning.

Then she spotted Drew, apart from the crowd, leaning against the wall beside the hearth, watching her with a lazy smile on his lips. He had one leg crossed over the other, one hand was in his front jeans pocket and he lifted his bottle of Mich, which had to be warm by now since he'd been nursing it for so long. She snapped, flashed the camera, making him laugh. He posed for her, pulling that hand out of his pocket and flexing his muscles. Of course it was impossible to see his real physique given the roomy plaid flannel shirt. He put his leg up on the seat of a nearby chair, gave her a profile and lifted the beer bottle—she liked it. He grinned, scowled, stuck his tongue out, blew raspberries at the camera—she snapped and laughed. Then he crooked his finger at her for her to come closer and she took pictures as she went. When she got real close he pulled the camera away.

"Let's get out of here," he whispered. "Somewhere we can talk."

"Can't we talk here?" she asked.

He shook his head. "Listen," he said.

She listened—the jukebox. Only the jukebox. He turned her around. Every single eye was on them. Watching. Waiting. She turned back to Drew. "Everyone knows," she said. "We are the only single people, we're both single and miserable—"

"Single," he said. "I'm not miserable and I know you intended to be miserable, but that's not really working out for you. So?" he asked with a shrug. "Wanna just throw caution to the wind and see if you can enjoy the rest of the evening?"

"I can't enjoy it here?"

"With all of them watching you? Listening?" he asked with a lift of the chin to indicate the bar at large.

When she turned around to look, she caught everyone quickly averting their eyes and it made her laugh. She laughed harder, putting her hand over her mouth.

"Don't do that," he said, pulling her hand away. "You have an amazing smile and I love listening to you laugh."

"Where would we go?"

"Well, it's only ten. I could take you to Eureka or Fortuna—there's bound to be stuff going on, but I'd prefer to find somewhere there's not a party. I could show you the cabin Erin turned into a showplace, but I don't have any 'before' pictures. Or we could take a drive, park in the woods and make out like teenagers." He grinned at her playfully. Hopefully.

"You're overconfident," she accused.

"I've been told that. It's better than being underconfident, in these circumstances at least."

"I have to speak to Uncle Nathaniel," she said.

He touched her cheek with the knuckle of one finger. "Permission?"

She shook her head a little. "Courtesy. I'm his guest. Grab our coats."

The walk across the bar to her uncle was very short and in that time she realized that Drew wasn't overconfident—*Glen* was overconfident. He preened, and had always managed to strike a pose that accentuated his height, firm jaw, strong shoulders. Drew clowned around. Laughed. Drew seemed to be pretty easygoing and took things as they came. But she'd known him for two whole hours. Who knew what secrets he harbored?

But what the hell, Sunny thought. *I can experiment with actually letting a male person get close without much risk—I'm never going to see him again. Who knows? Maybe I'll recover after all.*

"Uncle Nate," she said. "I'm going to go with Drew to see if anything fun is happening in Fortuna or Eureka. If you're okay with that."

"Well," he said. "I don't actually know—*ow!*"

Annie slugged him in the arm. "That's great, Sunny," she said. "Will you come back here or have Drew take you home?"

She shrugged and shook her head. "I don't know. Depends on where we are, what's going on, you know. Listen, if the cells worked up here, I'd call, but…"

"Your cell from Fortuna or Eureka to my home phone works. Or to Jack's landline. We'll be here till midnight," Nate said. Then he glared briefly at Annie. "Jack, can you give her your number?"

"You bet," Jack said, jotting it on a napkin. "I've known Drew and his family a couple of years. You're in good hands, Sunny."

"Does he have four-wheel drive?" Nate asked.

Sunny grinned. "Oh, you're going to be a fun daddy, yessir." Then she walked back to Drew and let him help her slip on her jacket.

"Where did you say we were going?" Drew asked.

"I said Fortuna or Eureka, but I want to see it—the cabin."

He grabbed his own jacket. "Hope I didn't leave it nasty."

"And is that likely?" she wanted to know.

"Depends where my head was at the time," he said. He rested her elbow in the palm of his hand and began to direct her out of the bar. As they were leaving he put two fingers to his brow and gave the gawkers a salute.

Sunny was trying to remember, what was the first thing Drew had said to her? She thought it was something simple, like "Hi, my name is Drew." And what had been Glen's opening line? With a finger in her sternum he had said, "Yo. You and me."

Five

"I'm not sure that was the best thing to do," Nate Jensen said right after Sunny and Drew left. "I'm supposed to be looking after her, and I let her go off with some guy I don't even know."

"She was *laughing!*" Annie stressed. "Having fun for the first time in so long! She didn't need your permission, Nate. She was being polite, telling you where she was going so you wouldn't worry."

"You did fine," Jack said. "Drew's a good guy. A doctor, actually—in his residency now."

"But is he the kind of guy who will take advantage of a girl with a broken heart?" Nate asked. "Because my sister…"

"I don't know a thing about his love life," Jack said. "He said he'd had a breakup, so that might make them sympathetic to each other. I'll tell you what I know. Every time I've talked to him he's seemed like a stand-up guy. His brother-in-law was a disabled marine in a nursing home for a few years before he died, and Erin said that Drew, along with the rest of the family, helped take care of him. Erin thinks that had an impact on him, drew him to medicine. And...he has four-wheel drive. That should put your mind at ease."

"She *was* smiling," Nate admitted. "You should'a been there last year. Sitting in that church, waiting for the wedding to start. Just like in all things, the rumors that the groom didn't show started floating around the guests, maybe before Sunny had even heard it. It was awful. How do you not know something like that is coming? How could she not know?"

Jack gave the bar a wipe. "You can bet she's been asking herself that question for about a year."

"Tell me about the photography business," Drew said as they drove.

"You don't have to ask that," she said. "I can tell you're a gentleman and that's very polite, but you don't have to pretend to be interested in photography. It bores the heck out of most people."

He laughed at her. "When I was a kid, I took pictures sometimes," he said. "Awful pictures that were developed at the drugstore, but it was enough to get me on the yearbook staff, which I only wanted to be on because Bitsy Massey was on it. Bitsy was a cute little thing, a cheerleader of course, and she was on the yearbook committee—most likely to been sure the lion's share of the pictures were of her. I was in love with her for about six months, and she never knew I was alive. The only upside to the whole thing? I actually like taking pictures. I admit, I take a lot with my cell phone now and I don't have any aspirations to go professional, but I wasn't just being polite. In fact," he said, reaching into his pocket for his cell, "I happen to have some compound fractures, crushed ankles, ripped out shoulders and really horrible jaw fractures if you'd like to—"

"Ack!" she yelled, fanning him away with her hand. "Why in the world would you have those?"

"Snap 'em in E.R., take 'em to report and explain how we treated 'em and have the senior residents shoot us down and call us fools and idiots. So, Sunny—how'd it happen for you—picture taking? A big thug named Rock who liked to pose for you?"

"Nothing of the sort," she said indignantly. "I got a camera for Christmas when I was ten and started taking pictures. It only takes a few good ones before you realize you *can.* Take good pictures, that is. I figured out early what they would teach us about photography in college later—to get four or forty good pictures, just take four hundred. Of course, some subjects are close to impossible. Their color, angles, tones and shadows just don't work, while others just eat the camera, they're so photogenic. But…" She looked over at him. "Bored?"

"Not yet," he answered with a grin.

"It was my favorite thing," she said. "My folks kept saying there was no real future in it and I'd better have a backup plan, so I majored in business. But friends kept asking me to take pictures because I could. Pretty soon I had the moxie to ask them to at least pay the expenses—travel costs like gas for the car, film, developing, mounting, that sort of thing. Me and my dad put a darkroom in the basement when I was a junior in high school, but right after that we went digital and got a really good computer, upscale program and big screen. I built a website, using some of my stock for on-line advertising, and launched a price list that was real practical for people on a budget—but the product was *good*. My darkroom became a workroom. I could deliver finished portraits in glossy, matte, texture, whatever they wanted, and I could do it quickly. Friends told friends who told friends and by my sophomore year I was booked every weekend for family reunions, birthday parties, christenings, weddings, engagement parties, you name it. The only thing I didn't have when I dropped out of school to do this full-time was a studio. Since I did all my shooting on location at the site, all I needed in a studio was a desk, computer, big-screen monitor, DVD player and some civilized furnishings, plus a whole lot of albums and DVDs and brochures of photo packages. The money was good. I was set up before I was set up. I was lucky."

"I bet you were also smart," Drew said.

She laughed a bit. "Sort of, with my dad running herd on my little business all the time. He wasn't trying to make me successful, he was looking out for me, showing me the pitfalls, helping me not fail. When it became my means of income, I think he was a little ambivalent about me quitting college. And my mom? Scared her to death! She's old-fashioned—go get a practical job! Don't bet on your ingenuity or worse, your talent!"

"Your guy," Drew asked. "What did he do?"

"Highway Patrol. He liked life on the edge."

"Did he like your photographs?"

Without even thinking she answered, "Of him. He liked being in front of the camera. I like being behind it."

"Oh, he was one of the photogenic ones?"

"He was," she admitted. "He could be a model. Maybe he is by now."

"You don't keep in touch?"

"Oh, no," she said with a mean laugh.

"Not even through friends?"

"Definitely not through friends." She turned to look at him. "You? Do you keep in touch?"

He shrugged but his eyes were focused on the road. "Well, she's going to marry one of the residents at the hospital. We're not in the same service—he's general surgery. But she turns up sometimes. She's polite. I'm polite." He took a breath. "I hate that. I don't know how she feels, but I don't feel polite."

"So you are angry," she said, a note of surprise in her voice.

"Oh, hell yes," he replied. "It's just that sometimes the line is blurred, and I get confused about who I'm angriest with—her or me. She knew what she was signing up for, that residents don't have a lot of time or money or energy after work. Why couldn't we figure that out without all the drama? But then, I'm guilty of the same thing—I was asking way too much of her. See? Plenty of blame to go around."

There was quiet for a while. The road was curvy, banked by very tall trees heavy with snow. The snow was falling lightly, softly. The higher they went, the more snow there was on the ground. There were some sharp turns along the road, and a few drop-offs that, in the dark of night, looked like they were bottomless. He drove slowly, carefully, attentively. If he looked at her at all, which was rare, it was the briefest glance.

"Very pretty out here," she said quietly.

He responded with, "Can I ask you a personal question?"

She sucked in her breath. "I don't know...."

"Tell you what—don't answer if it makes you the least bit uncomfortable," he suggested.

"But wouldn't my not answering tell you that—"

"Did you fall in love with him the second you met him? Like right off the bat? Boom—you saw him, you were knocked off your feet, dead in love?"

No! she thought. "Yes," she said. She looked across the front seat at him. "You?"

He shook his head first. "No. I liked her right away, though. There were things about her that really worked for me, that work for a guy. Like, for example, no guessing games. She was very upfront, but never in a bitchy way. Not a lot of games with Penny, at least up until we got to the breaking-up part of our relationship. For example, if we went out to dinner, she ordered exactly what she liked. If I asked her what she'd like to do, she came up with an answer—never any of that 'I don't care' when she really did care. I liked that. We got along, seemed like we were paddling in the same direction. I wanted to be a surgeon, and she was a nurse who liked the idea of being with a doctor, even though she knew it was never easy on the spouse. When I asked her if she wanted to move in with me before the residency started she said, 'Not without a ring.'" He shrugged. "Seemed reasonable to me that we'd just get married. I'm still real surprised it didn't work out that way. I really couldn't tell you exactly when it stopped working. That's the only thing that scares me."

She stared at his profile. At that moment she decided that if she ever broke a bone, she'd want him to set it. "But by then you were madly in love with her, right? By the time you got to the ring?"

"Probably. Yeah, I think so. The thing is, Penny

seemed exactly right for me, exactly. Logical. Problems that friends of mine had with wives or girlfriends, I didn't have with Penny. Guys envied me. I thought she was the perfect one for me."

She heard Glen's voice in her head. *I thought you were the best thing for me, the best woman I could ever hook up with for the long haul....*

"Until all this fighting started," he went on. "Things had been so easy with us, I didn't get it. I thought it was all about her missing her friends, me working such long hours, that kind of thing. I'm still not sure—maybe it was about another guy and being all torn up trying to decide. But really, I thought everything was fine."

"What is it with you guys?" she said hotly. "You just pick out a girl who looks like wife material and hope by the time you get to the altar you'll be ready?"

Drew gave her a quick glance, a frown, then looked back at the road. And that's when it happened—as if it fell from the sky, he hit a buck. He knew it was a buck when he saw the antlers. He also saw its big, brown eyes. It was suddenly in front of the SUV—his oldest sister's SUV that he had borrowed to go up to the cabin. Though they weren't traveling fast, the strike was close, sudden, the buck hit the front hard, was briefly airborne, came down on the hood, and rolled up against the windshield with enough force for the antlers to crack it, splinter it.

Drew fought the car, though he could only see clearly out of the driver's side window. He knew that to let the SUV go off the road could be disastrous—there were so many drop-offs on the way to the cabin. He finally brought the car to rest on the shoulder, the passenger side safely resting against a big tree.

Sunny screamed in surprise and was left staring into the eyes of a large buck through the webbed and cracked windshield. The deer was lying motionless across the hood.

Drew turned to Sunny first. "Sunny..."

"We hit a deer!" she screamed.

"Are you okay? Neck? Head? Back? Anything?" he asked her.

She was unhooking her belt and wiggling out of it. "Oh, my God, oh, my God, oh, my God! He's dead! Look at him! He's dead, isn't he?"

"Sunny," he said, stopping her, holding her still. "Wait a second. Sit still for just a second and tell me—does anything hurt?"

Wide-eyed, she shook her head.

He ran a hand down each of her legs, over her knees. "Did you hit the dash?" he asked. "Any part of you?"

She shook her head. "You have to help the deer!" she said in a panic.

"I don't know if there's much help for him. I wonder why the air bags didn't deploy—the SUV must've swept the buck's legs out from under him, causing him to directly hit the grille, and since the car kept moving forward, no air bags. Whew, he isn't real small, either."

"Check him, Drew. Okay?"

"I'll look at him, but you stay right here for now, all right?"

"You bet I will. I should tell you—me and blood? Not a good combination."

"You faint?"

She nodded, panic etched on her face. "Right after I get sick."

He rolled his eyes. That was all he needed. "Do not get out of the car!"

"Don't worry," she said as he was exiting.

Drew assessed the deer before he took a closer look at the car. The deer was dead, bleeding from legs and head, eyes wide and fixed, blood running onto the white snow. There was some hood and grille damage, but the car might be drivable if he didn't have a smashed windshield. It was laminated glass, so it had gone all veiny like a spiderweb. He'd have to find a way to get that big buck off and then, if he drove it, he'd have a hard time seeing through the cracked glass.

He pulled out his cell phone and began snapping pictures, but in the dark it was questionable what kind of shots he'd get.

He leaned back in the car. "Can I borrow your camera? It has a nice, big flash, right?"

"Borrow it for what?"

"To get some pictures of the accident. For insurance."

"Should I take them?" she asked.

"I don't know if you'll have time before you get sick and faint."

Blood. That meant there was blood. "Okay—but let me show you how." She pulled the camera bag from the backseat, took the camera out and gave him a quick lesson, then sat quietly, trying not to look at the dead deer staring at her as light flashed in her peripheral vision.

But then, curious about where Drew was, she looked out the cracked windshield and what she saw almost brought tears to her eyes. With the camera hanging at his side from his left hand, he looked down at the poor animal and, with his right hand, gave him a gentle stroke.

Then he was back, handing her the camera. "Did you pet that dead deer?" she asked softly.

He gave his head a little nod. "I feel bad. I wish I'd seen him in time. Poor guy. I hope he doesn't have a family somewhere."

"Aw, Drew, you're just a tender heart."

"Here's what we have to do," he said, moving on. "We're going to have to walk the rest of the way. Fortunately it's only a couple of miles."

"Shouldn't we stay with the car? I've always heard you should stay with the car. What if someone comes looking for us?"

"It will be too cold. I can't keep it running all night. And if anyone gets worried by how long we're gone, they're going to look in Fortuna or Eureka. Or at least the route to those towns, which is where you told them we were going." He lifted a brow. "Why do you suppose you did that?"

She shook her head. "I didn't want my uncle Nate to think we were going somewhere to be alone. Dumb. Very dumb."

"I need a phone, a tow truck and a warm place to wait, so here's what's going to happen. Hand me the camera case." She zipped it closed and he hung it over his shoulder. "There's a big flashlight in the glove box. Grab it—I'll have to light our way when we clear the headlights. Now slide over here and when you get out, either shield or close your eyes until I lead you past the deer, because the way my night's going if you get sick, it'll be on me."

She wrinkled her nose. "I smell it," she said. "Ick, I can *smell* it!"

"Close your eyes *and* your nose," he said. "Let's get past this, all right?"

She slid over, put her feet on the ground and stood. And her spike heels on her boots sank into the frozen, snowy ground. "Uh-oh," she said.

"Oh, brother. So, what if I broke the heels off those boots? Would you be able to walk in them?"

She gasped! "They're six-hundred-dollar Stuart Weitzman boots!"

He looked at her levelly for a long moment. "I guess the photography business is going very, very well."

"I had to console myself a little after being left at the church. Giving them up now would be like another... Oh, never mind..."

"You're right," he said. "I must have lost my mind." He eased her backward, lifted her onto the seat with her legs dangling out. Then he positioned the heavy camera bag around his neck so it hung toward the front. Next he turned his back to her, braced his hands on his knees and bent a little. "Piggyback," he said. "Let's move it."

"I'm too heavy."

"No, Sunny, you're not."

"I am. You have no idea how much I weigh."

"It's all right," he said. "It's not too much."

"I'll go in my socks. It's just a couple of miles..."

"And get frostbite and from then on you'll be putting your prosthetic feet into your Stuart Weitzmans." He looked over his shoulder at her. "The sooner we do this, the sooner we're warm and with help on the way."

Sunny only thought about it for a second—she was getting cold and she liked her feet, didn't want to give them up to frostbite. She grumbled as she climbed on. "I was just willing to leave Jack's so we could talk without everyone watching. I haven't really talked to a single guy in a year."

"Close your eyes," he said. "What does that mean, 'really talked to a single guy'?"

"Obviously I ran into them from time to time. Bag boys, mechanics, cable repairmen, cousins to the bride or groom… But after Glen, I had sworn off dating or even getting to know single men. Just not interested in ever putting myself in that position again. You know?"

"I know," he said a bit breathlessly. He stopped trudging up the hill to catch his breath. Then he said, "You lucked out with me—there's no better way to see a person's true colors than when everything goes to hell. Wrecked car, dead deer, spiked heels—it qualifies." He hoisted her up a bit and walked on.

"I'd like to ask you something personal, if you're up for it," she said.

He stopped walking and slid her off his back. He turned toward her and he was smiling. "Sunny, I can't talk and carry you—this top-of-the-line camera is heavy. Here's what you can do—tell me stories. Any stories you want—chick stories about shopping and buying six-hundred-dollar boots, or photographer stories, or scary stories. And when we get to the cabin, you can ask me anything you want."

"I'm too heavy," she said for the umpteenth time.

"I'm doing fine, but I can't carry on much of a conversation. Why don't you entertain us by talking, I'll walk and listen." And he presented his back again so she could climb on.

She decided to tell him all about her family; how her mother, two aunts and Uncle Nate had grown up in these mountains; and how later, when Grandpa had retired and left the veterinary practice to Uncle Nate, they all went back for visits. Grandma and Grandpa lived in Arizona as did Patricia and her two sons. Auntie Chris lived in Nevada with their two sons and one daughter and Sunny, an only child, lived in Southern California.

"Am I heavier when I talk?" she asked him.

"No," he said, stopping for a moment. "You make the walk shorter."

So she kept going. She talked about the family gatherings at the Jensen stables, about how she grew up on a horse like her mom and aunts had. But while her only female cousin and best friend since birth, Mary, had ridden competitively, Sunny was taking pictures. She spoke about fun times and pranks with her cousins.

She told him how Nate and Annie had met over an abandoned litter of puppies and would be married in the spring. "I'll be a bridesmaid. It will be my third time as a bridesmaid and a lot of my girlfriends are getting married. I've never before in my life known a single woman who was left at the altar. I keep wondering what I did wrong. I mean, Glen worked out like a madman and he wanted me to work out too, but you can't imagine the exercise involved in carrying a twenty pound camera bag, running, stooping, crouching, lifting that heavy camera for literally hours. I just couldn't get excited about lifting weights on top of that. He said I should think about implants. I hate surgical procedures of any kind. Oh, sure, I've always wanted boobs, but not that bad. And yes, I'm short and my butt's too big and my nose is pointy…. He used to say wide hips are good for sex and nothing else. That felt nice, hearing that," she said facetiously. "I tried to take comfort in the sex part—maybe that meant I was all right in the sack, huh?

And I'm bossy, I know I'm bossy sometimes. I liked to think I'm efficient and capable, but Glen thought it was controlling and he said it pissed him off to be controlled by a woman. There you have it—the recipe for getting left at the altar."

Then she stopped talking for a while. When she spoke again, her voice was quiet and his tread actually slowed. "I'd like you to know something. When we first met and I was so snotty and rude, I never used to be like that. Really. I always concentrated on being nice. That's how I built my business—I was nice, on time, and worked hard—that's what I attribute most of my success to. Seriously. That whole thing with Glen.... Well, it changed me. I apologize."

"No apology necessary," he said breathlessly. "I understand."

Then she was embarrassed by all her talking, talking about boobs and hips and sex to a total stranger. Blessedly, he didn't make any further comment. It wasn't long before she could see a structure and some lights up ahead. He trudged on, breathing hard, and finally put her down on the porch that spanned the front of a small cabin.

She looked up at him. "It's amazing that you would do that. I would have left me in the car."

He gave her a little smile. "Well, you wanted to see the cabin. And now you will. We'll call Jack's, let everyone know what happened, that we're all right, and I'll light the fire, so we can warm up. Then I have a few things to tell you."

Six

Drew immediately started stacking wood in the fireplace on top of some very big pinecones he used as starters.

Sunny looked around—showplace, all right. She appreciated the plush leather furniture, beautiful patterned area rug, spacious stone hearth, stained shutters, large kitchen. There were two doors off the great room—bedrooms, she assumed. It wasn't messy, though books and papers were stacked on the ottoman and beside the long, leather sofa, and a laptop sat open on the same ottoman. There was a throw that looked like it might be cashmere that was tossed in a heap at the foot of the sofa.

"Should I go ahead and call Jack's?" she asked him.

He looked over his shoulder at her and smiled. "No hurry. No way I'm getting a tow truck tonight, on New Year's Eve. In fact, I wouldn't count on New Year's Day either—I'm probably going to have to get my brother-in-law to drive up here in his truck to get me and tow Erin's car home. We're not late yet, so no one's worried." He lit a match to the starter cones and stood up as the fire took light. He brushed the dirt off his hands. "I hate to think about you being rescued too soon. I think we still have some things to talk about."

"Like?"

He stepped toward her. There was a softness in his eyes, a sweet smile on his lips. "You wanted to ask me something personal. And I have to tell you something." His hands were on her upper arms and he leaned down to put a light kiss on her forehead. "You're not too short. You're a good height." He touched her nose with a finger, then he had to brush a little soot off of it. "Your nose looks perfect to me—it's a very nice nose. And your chest is beautiful. Inviting, if you can handle hearing that from a man who is not your fiancé. I was never attracted to big boobs. I like to look at well-proportioned women. More than that, women in their real, natural bodies—implants might stay standing, but they're not pretty to me." His hands went to her hips. "And these?" he asked, squeezing. "Delicious. And your butt? One of the best on record. On top of all that I think you have the greatest laugh I've heard in a long time and your smile is infectious—I bet you can coax excellent smiles out of photo subjects with it. When you smile at me? I feel like I'm somebody, that's what. And the fact that you were a little ornery? I'm okay with that—you know why? Because when someone does something that bad to you, they shouldn't just get away with it. It hurts and turns you a little mean because it's just plain unfathomable that a guy, even a stupid guy, can be that cruel. I'm really sorry that happened, Sunny. And I hope you manage to get past it."

She was a little stunned for a moment. No one had ever talked to her like that, not that she'd given anyone a chance with the way she pushed people away. But he was so sexy and sweet it was *killing* her. "Just out of curiosity, what would you have done?"

"If I was left in my Vera Wang?" he asked, wide-eyed.

She laughed in spite of herself. "No, if you realized you didn't want to get married to the woman you were getting married to!"

"First of all, it would never have gotten that far if I wasn't sure. Invitations would never be mailed. Getting married isn't just some romantic thing—it's a lot of things, and one is a serious partnership. You have to be in the same canoe on at least most issues, but it's okay to be different, I think. Like my sisters and their guys? I would never have coupled them up, they're so different from their guys. But they're perfect for each other because they have mutual respect and a willingness to negotiate. They keep each other in balance. Plus, they love each other. Jesus, you wouldn't believe it, how much they're in love. It's almost embarrassing. But when they talk about being married, it's more about how they want their lives to go, how they want their partnership to feel."

"And you were that way with…Penny?" she asked.

"I thought I was," he said. "Thought she was, too."

"What if you're wrong next time, too?" Sunny asked.

"Is that what you're afraid of, honey?" he asked her gently.

"Of course! Aren't you?"

He stared at her for a second, then walked into the kitchen without answering. "Let's hope good old Erin stocked something decent for a cold winter night, huh?" He began opening cupboards. He finally came out with a dark bottle of liquid. "Aha! Brandy! Bet you anything this isn't Erin's, but Aiden's. But it's not terrible brandy—at least it's Christian Brothers." He lifted the bottle toward her.

"Sure, what the hell," she said, going over to the sofa to sit. She raised the legs of her jeans, unzipped her boots and pulled them off. She lifted one and looked at it. Now why would she bring these to Uncle Nate's stable? These were L.A. boots—black suede with pointy toes and spike heels. The boots she normally brought to the stable were low-heeled or cowboy, hard leather, well-worn. The kind that would've made it up that hill so she wouldn't have to be carried.

She threw the boot on the floor. Okay, she had wanted to be seen, if possible, and judge the look on the face of the seer. Her confidence was pretty rocky; she needed to feel attractive. She wanted to see a light in a male eye like the one she had originally seen in Glen's—a light she would run like hell from, but still....

Drew brought her a brandy in a cocktail glass, not a snifter. He sat down beside her. "Here's to surviving a deer strike!" he said, raising his glass to her.

She clinked. "Hear, hear."

They each had a little sip and he said, "Now—that personal question? Since I can breathe and talk again."

"It's probably a dumb question. You'd never be able to answer it honestly and preserve your manhood."

"Try me. Maybe you're right about me, maybe you're not."

"Okay. Did you cry? When she left you?"

He rolled his eyes upward to find an answer. He shook his head just a bit, frowning. "I don't think so. Didn't cry, didn't beg." He leveled his gaze at her. "Didn't sleep either, and since I couldn't sleep I worked even more hours. I kept trying to figure out where I'd gone wrong. For two years we seemed to be fine and then once the ring was on the finger, everything went to hell."

"So what *did* you do?" she wanted to know.

"I did my chores," he said. "All the things she wanted me to do that when I didn't, drove her crazy. There were little rules. If you're the last one out of the bed, make it. If you eat off a plate, rinse it and put it in the dishwasher. If something you take off is dirty it doesn't go on the floor, but in the hamper. I thought if she came back, she'd see I was capable of doing the things that were important to her."

That almost broke her heart. "Drew…"

"In medicine we have a saying, if you hear hoofbeats, don't expect to see a zebra. I was thinking horses—it's pretty common for surgeons to have relationship problems because of the pressure, the stress, the time they have to spend away from home. Horses. I brought her with me to my residency program, took her away from her mom, away from her job and girlfriends, and then I had even less time for her than I'd had as a med student. And we fought about it—about my hours, her loneliness. But when she left me, she didn't go back home. It took me so long to figure that out. I thought it meant she was still considering us. She moved a few miles away. Not because I was still a consideration, but because there was a guy. I never suspected a guy. I didn't even know about him for six months after we broke up. It was a zebra all along."

"Ow. That must have hurt you bad."

He leaned toward her. "My pride, Sunny. At the end of the day, I missed her, hated giving up my idea of how we'd spend the rest of our lives, but it was mostly my pride that was hurt. I'm real grateful to Penny—she walked away while all we had at stake was some cheap, hand-me-down furniture to divide between us. If we weren't going to make it together, if she wasn't happy with me, I'm glad she left me before we invested a lot more in each other. See," he said, taking Sunny's hand in his, "I think I put Penny in charge and I went along, and that wasn't fair. When a man cares about a woman, he owes it to her to romance her, pursue her, *convince* her. I learned something there—you don't just move along toward something as serious as marriage unless just about every emotion you have has been engaged. Like I said, we grew on each other. Lots of times I asked myself why I thought that was enough."

"But what I want to know is, will you ever be willing to risk it again?" she asked.

"Yes, and I look forward to it," he answered.

"You're just plain crazy! A glutton for punishment!"

"No, I'm reformed. I always heard it was a good idea to fall in love with your best friend and I bought that. I thought if you could meet someone you really liked and she also turned you on, all the mysteries of life were solved. I still think you'd better be good, trusted friends with the person you marry, but by God, there had better be some mind-blowing passion. Not like when you're sixteen and carry your brain in your… Well, you know. But next time, and there will be a next time, I want it all—someone I like a lot, trust, someone I respect and love and someone I want so bad I'm almost out of my mind."

"Do you think you'll ever find that?" Sunny asked.

"The important thing is that I won't settle for less.

Now, you've had a year to think about it—what's your conclusion about what happened?"

She pursed her lips and frowned, looked down for a second, then up. "I was about to marry the wrong guy and he bolted before he could make the biggest mistake of his life. But don't look at me to thank him for it— the mess he left was unbelievable. Over a hundred gifts had to be returned, my parents had paid for invitations, a designer gown, flowers and several big dinners—including the reception dinner. Flowers were distributed to the wedding party so they wouldn't just be wasted… It was horrendous."

"Have you ever wondered," he asked her, "what one thing would make that whole nightmare a blessing in disguise?"

"I can't imagine!" she said.

Funniest thing, he thought. *Before tonight, neither could I.*

He moved very slowly, scooting closer to her. He lifted the glass of brandy out of her hand and placed both hers and his on the coffee table. He put his hands on her waist and pulled her closer, leaning his lips toward hers. He hovered just over hers, waiting for a sign that she felt something, too; at least a stirring, a curiosity, that would be enough for now. Then slowly, perhaps reluctantly, her hands slid up his arms to his shoulders and that was just what he needed. He covered her mouth with his in a hot, searing kiss. He wanted to see her face when he kissed her, but he let his eyelids close and allowed his hands to wander around to her back, pulling her chest harder against his, just imagining what more could happen between them.

The kiss was warm and wet and caused his heart

to thump. He'd had quite a few brief fantasies linked to desires. Earlier, out by the Christmas tree in town, he'd had a vision of kissing her and then licking his way down her belly to secret parts that would respond to him with powerful satisfaction. He wanted nothing as much as to lie in her arms, skin on skin, and explore every small corner of her beautiful body.

But that wasn't going to happen now. Not tonight. Not tomorrow.

He pulled away reluctantly.

"I haven't been kissed in a year," she whispered. "I had decided I wasn't ever going to be kissed again. It was too dangerous."

"No danger here, Sunny. And you'll be happy to know you haven't lost your touch. You're very good at it." He looked into those hypnotic blue eyes as he pushed a lock of her hair over her ear. "If I had married Penny, if Glen had shown up when he was supposed to, I wouldn't be kissing you now. And I have to tell you, Sunny, I can't remember ever feeling so good about a kiss…"

She could only sigh and let her eyes drift closed. "We are a bad combination," she whispered.

"I can't believe that…"

"Oh, believe it." She opened her eyes. "You were a guy who just went along with what a woman wanted and I was a woman who, without even thinking about it too much, pushed a man into a great big wedding he didn't want." She swallowed and her eyes glistened. "I hate to admit this to anyone, but Glen kept telling me things—like he just wasn't comfortable with the size of that wedding, and he wasn't sure our work schedules would be good for us, or this or that. I told him not to worry, but I never changed anything. I kept saying I couldn't—that photographers work weekends. But that's not really true, they don't have to work *every* weekend. Portraits for events like anniversaries and engagements can be done before the parties are held, belly shots and babies can be done on weekdays. But the important thing is that until five minutes ago, I wasn't willing to admit our breakup had anything to do with me. And I might be admitting it to you because I'll probably never see you again."

"Listen—I might have been a go-along kind of guy, but I was never that spineless. Glen let it go too far. He doesn't get off that easy."

She gave him a weak smile. "I'm glad I met you. I didn't want to meet a guy, get to know a guy, and I sure didn't want to like a guy, but… Well, I'm not sorry."

"You know what that means, don't you?"

She shook her head.

"After you go through something like a bad breakup and you meet someone new, you check it out and you either find someone better for you, or you recognize right off that you haven't found the right one yet. But at least you keep moving forward until the guy and the life that's right for you comes into focus. And until that happens, we get to kiss."

"You're an opportunist. I could smell it on you the second I met you."

"Now you call your uncle and tell him about the deer accident, tell him we're safe and warm and I'll be looking for a tow truck in the morning. If you want him to, you can ask him if he'll come and rescue you. He can come now or later. A little later or much, much later. You could even stay the night, if you felt like it."

"No I couldn't," she said with a laugh.

"Then will you ask him to wait till after midnight? It's not that far off."

"I think I'll just wait awhile to call," she said. "If I know my uncle, he'll be on the road as soon as he gets my call."

That made Drew smile. "I know I'm probably a poor substitute for the guy you wanted to be kissing at midnight, but—"

"Actually, Dr. Foley, I think maybe you're a big improvement. And I might've gone a long time without knowing that."

Sunny waited a little bit and then called her uncle, letting him know where she was, what had happened and that she was fine. While she was on the phone, Drew quickly downloaded the pictures of the bloody deer onto his laptop and deleted them from her camera. Then, while the fire roared, they sat on the leather sofa, very close together, with their feet propped up on the ottoman. At times their legs were on top of each other's. They kissed now and then. Other times they talked. Sunny didn't say too much more about Glen, and she didn't want to hear any more about Penny.

She didn't tell him that Glen wasn't always nice to her. Oh, it went a bit further than the comment about the wide hips. Glen was the kind of guy who stayed out too late "unwinding" after work, criticized her appearance as being not sexy enough for his tastes and when they did have time together, he was never happy with how they were going to spend it—almost as if he'd rather she be working. She had thought about snatching his phone and looking at old text messages, listening to voice mails, but she was a little afraid of what she might find so she convinced herself she was being paranoid. By the time she realized it wasn't such a positive match, she was wearing a ring and had made deposits on wedding stuff.

It was too late.

But what she did want to ask Drew was, "What makes you think you'll do any better the next time you have a relationship?"

He turned to her with a smile and said, "Good! I really wanted you to ask me that." He ran the knuckle of his index finger along her cheek. "Do you have any idea what attracts men and women to each other?"

She just shook her head. "I thought it was a learned behavior...."

"Maybe, but I bet it's more. I bet it's a real primal mating thing that has no logical explanation. Like you see someone and right away, *bam,* you gotta be with that person. And I bet sometimes all the other elements fall into place, and sometimes they don't. That kind of unexplainable thing—you see a woman on the other side of the room and your heart just about leaps out of your chest. You go brain-dead and you're on automatic. All of a sudden you're walking over to her and you don't know why, you just know you have to get closer. Everything about her pulls you like a magnet. You feel kind of stupid but you just walk up to her and say, 'Hi, my name is Drew' and hope for the best, even though she's looking at you like you're an idiot."

"Slick," she said. "Have you actually been able to use that technique very often?"

"I've never even tried it before, I swear. Listen, it's kind of embarrassing to admit this, but that never happened with Penny. It was comfortable, nice, that's all. No fireworks, no mind-blowing passion…"

"But you said it was good with her! You said sex was good."

"I might be kind of easy to please in that department. The worst sex I ever had was actually pretty good. I want what *else* there is! How did what's-his-name reel you in?" he asked.

Yo. Me and you!

"He wasn't too slick, as a matter of fact. He thought he was. I never told him his great pickup line didn't impress me. Thing was, he was cute. And I worked all the time. I hadn't been out on a date in a long time and he was…" She shrugged. "Handsome and interested." She tilted her head and smiled at him. "I think I'm telling you all these things because you're safe."

His large hand closed over her shoulder. "I don't want to be safe," he said. "And I want to see you again."

"Want to go off, live our solitary lives and meet back here for New Year's Eve every year…kind of like a take-off on *Same Time, Next Year*?"

"Did you know what Jack had planned for midnight?" Drew asked. "Did you write your resolution?"

She shook her head, then nodded. "I wrote that I had to stay away from men. He put it in the fishbowl."

"At midnight everyone was going to pull out a resolution, ending up with someone else's. Really corny, don't you think?" he asked her, reaching into the pocket of his jeans. "It's going to be for laughs, not for real. Some skinny girl could get a resolution to lose twenty pounds. But I wrote this one before I knew much about you." He presented a slip of paper. "Look, Sunny—it's midnight."

"No, it's not," she said. "It's like three minutes till."

"We can stretch it out," he said, handing her the paper. "I have no idea why I stuck this in my pocket. I put a different one in the fishbowl."

She took it, opened it and read, "Start the new year by giving a new guy a chance."

Her cheeks got a little pink. She was flattered, she was feeling lusty and attracted, but… "But, Drew, I'm not going to see you again."

"If you want to, you will…"

"You're just looking for a replacement fiancée," she said. "And long-distance relationships are even harder to keep going than the close kind."

"We can start with football tomorrow. I have beer and wings. Unfortunately I have no car, but I bet you can wrangle one from the uncle."

"That's cute, but—"

"It's midnight," he said, closing in on her. His lips hovered right over hers. "Sunny, you just do something to me."

"Thanks," she said weakly. "Really, thanks. I needed to think I was actually attractive to someone."

"You're way more than that," he said, covering her mouth in a deep and powerful kiss. He put his arms around her waist and pulled her onto his lap, holding her against him. His head tilted to get a deeper fit over her mouth, their tongues played, her fingers threaded into his hair. At long last their lips parted. "Let's just give it a try, see where it goes."

"Can't work. I live in the south. L.A. area.…"

"Me, too."

She jumped, startled. She slid off his lap. "You said Chico…"

"No, I didn't. My family is in Chico. I lived there while I went to med school, while I dated Penny, but I don't live there anymore. I'm in residency at UCLA Medical."

She slid away from him. "Uh-oh..."

He shook his head. "I'm just saying we keep getting to know each other, that's all. Neither one of us is likely to keep moving forward in a relationship that doesn't feel good. We're wiser—we know too much now. But for God's sake, Sunny, what if it's good? You gonna walk away from that?"

"I don't want to take any chances!"

"I don't blame you," he said. "It's midnight. Kiss in a new year. And just think about it."

She looked into his eyes for a long moment, then she groaned and put the palms of her hands on his bristly cheeks and planted a good, wide, hot one on his mouth.

Against her open mouth he said, *"Yeah!"* Then he moved against her mouth, holding her tight, breathing her in, memorizing the taste of her.

A car horn penetrated the night. "Awww," he groaned. "Your uncle broke every speed limit in Humboldt and Trinity Counties."

"I told him to stay at Jack's till midnight, but I knew he wouldn't listen," she said. She pulled away from him, slid down the couch and reached to the floor for her boots. Without looking at him she said, "Listen, thanks. Really, thanks. I needed to drop the rage for a while, have a real conversation with a guy, test the waters a little bit. Kiss—I needed to kiss." She zipped the first boot. Then she looked at him. "I'm just not ready for more."

"But you will be," he said. "I can hang loose until you're more comfortable."

"I'll think about that," she said, reaching for the other boot.

The horn sounded again.

"He's going to be pounding on the door real soon," she said, zipping the boot.

"Will you come back tomorrow?" he asked.

She shook her head. "I need to think. Please understand."

"But how will I find you? How will you find me?"

"Doesn't Jack know your family? Don't they know where you are?"

He grabbed her just as the horn blasted another time. He held her upper arms firmly but not painfully, and looked deeply into her eyes. "The second I saw you I lost my mind and wanted to sit right down by you and talk to you. I wanted a lot more than that, but I'm no caveman. Sunny, all I want is to know more about you, to know if there's an upside to our mistakes—like maybe the right ones were meant to come along just a little later. I'd hate to stomp on a perfectly good spark if it's meant to be a big, strong, healthy flame. I—"

There was a pounding at the door.

Sunny sighed and pulled herself from his grip. "Well, here's a bright side for you," she said. "I'm going to kill my uncle."

Seven

Sunny threw open the door and glared at her uncle Nathaniel. "Not real patient, are you?"

Nate had his hands plunged into his jacket pockets to keep warm. He glared back. "A—you didn't go where you said you were going to go. And B—you didn't come out when I honked. Something could have been *wrong!*"

"A—I'm twenty-five and can change my plans when it suits me. And B—something could have been *right!*" She turned toward Drew. "Thank you for everything. I'll get this lunatic out of here."

"Sunny," Drew said. "UCLA Medical. Orthopedics Residency. I stand out like a sore thumb. I'm the one the senior residents are whipping and screaming at."

She smiled at him. "I'll remember. I promise."

Sunny grabbed her jacket, her camera bag and pulled the door closed behind her as she left. Nathaniel let her pass him on the porch. She stomped a little toward the truck until her skinny heels stuck into the snow-covered drive and she had to stop to pull them out.

"Must've been tough, walking from that wrecked car to the cabin in those boots," Nate observed.

She glared over her shoulder at him. "He carried me."

"Are you kidding me?" Nate said. "It was two miles!"

"Piggyback," she said, trying to balance her weight on the balls of her feet until she got to the truck. She pulled herself up into the backseat of the extended cab with a grunt.

Annie, who sat in the front of the truck, had her arms crossed over her chest. When she looked into the backseat, there was a frown on her face. "Are you all right?" she asked grimly.

"Of course, I'm all right," Sunny said. "Are you angry with me, too?"

"Of course not! I'm angry with Nathaniel!"

"Because...?"

"Because you were laughing with Drew Foley and I didn't want to crash your party!"

Sunny laughed lightly. "Oh, you two," she said. "It wasn't a party," she said just as her uncle was getting behind the wheel. "It was supposed to be a tour of the cabin, but it turned into a deer accident and a two-mile trek. Poor Drew. He had to carry me because of my stupid boots."

"But were you ready to leave?" Annie asked, just as Nate put the truck in gear.

No, Sunny thought. Not nearly ready. She loved everything about Drew—his voice, his gentle touch, his empathy for kids and animals, his scent.... Oh, his scent, his lips, his *taste*. But she said, "Yeah, sure. Thanks for coming for me. Sorry if I was a bother."

"Sorry if I was a lunatic," Nate said, turning the truck around. "I have a feeling if I have daughters, Annie will have to be in charge."

"First smart thing you've said in an hour," Annie informed him.

"Well, I have a responsibility!" he argued.

Sunny leaned her head forward into the front of the cab, coming between them. "You two didn't have your New Year's kiss, did you? Because whew, are you ever pissy!"

"Some people," Annie said, her eyes narrowed at Nate, "just don't listen."

Winter in the mountains was so dark; the sun wasn't usually up before seven in the morning. But Sunny was. In fact, she'd barely slept. She just couldn't get Drew out of her mind. She got up a couple of times to get something from the kitchen, but she only dozed. At five-thirty she gave up and put the coffee on.

By the time it was brewing, Annie was up. Before coming into the kitchen she started the fire in the great room fireplace. She shivered a bit even though she wore her big, furry slippers and quilted robe.

"Why are you up so early?" Sunny asked, passing a mug of coffee across the breakfast bar.

"Me? I'm always up early—we have a rigid feeding schedule for the horses."

"This early?"

"Well, I thought I heard a mouse in the kitchen," Annie said with a smile. "Let's go by the fire and you can tell me why *you're* up."

"Oh, Annie," she said a bit sadly, as she headed into the great room. "What's wrong with me?"

"Wrong?" Annie asked. She sat on the big leather sofa in front of the fire and patted the seat beside her. "I think you're close to perfect!"

Sunny shook her head. She sat on the sofa, turned toward Annie and pulled her feet under her. "I made up my mind I wasn't getting mixed up with another guy after what Glen did to me, then I go and meet this sweetheart. He's pretty unforgettable."

"Oh? The guy from the bar?"

Sunny sipped her coffee. "Sounds funny when you put it that way. Drew—a doctor of all things. Not a guy from a bar. He was up at his sister's cabin to study and only came into town to get a New Year's Eve beer. I never should have run into him. And even though he's totally nice and very sweet, I promised him I'd never get involved again, with him or anyone else. I told him I just wasn't ready."

"Smart if you ask me," Annie said, sipping from her own steaming cup.

"Really?" Sunny asked, surprised. Wasn't this the same woman who lectured her about letting go of the anger and getting on with her life?

Annie gave a short laugh. "After what happened to you? Why would you take that kind of chance again? Too risky. Besides, you have a good life! You have work you love and your parents are completely devoted to you."

"Annie, they're my parents," she said. "They're wonderful and I adore them, but they're my parents! They don't exactly meet all my needs, if you get my drift."

Annie patted Sunny's knee. "When more time has passed, when you feel stronger and more confident, you might run into a guy who can fill some of the blank spots—and do that without getting involved. Know what I mean?"

"I know what you mean," Sunny said, looking down. "Problem is, those kind of relationships never appealed to me much."

"Well, as time goes on…" Annie said. "I imagine you'll get the hang of it. You're young and you've been kicked in the teeth pretty good. I understand—you're not feeling that strong."

Sunny actually laughed. "I had no idea how strong I was," she said. "I got through the worst day of my life. I helped my mom return over a hundred wedding gifts…" She swallowed. "With notes of apology."

"You're right—that takes strength of a very unique variety. But you told me you don't feel too confident about your ability to know whether a guy is a good guy, a guy you can really trust," Annie said.

Sunny sighed. "Yeah, it's scary." Then she lifted her gaze and a small smile flitted across her mouth. "Some things are just obvious, though. You know what Drew said is the best and worst part of his job as an orthopedic surgery resident? Kids. He loves being able to help them, loves making them laugh, but it's really hard for him to see them broken. What a term, huh? Broken? But that's what he does—fixes broken parts."

"That doesn't mean you'd be able to count on him to come through for the wedding dance…" Annie pointed out.

But Sunny wasn't really listening. "When that deer was lying on the hood of the SUV I tried not to look, but he was taking pictures for the insurance and I had to take a peek out the windshield. He gave the deer a pet on the neck. He looked so sad. He said it made him feel bad and he hoped the deer didn't have a family somewhere. Annie, you grew up around here, grew up on a farm—do deer have families?"

"Sort of," she said softly. "Well, they breed. The bucks tend to breed with several doe and they run herd on their families, keep 'em together. They—"

"He's got a soft spot," Sunny said. "If I ever gave a

new guy a chance, it would be someone with a soft spot for kids, for animals...."

"But you won't," Annie said, shaking her head. "You made the right decision—no guys, no wedding, no marriage, no kids." Sunny looked at her in sudden shock. "Maybe later, when much more time has passed," Annie went on. "You know, like ten years. And no worries—you could meet a guy you could actually trust in ten years, date a year, be engaged a year, get married and think about a family... I mean, women are now having babies into their forties! You have lots of time!"

Sunny leaned toward her. "Did you hear me? He loves helping kids. He carried me to the cabin—two miles. He petted the dead deer! And he should have broken the heels off my Stuart Weitzmans so I could walk in the snow, but he carried me instead because I just couldn't part with—" Sunny looked at Annie with suddenly wide eyes. "What if he's a wonderful, perfect, loving man and I refuse to get to know him because I'm mad at Glen?"

Annie gave Sunny's hand a pat. "Nah, you wouldn't do that. You're just taking care of yourself, that's all. You don't have a lot of confidence right now. You're a little afraid you wouldn't know the right guy if he snuck up on you and kissed you senseless."

Sunny touched her lips with her fingertips. "He kisses *great*."

"Oh, Sunny! You let him *kiss* you?"

Sunny jumped up so fast she sloshed a little coffee on her pajamas. "I have plenty of confidence, I always have," she said. "I started my own business when I was twenty and it's going great. I know I get help from my dad, but I was never unsure. And I can't even think about being alone another ten years! Or sleeping with guys I don't care about just to scratch an itch—bleck!"

Annie shrugged and smiled, looking up at her. "All part of protecting yourself from possible hurt. I mean, what if you're wrong? Scary, huh?"

"Oh, crap, one hour with Drew and I knew what was wrong with Glen! I just couldn't…" She stopped herself. She couldn't stop that wedding!

"You said it yourself—you shouldn't get mixed up with another guy," Annie reminded her softly. "You wouldn't want to risk getting hurt." Annie stood and looked Sunny in the eyes. "Give it eight or ten years. I'm sure the right guy will be hanging around just when you're ready."

Sunny stiffened so suddenly she almost grew an inch. She grabbed Annie's upper arm. "Can I borrow your truck? I have something important to do."

"In your pajamas?" Annie asked.

"I'll throw on some jeans and boots while you find your keys," she said.

Sunny dashed to the kitchen, put her coffee mug on the breakfast bar and as she was sailing through the great room Annie said, "Sunny?" Sunny stopped and turned. Annie took a set of keys out of the pocket of her quilted robe and tossed them.

Sunny caught them in surprise, then a smile slowly spread across her face. *Who carries their car keys in their robe?* "You sly dog," she said to Annie.

Annie just shrugged. "There are only two things you have to remember. Trust your gut and take it one day at a time." Annie raised a finger. "One day at a time, sweetheart. Nice and easy."

"Will you tell Uncle Nate I had an errand to run?"

"You leave Uncle Nate to me," Annie said.

* * *

By the time Sunny was standing in front of the cabin door, it still was not light out. It was only six-thirty, but there were lights on inside and the faintest glow from the east that suggested sunrise. Drew opened the door.

"We never open the door that fast in L.A.," she said.

"There weren't very many possibilities for this part of town," he said. And he smiled at her. "I'm pretty surprised to see you. Coming in?"

"In a minute, if you still want me. I have to tell you a couple of things."

He lifted a light brown brow. "About my nose? My hips?"

"About me. First of all, I never lie. To anyone else or to myself. But my whole relationship with Glen? I wouldn't admit it to anyone, but it was one lie after another. I knew it wasn't going well, I knew we should have put on the brakes and taken a good, honest, deep look at our relationship. But I couldn't." She glanced down, then up into his warm brown eyes. "I couldn't stop the wedding. It had taken on a life of its own."

"I understand," he said.

"No, you don't. It was the wedding that had become a monster—a year in the making. Oh, Glen should take some responsibility for going along with it in the beginning, but it was entirely my fault for turning off my eyes, ears and *brain* when it got closer! I'd invested in it—passion and energy and money! My parents had made deposits on everything from invitations and gowns to parties! And there was an emotional investment, too. My friends and family were involved, praising me for the great job I was doing, getting all excited about the big event! Not only did I feel like I was letting everyone down, I couldn't give it up."

"I understand," he said again.

"No, you don't! The wedding had become more important than the marriage! I knew I should snoop into his text messages and voice mails because lots of things were fishy, but I didn't because it would ruin the wedding! I should have confronted our issues in counseling, but I couldn't because I knew the only logical thing to do was to postpone the wedding! The wedding of the century!" A tear ran down her cheek and he caught it with a finger. "I knew it was all a mistake, but I really didn't see him not showing up at the last minute as a threat, so that made it easy for me to lie when everyone asked me if there were any clues that it would happen." She shook her head. "That he would leave me at the altar? I didn't see that coming. That we weren't right for each other? I managed to close my eyes to that because I was very busy, and very committed. That's the truth about me. There. I traded my integrity for the best wedding anyone had ever attended in their life! And I've never admitted that to anyone, ever!"

"I see," he said. "Now do you want to come in?"

"Why are you awake so early?" she asked with a sniff.

"I don't seem to need that much sleep. I'd guess that was a real problem when I was a kid. Sunny, I'm sorry everything went to hell with your perfect wedding, but I'm not threatened by that. I'm not Glen and I have my own mistakes to learn from—that wouldn't happen with me. And guess what? You're not going to let something like that happen again. So the way I see it, we have only one thing to worry about."

"What's that?" she asked.

"Breakfast. I was going to have to eat canned beans

till you showed up. I don't have a car. Now you can take me to breakfast." He grinned. "I'm starving."

"I brought breakfast. I grazed through Uncle Nate's kitchen for groceries," she explained. "I wasn't going to find anything open on the way over here."

"You are brilliant as well as beautiful. Now we only have one other thing to worry about."

"What?"

"Whether we're going to make out like teenagers on the couch, the floor or the bed after we have breakfast."

She threw her arms around him. "You should send me away! I'm full of contradictions and flaws! I'm as much to blame for that nightmare of a wedding day as Glen is!"

He grinned only briefly before covering her mouth in a fabulous, hot, wet, long kiss. And after that he said, "Look. The sun's coming up on a new day. A new year. A new life. Let's eat something and get started on the making out."

"You're not afraid to take a chance on me?" Sunny asked him.

"You know what I'm looking forward to the most? I can't wait to see if we fall in love. And I like our chances. Scared?"

She shook her head. "Not at all."

"Then come in here and let's see if we can't turn the worst day of your life into the best one."

* * * * *

BACKWARD GLANCE

One

John drove past Jess Wainscott's house regularly, his eyes always sharpened for a glimpse of her daughter, Leigh. It had been almost five years. He hated that he looked for her; he wanted to be over her. He looked in spite of himself—and he wasn't over her in the least.

Today he wasn't just driving past. Jess had called him to do a job. John owned his own business in Durango—McElroy Property Services—which included home maintenance and repairs, landscaping and a very fine nursery, and Jess wanted to know if now—early March—was too early to plant a flowering plum tree. Though his business had incidentally or accidentally become successful, he still considered himself a handyman and lawn maintenance person. He could not only bring her a flowering plum, but also change the faucet on the sink, hang wallpaper, install a hot tub, pour a cement patio. Or have one of his employees do it.

"No, it's not too early," he had said. "Not as long as you're willing to protect it from a possible late freeze and pay the price of having some poor slob try to dig into the hard ground."

"Only if that poor slob is you," she cheerfully replied. "I really have my heart set on seeing those blossoms outside my bedroom window this spring." And then she had sighed. John had never before heard a wistful sound from Jess. Sentimentality was not in her repertoire.

Jess Wainscott was sixty and had been widowed for eight years. At fifty-two, a ripe age for a woman of sound health and strong looks, she had lost her mate, but not her vitality. Jess chaired both the Friends of the Library board of directors and the Women's Council of the First Presbyterian Church. Additionally, she served on many committees and worked for several charitable causes. She could be found at almost every art fair, fund-raiser, ball game, black-tie dinner or barbecue in town. And she skied, which was where John saw her most often, because he was on the volunteer ski patrol.

"Cal told me if he came back after death he'd be a hummingbird and suck the nectar out of the blossoms outside my bedroom window," she told John. John grunted as he hauled the can holding the plum tree from the back of his pickup. He let it drop with a bang. "I have to get something planted and see if he was putting me on."

"You've been widowed quite a few years, Jess," John pointed out. She was the fourth and newest member of a group of vivacious women who referred to themselves as the widows' brigade. They were best friends, seen together all over town, and John did handiwork for all of them. Peg, Abby, Kate and Jess. He had many clients, not all widows, but these four women were his favorites. They all overpaid him, pestered him, tried to feed him like a son.

"Eight years," she said. "I tend to procrastinate," she laughed. "Until now, I didn't want his interference."

The cars lining the driveway indicated that Jess had company. "Meeting of the brigade?" he asked.

"Tuesday. Garden club. Or is it mah-jongg day? I never remember. We hardly ever do what we planned to do, anyway. Usually we just try to have something to do while we gossip," she said. She followed John to the side of the house where the tree would be planted and asked him questions the whole time he dug. Had he led the ski patrol again last winter? Did the nursery do much business winters? What softball team would he be on this summer so she could watch for one of his games? Did he still have that condo for rent at Purgatory? Not just questions. Also statements. The yard needed to be resodded. She was thinking of moving the piano upstairs. Leigh, her daughter, would be arriving soon.

The shovel paused in midair.

"My daughter, Leigh. Surely you've met her on one of her visits. She was here for two or three months the summer Cal died. She spent another whole summer here a few years…ah, five years ago, I guess. Maybe you met her then."

"I…ah, might've. Yeah. Maybe."

"Oh, you'd remember, John. She's very striking. Rather unforgettable, actually."

Yes. Unforgettable. Completely. His brow began to bead with sweat. The temperature was fifty-two degrees, and there was still snow here and there in crevices around yards, at the edges of driveways, sidewalks, but he was sweating. His heart rate had been about one-ten from digging; the mention of Leigh Wainscott Brackon had caused it to shoot to two-sixty.

"You never mention her," he said.

"Don't I? Oh, nonsense, you just haven't been paying attention. I hardly talk about anything else."

But not to him. They didn't move in the same social circles, have mutual friends, or seek common amusements. Their only common trait was that they were equally well-known in town, for entirely different reasons. Everyone knew John McElroy because he was in charge of the volunteer ski patrol and A-Number-One Mr. Fix-it, and everyone knew Jess Wainscott because she belonged to every club, charity and social group in Durango. One of the town matrons and the town's best handyman. And although they liked each other fine, they weren't exactly friends.

Every time Jess called him out on a chore, he hung on her every word. Leigh never came into the conversation; it wasn't as though he would have missed it. The few times he had done indoor jobs, he had scanned the place for pictures, and there was only an old one—Leigh in her twenties. The same picture that had been there when he cleaned Jess's chimney, put up her new chandelier, unplugged the kitchen drain. It seemed to move around a lot, but there was never a new one. "Does she ski?" he asked, as if he didn't know.

"Leigh does many remarkable things, although athletically she isn't accomplished. She's kind of…uncoordinated. She hasn't been out here for a long time. Well, two years ago last October, and then only for a couple of days. She prefers that I visit her, since she has so many obligations, and she has plenty of room. Los Angeles is a nice place to get a tan in winter. That's about all I care to do there, anyway."

Los Angeles? It had been Los Altos when she was at

Stanford University. But she had said there was a job at UCLA if she wanted it. He shook these thoughts from his mind. God, so long ago. She'd never looked back; what had she decided their relationship was? Dalliance? Panic attack? Mistake? He'd written her at her office, only to have letters returned. He'd called; a secretary took messages. Her home phone number in Los Altos, which had been difficult to find, was changed. Shovel ready, he mentally scanned those events while he dug, and dug hard.

He plunked the tree into the hole and started pushing dirt in around it. "If she's coming for a long visit, I'll probably meet her," he said. He thought about getting drunk later.

"I'm practically forcing her to come. I've been trying to get her back here for a long, long time. Now the darnedest thing has come up. You just won't believe it. It seems I've developed some kind of heart problem." His eyes shot to her face; Jess was a breathtakingly robust sixty-year-old woman with the appearance of absolutely rude good health. Her hair had been thick gray for as long as he'd known her; her face was healthily tanned and only slightly wrinkled at the corners of her clear, intelligent blue eyes. Her cheeks were pink, her lips cherry red, and she looked smashing on skis. If it weren't for her shock of silver hair, she could pass for forty, maybe forty-five. She shrugged off his look of concern. "Not unheard of at my age."

"That's awful. What's Doc doing about it?"

"Heavens! Tom Meadows doesn't even know," she said, which instantly made John suspicious. Tom Meadows was seen with the widows often…with one or all of them. He must be some kind of late-in-life beau.

"You're not seeing Doc about this?" he asked. He had just assumed Doc was everyone's Doc.

"Well, now, Tom is a fine doctor, I'm sure, but he isn't a cardiologist."

"I really hate to hear this, Jess. Please, be careful. Do as you're told."

"Well, I'd rather it were something like a testy heart than all the things it could be. I've always been just a bit ticked off at Cal for the abrupt way he left us, but all things considered, if I could just nod off in the garden, I would rather do that than be sick. I feel all right, you see. I've just been diet-restricted as all hell. Can't eat anything truly enjoyable. However, besides eliminating strenuous exercise like skiing, my lifestyle is unchanged. I do watch cholesterol much better now. I thought I had watched it before, but now I watch. And I take long walks."

"Is it bad?"

"Bad tickers are getting to be a regular thing, John," she said philosophically. "They can check your cholesterol at the grocery store. Now that they know so much about hearts, seems no one just drops dead anymore— everyone is getting a bypass or something. The fact is, if I'm very conscientious I could live long enough to become a nuisance. On the other hand, I shouldn't get hooked on any serial novels right now."

"Jess!"

She laughed at him. A resounding, loud, hilarious laugh—typical. It made him flinch; he worried she might keel over. "You know, John, you could drop dead tomorrow, too. The only difference is that if I do, it won't be completely unexpected. I want to get that girl home and straightened out. She needs a keeper, that one.

Lord, raising her was a job for ten mothers. Come in and I'll write you a check. You can have a glass of wine with the girls and me—it's my medication." For a moment he thought she had read his mind. The news that Leigh was coming had caused him to think he could use a glass—or ten. "It's the only nice thing about a tricky heart—a glass in the afternoon, a glass in the evening."

"I have to pass on the wine," he said. "But I'll take the check."

He followed her up the stairs to the redwood deck surrounding her large home, then in the back door to the kitchen. There, as predicted, were the other women at the kitchen table. What they were doing today was unclear; nothing but writing paper and coffee cups covered the surface between them. They could be planning a cotillion or writing book reviews for the local paper. Once, when he'd seen them around a table with writing tablets and impetuously inquired about their current project, they had said they were writing their wills. He hadn't asked since. "Hi, John," he heard three more times.

"Will you promise to drop by when Leigh and the boys are here?"

"Boys?" His voice had gone an octave higher. He had to concentrate to keep the shock from showing all over his face. So, Leigh had achieved motherhood. That had been one of her chief desires, children. At the time he had been with her, having children had been low on his list of wants, but hearing she had sons caused a pang of envy. Was Jess going to insist she'd been talking about "the boys" all these years, too?

"Mitch and Ty, my grandsons," she replied, digging into her purse for her checkbook. "You'd hit it off, I think. They're absolute hellions. Unlike their mother, they're quite athletic." She wrote his name on the line. "I wouldn't say Leigh is a bad mother. She adores them. But her mind wanders, and she's frequently off in la-la land. She's really no fun for little boys to play with. She's too prissy. She's the kind of woman who's…brilliant, but without a lick of sense, you know?"

He knew.

"I think she has burnout," Jess was saying as she wrote the check. "Pressures, deadlines, complications, work work work. Her housekeeper quit, leaving Leigh in charge, and Leigh's a slob. My fault. With all she learned, she was too busy to straighten up. Gad. Leigh never takes time off unless she's completely frazzled."

Like last time, he thought. "How old are your grandsons?" he asked.

"Four," she supplied, fishing her wallet out of her purse. "Twin boys." She flipped open the picture section of her wallet. John didn't audibly gasp, but his heart did flip around in panic. "I can't believe I haven't bragged about them, but maybe I just bore other people."

"She is an awful show-off about those boys," Kate said.

"We don't exactly get sick of hearing about them," Peg said, "but a change of subject once in a while wouldn't hurt."

John looked at the pictures. One was blond and blue eyed, one dark. Interesting. Leigh was blond and blue eyed. He himself, it so happened, had very dark brown hair and brown eyes. He gulped. "They look older than four," he tried a bit breathlessly, baiting her, his heart not only hammering, but racing. He hoped his voice didn't sound terribly unnatural.

"Oh, no, they just turned four." He almost fainted. His eyes did a long blink. "End of January, I think... Yes, the twenty-eighth."

His eyes actually closed while he calculated, but he didn't drum his fingers one at a time; he wasn't the snap at math that Leigh was. At anything, for that matter. Seven months from the time he met her. An old pain shot through him and hurt slightly more. Oh, no. Oh, no. She had already achieved motherhood. And hadn't known? She couldn't have. She wouldn't have gotten involved with him if she...

"I wonder if I could impose on you to take them fishing or something? We have a fundamental absence of men here."

"Yeah. Sure," he said, suddenly exhausted. His eyes began to blur, and he acknowledged the remarkable presence of threatening tears. God, how he had loved her. "Let me know if there's anything more you need," he said, pocketing the check, dying to get back to his truck. He usually loved hanging around with the women, but this time he couldn't chance it. He could barely breathe. "And for God's sake, take care of yourself, Jess."

"I do need a crew, beginning soon, to spruce up the place. I'm planning to have a very large party here in mid-June, and I want some extensive landscaping and building done. I'm going to wait for Leigh to get here— just a couple of days from now—and get her input before I start, since she's going to live here for several months...though I do hope she stays on permanently now. You can do it, can't you? Handle a big job?"

"Permanently?" He nearly choked. "She's coming to live here permanently?"

She laughed, and the women joined her, stifling their chuckles. "Well, I admit I'm only calling it a long visit, but I fully intend to hang on to her this time. She loves Durango. No reason she can't stay. It's the perfect place to raise kids, and Leigh knows that."

"Sure," he said weakly. Imagine having her around all the time, running into her at the grocery store, at the Jaycee's Spring Art Fair…at the Steak House.

"Will you be able to do the yard this spring, John?"

"Yeah. Sure. Gotta run. Busy day. Lotta calls. Take it easy, ladies."

"Bye, John," was said, times four.

He let the back door slam shut, took the steps down from the deck two at a time and loped to his truck. At last he was alone. He waited a minute to start the engine. Leigh was burned-out and frazzled, he thought. That was what had been itching in her before, when he'd hoped it was him. It hadn't been, obviously.

Jess saw him sitting in his truck in front of the house as she watched from the living-room window. Abby came up behind her and reached over her shoulder to pull back the curtain for a better look.

"Don't do that," Jess whispered. "What if he sees us watching him."

"You don't have to whisper," Kate said. "He can't hear us."

"So? What do you think?" Jess asked.

"He just about fainted when you told him she had kids, but that doesn't mean anything. How did he react when you said she was coming home?"

"Oh, like he wanted to get in the hole he was digging."

"I don't think you'll know anything for sure until you see them together. Wouldn't it be just as easy to come right out and ask her if she just happened to be in love with our favorite handyman about five years ago when she was here for the summer getting pregnant?"

Jess scowled. "It's just not that simple. She nearly had a nervous breakdown. I was worried about her survival. Now I'm worried about her future and the future of those little cuties. But don't you think John would be good for them even if it's not him?"

"He'd be good for anyone." Peg sighed. "Oh, to be forty years younger."

"Look at him. He's just sitting there. He's in shock. I'd say that's a good sign," Kate said. "Doesn't that seem like a good sign?"

"He's in shock? That could be a bad sign," said Abby.

"Oh, to put a man in shock." Peg sighed. "Just once more."

"I just don't know if this is going to work," Jess mused, watching the truck just sit there.

"Logically, I don't think anyone can be tricked into getting married," Kate said.

"Of course they can't," Jess said. "I wouldn't even attempt that. I thought I'd just trick them into being together again. If they still care for each other, they'll do the getting married part themselves."

"They didn't before."

"Well…things were different then."

"Not as different as things are now," Kate said.

Two

John couldn't move. He would drive away in a minute, but not until his breathing began to smooth out and his heart quit leaping around.

Five years ago—just about the first of June, when everything was gloriously green, when Durango, Colorado, was as fresh and alive as a new baby—he had met her. Leigh, twenty-seven, long limbed, intelligent, monied, home to see her mother for a long visit. She had filed for divorce after a year-long separation from her husband. It was uncontested, mutually desired and would be no-muss, no-fuss, simple and quick. A mere formality, said Leigh, since she and her estranged husband had always been more student and teacher than husband and wife.

John had seen her in the Steak House, sitting alone at the bar, having a glass of white wine. She looked like one of a million long-legged beauties who visited Durango, except it was June. Most of the female visitors possessed of such blatantly powerful and photogenic looks made their appearance during ski season. Durango was a veritable smorgasbord of feminine delight. He introduced himself with nothing in mind but killing time with a knockout woman. That was when he found out she was Jess's daughter. He had done some repair and landscaping work for Jess Wainscott. So he had a couple of beers while Leigh mostly just twirled the stem of her wineglass in her fingers. They shared chitchat, and John began to tumble into incredible love. Then and there.

Her soon-to-be-ex-husband was a molecular biologist at Stanford University, a genetic engineer. She had met him when she was very young and doing some research for an advanced degree. She married him and began to work on his research projects with him, for him. John had thought she meant she had been his secretary. Although some members of his family were impressively educated, he didn't hang out with scientists.

Every time Max Brackon got a new project and new budget, Leigh explained, he hired his wife. Now she was home for a rest; she intended to change her lifestyle. A great deal was missing from her life.

So he asked her out.

"On a date? Should I be dating?" she asked.

"It's okay during a legal separation," he told her, as if he knew. All he really knew was a need to be with her.

"I need to be socialized," she said. "With Max, you see, I was isolated and I haven't—yes," she finally said. He told her to meet him Friday night for a drink, same time, same place. "Do you think I should tell my mother?" she asked him.

"Well, sure…I guess. Why not? Or you could always tell her you've joined the Sierra Club because you've begun to love the environment." He'd been kidding. Sort of. Even though he didn't know much about

Leigh, he wasn't sure Jess would approve of her dating the handyman.

Affairs probably always started that way, he thought now. A little bit by accident. He had expected her to change her mind, but she hadn't. They started by exchanging details of their failed relationships—John had had a serious relationship when he was twenty-one. He had met a San Francisco girl while he was in the navy and brought her to Durango to live with him. That put a few gray hairs on his mother's head. But it didn't last long. She didn't like small-town life and had really wanted to be a rock star, even though she couldn't sing or play an instrument. She left him a note; it didn't take him all that long to get over her. He expected he might catch her on MTV one of these days, wearing underwear for a costume and belting out some deranged sonnet...off tune. Since then, he admitted unself-consciously, he dated women who were just in town on vacation.

Commitment, said John, was not his bag.

Leigh had married a very successful, well-known stimulating older man. A scientist. A genius. She had been too young, she knew, and he had been too old. But her circumstances had been somewhat unusual—she didn't immediately explain how—and she had married her teacher, a father figure. "Did you know," she had asked John, "that my father did medical research? Biochemistry. Mom and Dad moved here to attempt retirement, although my dad just couldn't seem to slow down. My dad was pretty famous."

That had no impact on John; he didn't peruse any scientific journals. He hadn't attended one day of college and had no desire to get any smarter.

Now, Leigh had said, she realized her mistake. She wanted children and friends, for example, and her husband didn't feel so inclined at his age. His work was as demanding as any unruly child, and he really couldn't keep up a social life. In fact, Leigh's husband was not terrifically interested in having a wife. Assistant, protégé, student—yes. Wife? The only kind of wife he could conceive of was one with goals like his, schedules like his, and who would not distract him from his research, which was his first wife. He was too busy for marriage, really. He was married to his job.

Even when they had separated, drifted apart, Max still called her to come to the lab to do this or that for him; he couldn't count on anyone else the way he could count on her. She had finally filed divorce papers and come to Durango because, "He seems as disinterested in our divorce as he was in our marriage. It's as if he hasn't noticed. At least if I'm here with my mother he can't call me to come in to the lab."

How anyone could take Leigh for granted was beyond John. He was already so shaken with adoration by their first date he believed he was in love. Well, maybe not love. But boy, he was in something. He almost had to sit on his hands at the bar to keep from fondling her. He knew he was going to love the way her skin felt, smelled, tasted.

For starters, the very sound of her voice sent him drifting; he loved her voice. Her skin was clear and fair, her eyes sparkled and her laugh was like music. He was falling.

"If you knew my father and how like him I am," Leigh had gone on, "you would know what utter chaos our marriage really was. My mother predicted long ago that Max wouldn't favor our marriage with even a cursory glance and it would simply disappear. Mother, you see, is not like my father. She is an absolute rock with great common sense. She was the anchor in the raging sea that was my father's enormous intelligence. She's very intelligent, but not in the showy, extreme way my father was. She always knew the best thing for me would be an anchor, not a sail. She advised me not to marry someone so like my father, but I didn't listen."

John had given her a bewildering frown and ordered another beer, letting her talk, intrigued by her expensive vocabulary. Then they had necked in his truck after drinks, indulging in kisses that were long, wet and the most exhilarating he had ever known. And he had known a few.

John had often pondered the whole concept of the physical chemistry between a man and a woman. It was like the meshing of fine gears, like waxing skis or tuning up a Porsche...and he said so. "What a great match of taste, texture, smell," he had said.

"Pheromones," she had replied.

John had more fun exploring the phenomenon than discussing it and closed her mouth with his. Whether it was pheromones or dumb luck, it could grab you by the neck and drag you across the room. That was how it had been with Leigh from the start, as it had never been with any other woman, ever. Though she was beautiful, it hadn't been her picture-perfect looks that had drawn him closer. In fact, he liked beauty but hated vanity. Leigh, he learned right away, didn't put much stock in her appearance. He had wanted her instantly; he wanted her still.

Jess never did know that Leigh was seeing a man in

Durango. With the Sierra Club as a cover, Leigh could disappear for "hikes," "trail rides" and "camping trips" that took days. It was the closest thing to paradise John had ever experienced. But, he wondered, didn't Jess suspect something?

"She works very hard at not interfering in my personal life," Leigh had said. "My dad was an intellectual, a Bohemian, more so than my mom…and I'm a spoiled and indulged only child. They treated me like an adult from the time I was three. I don't want her to start worrying about me now."

Over the next several weeks John began to understand that he had landed himself in a peculiar and extraordinary situation. When Jess had been twenty-one she had married a forty-year-old eccentric genius and produced one gifted child. Leigh. Cal, a very successful, prizewinning scientist, was so well-known and well traveled that Leigh had lived a privileged, highly educated life. She had graduated at the age of nineteen from Princeton and received a master's degree by twenty-one. Math and philosophy, a unique combination, were her specialties. She also spoke four languages, painted, sculpted, wrote poetry and plays, played the piano, to say nothing of all she had read.

Also she had two left feet and often seemed sidetracked by some huge idea; she lost things, missed turns, bounced checks. It made him laugh; she could work on some complex math theory containing more letters than numbers—not to mention strange symbols—but forget to balance her checkbook or make deposits. She was brilliant. John began to slowly understand that Leigh had been far more than Max's secretary; she had several degrees of her own, including a Ph.D. in Physics.

John, by contrast, had a high-school diploma and, when he met Leigh, was a ski bum who played Mr. Fix-it and Mr. Yardman from April to October so he could make just enough money to ski all winter. He was emotionally and materially unencumbered and led a loose, fast life. After Leigh left Durango, he found he was so much in demand that he hired young men with similar agendas to work in a little business that had since become a hefty operation. He had been raised in Denver by an airline mechanic and a housewife, and was the youngest of four boys. He did not like the big city and had never understood, nor cared to understand things like stock leveraging, quantum physics or DNA, nor did he read anything more complicated than the sports weeklies. But, boy, could he plant a flowering plum. If he died in summer, he would go to heaven with dirt under his nails.

They were together for just over two months. Through the high, green heat of summer he was amazed by how intensely he loved her. He knew that while Leigh had traveled the world and read *El Cid* in Spanish, she had never before had great sex. He knew because her response shocked her as much as it pleased him. Though multilingual, she had not been multi-that-other-thing before John—and she told him so. Breathlessly, she said, "I thought there was only one to a customer."

"How many do you want, doll? I'm in no hurry."

"Oh…John…is everyone this good at this?"

"No," he told her, kissing every place he could think of. "Just me with you—it's the only combination that works this good."

"Well," she corrected. He didn't hear.

The true meaning of arrogance, John discovered, was believing you were the cause of another person's passion or pleasure. He believed he had invented sex for Leigh. She could paint and sculpt, but he had been the first man to undress her outside, beside the lake, and rock with her on a floating dock.

Around the first of August, just as John was beginning to believe he could not live without her, a series of events conspired to tear them apart. In retrospect, he could see that it was nothing but lousy luck that arrived before he was ready to deal with it.

First, Max Brackon had a heart attack and Leigh went to him. Though it didn't change the facts of the divorce and she returned to Durango in less than a week, it exacerbated John's jealousy and fear that he wasn't smart enough to be loved by her. It made him irritable, unfair and critical. He began to find things seriously wrong with being in love with a genius.

One—she had very few practical skills, having been told by a quorum of professors throughout her life that she had more to offer the world than her skill at cleaning and cooking. She should exercise her cerebellum and let someone else do the drudge work. She could, therefore, theorize and build a microwave oven, but she couldn't cook vegetables in one.

"That's just plain lazy," said John. Perhaps he raised his voice.

"I am not lazy," she replied, just as hotly. "You can't call someone who has three degrees and gets a Ph.D. by twenty-three lazy."

"I thought it was just a master's," he replied.

"That was at twenty-one."

Two—she obviously thought that because of her higher than average IQ, she had higher than average needs and should be indulged. Whenever they began to talk about never being apart, she naturally assumed they would go wherever she went. "What can I do in Durango?" she had asked. "I'll have to go somewhere where I can be challenged. Boredom terrifies me more than anything. I have an offer from UCLA to work on a design for a newborn CAT scan device that can be used to detect a predisposition for Sudden Infant Death Syndrome. You could come to L.A."

"And do lawns?" he asked. "While you win the Nobel Prize in scientific discoveries? Maybe I should clean pools."

"You could do anything you like," she replied, not understanding him or his ego problem. "I would be happy to support you financially. It would be no problem."

"Yes, it would," he had said. How could a woman so smart be so completely insensitive to a man's feelings? A man's needs? It never occurred to him to be more considerate of what she might need.

Three—there appeared to be exactly one place in which they were totally compatible; in all other places they were different. She wanted children right away, the sooner the better. He didn't. He loved athletics; she didn't even run to answer the phone. He liked the mountains and fresh air; she had her nose in a book. He was physical; she was mental. He was night; she was day.

"It works here, like this," he whispered to her when they had just made love.

"Yes," she said, her eyes tearing, "but will this be enough? I didn't have this with Max, but here in Durango, with you, there's nothing to do after this! I need work, family, challenge, mental stimulation, intellectual activity."

Those were not things John could offer.

Things fell apart at the last breath of summer. Leigh gave him books he didn't read; she talked about scientific research he couldn't fathom. Ecology was the only subject on which they could converse without him feeling like an idiot. He had trouble prying her loose from some sheaf of papers to hike. Their differences became more obvious. Tense. Leigh often lost track of things. She could begin to make a pot of coffee, think of some odd mathematical equation she had read about or have an unfinished poem pop into her mind, and become consumed, forget to put the pot under the coffeemaker and flood the kitchen. She left Jess's car in Drive once because she had been thinking of something complex, and it rolled down a steep incline and into a ditch. The scatterbrain antics that had amused him at first began to strike him as inexcusable. It was like babysitting sometimes. John wasn't quite ready for the job but was definitely unprepared to give her up. The pain and frustration began to match the ecstasy.

Leigh became morose and restless all at once. She wanted to stay, wanted to go. Wanted to make love, but cried, sometimes during their loving. John couldn't stand to be so messed up over someone so messed up! Where were all the uncomplicated, silly, girlie girls? The ones looking for a man with muscles and no serious conversation?

In the panic of coming to the end of an affair they were filled with equal parts hunger and agony. It was exactly the kind of mood that made lovers demand impossible things of each other and suffer temporary insanity. He demanded she admit she couldn't cope with being in love with a ski bum who had no ambition beyond enjoying life as much as possible. She demanded he make an effort, at least, to fit into a world in which she would have the challenge she craved and he could fish, hunt, ski, boat and do anything he wanted on the money she would earn. He said he would cut his throat before he'd live off a woman, and she said she'd only die a painful death without intellectual stimulation. She needed long hours. Relaxation of the type he loved was harder for her than anything else in life. However impossible it was for him to understand, she relaxed by reading philosophy and physics.

John said that was garbage. And he honestly thought it was.

The way it ended was even more ridiculous than the rest of it had been. She said she was going to go back to Stanford to think things through, to at least get her divorce taken care of. And he said—it was still hard for him to believe—he actually said, "Good. Go. It was fun, but we're just from two different worlds. I'm not up to this, anyway."

When that made her cry, he didn't hold her and say he was sorry. He didn't try to take it back. For a brief moment he really believed he wanted someone "regular." That's what you think when you're twenty-seven and stupid.

Then, when she was gone, he had called, written, even braved asking Jess, "How are you getting on? Need anything done around the house?"

"No, my daughter was here, but she's gone home now," Jess had said, as if that were an answer.

John felt thoroughly rejected. After a hard-hitting four-month depression and more failed attempts to reach Leigh, he quickly married a pretty young woman named Cindy who was "regular" and whom, though he didn't know it at the time, he did not love. Their happiness had lasted only a month or so, although their divorce took much longer.

He often wished there was some way to find out if Leigh had really left because she wanted to or if he had driven her away.

When he thought about it rationally, he believed Leigh had been the smart one. They couldn't have made it work; she hovered above the average mind by about twenty feet. No matter how great their bodies worked together, it would have been unbearable to watch her grow bored and weary with someone like him—a simple man who didn't earn much money and couldn't discuss science. Unfortunately, he wasn't able to think about it rationally very often.

But now he knew she had twin sons, and he realized what else had been going on. That first night he met her, she had said one of her marital frustrations had been about children. Seven months after that first shared drink, after the first time they were intimate, she had had twins. She must not have been all that separated from her husband. She must have realized she was pregnant and taken herself guiltily home to Max, disconnecting from her summer affair. It made him feel slightly better to know that her inability to bridge the IQ gap hadn't been her only reason for leaving. Very slightly.

He was afraid to see her again, yet he wanted desperately to see her again. He was no braver. Also no smarter.

* * *

Jess was repotting a plant on her redwood deck. She could see her grandsons, Mitch and Ty, constructing a fort in the thick batch of trees behind the yard and garden. They had taken turns swinging on a rope swing; they had nailed boards together in a sad attempt to make a ladder up the crooked spine of a perfect tree-house tree. She predicted they would ask to sleep in a tent in the backyard before the end of the week. She would say no. But it was grand to know they were average. Active, curious, healthy, athletic boys... What a treasure. They could keep themselves busy and challenged. They could get into the same jams that all kids did—a ball through a window, swiped candy, a fight.

Leigh been such a handful to raise; she had been reading at the age of two, skipped grades and taken special classes and advanced lessons all through school. Leigh had been so relentlessly curious that she mixed cleaning supplies with fertilizers after she had picked the lock on the garden shed. It was amazing she hadn't killed herself; she had burned a hole through the floor.

Having her home was much like having Cal back. Ninety-five percent of the time Leigh was a joy and best friend—clever, funny, helpful. That other five percent she was like a wandering two-year-old. Jess hadn't yet encountered the five percent this visit; Leigh seemed to be improving at keeping her mind clear.

The first thing they had to get out of the way was the business of Jess's heart abnormality.

"I want to talk to your doctor," Leigh had said.

"No. This is my condition. It's manageable, and I will not have you involved. I've had a series of examinations, and I'm watching my cholesterol and my activities. I've been told I won't drop dead today, and I'm still a competent babysitter. In fact, if I'm careful of my diet, I'll probably be around to drive you crazy for years to come. I'm having another checkup in the fall. You're lucky I told you at all. And the only reason I did is that I really wanted to spend some time with you and the boys. Just in case."

"Is it angina?"

"What?"

"Mom," Leigh had said, "I could investigate, help with some treatment decisions…"

"Absolutely not. I'm well aware of your intelligence, but this is a matter that requires good instincts. You'll only get technical, pragmatic and annoying. Butt out."

"But I'm home because—"

"I hope you're home because you want to be, not just because you're afraid I'm short-term!"

"Mother," Leigh had begun.

"Daughter," Jess had mimicked.

Now Jess saw Mitch, the dark one, take a wide swing on the rope that hung from a high branch. A good, big swing. What a guy. And then she smelled a nasty smell and cursed under her breath. The five percent! She made quick work of the steps to the kitchen and found macaroni burning in the pan. Then she heard a sound and looked up; a damp spot was spreading on the ceiling. She cursed again. She missed Cal, but not enough to go through all this again.

"If I had a serious heart condition," she grumbled as she raced up the stairs, "this girl would kill me in no time. And if I ever get a really important heart condition, she will be the last to know!"

The tub was overflowing. "Leigh!" she shouted.

But of course she wasn't heard. Busy mind, blocked ears. She turned off the water and pulled the plug. The carpet was soaked, and her sneakers got so wet she sloshed. She went to the loft that had been Cal's study and saw Leigh, wearing her bathrobe, sitting in front of her computer screen, her fingers clicking keys at lightning speed. She touched Leigh's shoulder. "You've burned up a pan and flooded the bathroom!"

"Oh, Mom," Leigh said, startled and shaken. "Oh, I'm sorry! I really don't do that so much anymore, really! Damn, I'll clean it up, I'm so sorry... I'm... "

"Never mind," Jess sighed wearily.

"Where are the boys?" Leigh asked over her shoulder.

"The boys are just fine. You need more watching than they do!" Oh, Leigh, she thought, where is your brain?

Much later, while drinking her afternoon glass of wine on the deck, Jess said, "Do you realize how much better you are when you have a social life? That summer you joined the Sierra Club, you had fewer mishaps. I think the fresh air helps clear your head."

"I had mishaps that summer. Remember?" Leigh said.

"They weren't as obvious," Jess said.

"To you," Leigh argued. And then, on the subject of mishaps who were now four years old, "The loveliest thing happened, Mom. Max remembered Mitch and Ty. Wasn't that dear of him?"

"In his will?" Jess asked, amazed.

"Yes. I can't think why. He rarely saw them. He must have done it for me, knowing how much I wanted children. Do you suppose that means he finally forgave me? Perhaps he loved me more than I knew. Am I being sentimental?"

Jess couldn't resist the urge to touch her daughter's golden hair, braided and falling over her shoulder. Sometimes Jess tried to imagine Leigh's pain, her feelings of inadequacy or the way she suffered in rejection. Men were afraid to date her; women friends were equally rare. It could be such a lonely life, being a fast-tracker. "Oh, Leigh, the boys need a father."

Leigh actually looked away. She rarely let her emotions show, was actually still in the learning stages of even allowing herself to have emotions. Jess thought it had a lot to do with returning to Durango. "Let's not go over that again, Mom. I don't have a father to offer them, and I can't help it."

Well, I can, Jess thought. "I'll need your advice with something, darling. I want to have a huge party this summer, partly to welcome you and the boys home and introduce you to all my friends, and partly because I don't know if I'll ever feel this well again. I've wanted to landscape the whole blasted yard for years now—make it a wonderland. You'll help me, won't you?"

"When did you start reading this?" Leigh asked, picking up a copy of a bridal magazine. What on earth was her mother doing with a bridal magazine?

"That? Oh, I think Abby or Peg left a lot of them here. We planned both their girls' weddings together... What fun. Abby's daughter even left her gown here... You're about the same size. You ought to try it on sometime.

"Now, I want flagstone walks, a gazebo and a big barbecue pit. I'd like a couple of birdbaths or statues...

maybe even a fountain. Can you design something like that on your little machine?"

"I think so…yes. I'll have a go at it in the next day or two."

"When you have some plans, I want you to see this man who sometimes works for me—John McElroy. He's a very good builder and a landscape specialist. In fact, he's also great on skis and heads up the ski patrol. This winter I'll talk to him about teaching the boys."

Leigh focused an unusual amount of attention on the magazine, not responding to her mother.

"Why don't you make my last days easier and just marry him? I think he's stable enough to take care of you and the boys when I'm gone. He even looks a bit like Mitch."

Leigh was silent for a long time. "What an imagination you have," she finally said, sipping her wine and flipping the pages.

Three

"Hello, John."

He dropped a fifty-pound bag of compost on a pile of identical bags and whirled around to face her. All the anticipation and anxiety that had surrounded the thought of seeing her again seemed to drain out of him when the moment actually arrived. There she was. Beautiful as ever. Hardly aged. He was instantly self-conscious about whether he smelled of sweat and cow dung. This was not what he had planned. He'd known he would run into her at some point, but he hadn't been able to prepare for the experience. "Leigh," he said quietly. "Dr. Brackon."

She half smiled when he said her name, then flinched just slightly when he used her title. "I…ah…didn't mean to startle you. I'm sorry. I'm—"

"No, it's okay. I'm just surprised. It's been a long time."

"I've been back a couple of weeks. I'm living with my mother for now, maybe for good. She needs me, and I need a new kind of lifestyle. Jess…my mom…she has some kind of—"

"She told me." He took a handkerchief from his pocket and wiped the perspiration from his forehead. "She said she has a heart problem and was forcing you home."

"She didn't actually have to force me. I was ready to come. I wanted to come. I've been planning to for years. I just kept putting it off."

"This can't make your husband very—"

"Didn't she tell you about Max? Oh, my... I divorced him a long time ago and Max...well, he passed away about six months ago. He was sixty, Mom's age... Far too young."

"I didn't know," he said slowly. "I'm sorry."

"I don't know why I thought you'd know," she said in that slightly baffled, absentminded way of hers.

"How would I know?" he asked a bit more peevishly than he intended. Leigh had always been able to imply that everyone should be able to keep up with her thoughts. *I guess I thought we talked about that, and I didn't mean to take it for granted that you already knew when you didn't.* But he didn't want to get into all that again now. "What I mean is, we do a little work for Jess now and then, but she hasn't mentioned you... Not once. In fact, I'm sure she just mentioned your children for the first time when I took out a tree to her. Congratulations. I know children were one of the things you wanted."

"That's impossible, her not mentioning the boys. She never shuts up about them. You must not have noticed."

"I would have noticed!"

"Uh-oh," she nervously replied.

"So, you're back to help Jess and learn a new kind

of lifestyle," he said, the edge to his words unmistakable. "Haven't you already done that one?"

"Look, John, my mom wants some work done in the yard. And she wants it to be you who does the work. She obviously doesn't know how testy you can get, or she'd hire someone more agreeable." Leigh reached into her purse and pulled out a piece of paper that had a long list of items on it. "The job would mean you and I would run into each other quite a bit, since I happen to live there now. If you'd rather not, say so and I'll just get someone else." She stared him down. Maybe she didn't seem older, but she had gotten tougher somehow. Tougher underneath. More sure of herself. "So?"

After some long and serious eye contact he churlishly snapped the list out of her hand. He concentrated on it for a second. Brick gazebo, barbecue, flagstone walks, a birdbath with a fountain. He whistled. "A few things," he muttered. These people, it seemed, never ran out of big ideas, brains or money. It could get downright irritating.

"Yes, well, I realize it's quite a lot. My mom is so spontaneous. When she gets an idea like this, she wants it, and she wants it fast."

"For what? She isn't selling, is she?"

"No, no. She plans for me to have that house one day. She says she wants to throw a big summer party and invite half the town. She has two reasons. Reason one—because I have returned to live in Durango with the boys. Reason two—which I do not much like—she isn't sure how good she'll feel next summer. What do you know about this heart condition of hers?"

"How would I know anything?" he asked, walking to

the countertop that he used as a desk. "I'm the handyman, Leigh, not her priest."

"Pardon me," she returned, just as cranky. "I'm only trying to find out what I can. She wouldn't tell me anything, and I'm worried."

John felt a bit contrite. "Sorry." The last thing he wanted was to get all nasty with her. "I don't know anything, though I did ask. It seems Doc Meadows doesn't even know about it. Which means, I guess, that she's seeing someone else, but I wouldn't even hazard a guess as to who. I thought Doc was taking care of all the widows. But I guess not medically."

"She said she doesn't see Tom professionally because they're good friends. But when I called him and asked him if he had recommended a cardiologist, he was silent a long time before he said he hadn't. Then he suggested I quiz the widows' brigade on this alleged heart condition. Alleged? She's acting very strangely. I think there's more wrong than her heart, although I can't get a drop of information out of her. I've snooped through all her cupboards and can't find any prescription bottles, insurance receipts, anything. She's being absolutely impossible and won't let me get involved."

"What did the widows tell you?"

She shrugged. "To mind my own business and let Jess have her way for once. Abby West said that mother thing. 'Now, dear, your mother made many sacrifices for you as you were growing up. Why not just indulge her for a while?' To forestall an enormous fight, Mother promised me that if I would leave her alone and get settled in, she would tell me all about it later, before her next checkup. She's adamant that she will not discuss her condition this summer."

He smiled in spite of himself. "Mighty pigheaded, isn't she?"

Leigh tapped the list. "I think she's getting some of these repairs and improvements out of the way so as not to leave anything—you know, undone." She swallowed and looked away.

"What a thought," he mumbled.

"Jess is that way—efficient, compassionate. I just hope she's completely wrong about this heart thing. I don't think I can live without her. She's my anchor. The lead in my shoes. You know…I just don't have anyone to turn to the way I can turn to Jess."

"Let's not bury her yet. Let's think about her yard before we worry about her plot. This is a lot of new landscaping and building. Expensive."

"Can you do all this? A brick gazebo with a shake roof? Brick barbecue pit? Flagstone walks? If I give you a blueprint to follow?"

He made a face. "No, Leigh. I'm the builder and landscaper. I give you the plans, and you approve or alter them. See, this is my business."

"It's my yard."

"For gosh sakes," he blustered, "do we have to argue about the damn air?"

Deep breath. Times two.

"Okay," she relented. "Your plans, my alterations. Can you do it?"

"You're in luck. We're having a special."

"What kind of special?"

"The one where we do anything for money."

She smiled indulgently.

"It's going to cost a lot if you want it to look good."

"Mom doesn't care about money. She's very well-fixed and still getting royalties from my father's books. John? Does my mother…could she…have you…?" She gave up, then started over more slowly. "Does she know about that summer?"

"I don't know how she could. Why?"

"She asked me to ask you if you could either supervise or do most of the work yourself. She also happened to ask me if I couldn't just marry you and make her life easy."

He didn't think that was funny. "Did you tell her we've been over all that?"

"Of course not," she said. "That wouldn't be true. We never actually talked about marriage. We talked about being together, and even that was too much."

"Well, one of us was married, if you recall," he flung back.

She rolled her eyes in irritation. She'd been afraid of this, that he would really make her mad. She tried a change of subject. "You've really made something of this operation. The last time I saw it, it was a garage surrounded by a big old cyclone fence."

"When was that?"

"Oh, I don't remember the date," she lied. She remembered exactly. "You weren't here. You were on your honeymoon." Nuts. It was no longer going to be all his fault if they moved from general sniping into a full-fledged battle. So much for good intentions.

"My honey—! You came here? No one ever told me you came here!"

"Well, I didn't leave a message. You weren't here. You were indisposed, so to speak. So I left. Back to the yard—this whole thing is typical of Jess's spontaneous—"

"Why did you come here?" he asked.

"I said I would. I said I was going to get things together, straightened out. Don't you even remember?"

"That isn't what you said. You said you couldn't live here with me—I wasn't challenging enough!"

"Not you. There wasn't any work for me here. I had to have some kind of—"

"You said you had to go back to Stanford because—"

"Because that's where I lived. That's where my job was. My stuff. All my stuff was in Los Altos. I'd been offered a grant—I had to accept a grant to have a job. One of us had to have a job. You were a ski bum who occasionally cut grass for people. Besides, you said you were glad I was going away."

"Ski patrol, if you don't mind. Ski patrol and landscaping. It wasn't a big, fancy job maybe, but a couple of little, decent, ordinary jobs that regular people do. And I only said I was glad because I was too proud to say I couldn't stand it that you would just leave like that." He snapped his fingers. "Without a backward glance!"

"Without a—" She ran a hand over her hair. "Sorry if I offended," she sarcastically replied. "I needed a paying job somewhere. I was pregnant! The grant was offered by UCLA. I had to move, John."

"Oh. Oh, I get it. So, you just came by to say hello. It wasn't like you came back to see me or anything."

Leigh stared for a second and opened her mouth to speak, but it turned into a huff. She began again. Another huff. She put a hand on her hip. "I came back to see my mom and you. My divorce was final. I thought I'd ask again if you wanted to try L.A. But…if you didn't, I thought maybe we could work something out."

"Work something out?"

"A commute. I don't know. What's the difference, John? You weren't available. You were on your honeymoon!"

"I was on my honeymoon because I got married, which I did four months after you couldn't be bothered to answer any of my calls or letters."

"Calls and letters? You dummy! I didn't get any calls or letters!"

"I left messages! I wrote!"

"Well, I went back to Los Altos, packed up and moved. I didn't know I was supposed to somehow keep you unmarried. Most people get married because they want to, not because someone else doesn't answer the damn phone!"

"No one told me you moved! And don't call me a dummy! You know I already feel like a dummy just being in the same town with you, since your IQ is around four thousand and something! So, is there any particular reason why you didn't try writing or calling or something?"

"No, no particular reason," she shouted back. "Except I was a little busy. I was working on a scientific project, pregnant with twins and visiting with a psychologist to find out how in the world I had managed to be so smart and still mess up my life so badly! Now, I'd love to hang around and fight with you, but I have things to do! Are you going to do the damn yard for my mother? Or what?"

"Yes!" he shouted. "I'll be out tomorrow!"

"Great!" she shouted back, turning so dramatically that her long blond braid swung out so far behind her that it hit him in the nose. She stomped out the door.

John felt the scorching heat of red anger on his

cheeks. Oh, boy, how he remembered the steam in their arguments. He pounded the counter twice, hard enough to make all the pencils bounce.

He put his elbow on the counter, lowered his forehead into his hand and took a few deep breaths. Boy, did she look good. Twenty-seven was pretty and nubile, but there was something about a few years on a woman. A couple of kids, a little maturity, and something a bit more steady settled around the chest and hips. She had changed from lovely to lush. What kind of dummy would fight with her? He could have been a nice guy and maybe asked her out. They were, after all, both single now.

Was he crazy? Wasn't that what had started all this? Dating? The two of them came from two completely different worlds.

"John?"

He looked up. "I…ah…locked my keys in my car… I must not have been…you know."

A small laugh woofed out of him. He should have known. "You weren't paying attention. You were thinking about the mating cycle of the whooping crane or iambic pentameters." Or me. *Could you have been thinking about me, Leigh?* "Don't worry, I can get anything open."

"And I'm sorry about what just happened. The fight. I really didn't think that would happen," she said. "Anymore," she added.

"You weren't the only one at fault," he said. "Leigh, maybe we'd better get together, meet for a drink or dinner or something. We have this really messed-up karma, me and you, and if we don't get some of this straightened out, we're going to meet again in the next life as deadly enemies. Which would be okay if we ended up on opposing football teams, but if we're twin sisters or something, it could be disastrous. Maybe we ought to get it all talked out so we can press on as… friends. Huh?"

"Yes," she said in a breath, relieved. "Yes, that's what I wanted to do from the start—to make up and be friendly somehow. But you're the married one now."

"Me? No, I'm divorced, too. I've been divorced practically since I got married."

Her shocked expression was unmistakable. "I didn't know. I'm sorry."

"It was over before it started. We only lived together for a few months. Ski season," he added quietly, with the good grace to be somewhat embarrassed.

"Children?"

"Nope."

"Oh. Well, you said you didn't want children, so you're probably all right about that."

"I didn't want them back then. I was twenty-seven and self-centered. I was a skier with no ambition, for gosh sakes. I never thought about anything or anyone but myself. Surely you remember that."

She nearly smiled. That was the closest to an admission of imperfection or an apology as John had ever come. "We don't seem to have the best luck in romance, do we?"

"Well, how about if two unlucky people meet later?"

"I don't know…"

"You have someone? Some guy?"

She laughed in spite of herself. There were never any guys. Colleagues, project managers. Probably the only reason she'd accidentally married Max was fatigue;

they had worked so hard and long together, marriage had seemed a natural progression. John was practically the only "guy" she'd ever had. Briefly. "I have a couple of guys. Four-year-old guys," she said.

"How about if, for now, it's just you and me?"

Leigh sighed. "I'm still not very good at this sort of thing, John. I'm so clumsy in relationships. I don't mean to be, and I don't want to be… I'm very quick with mathematical problems. I just—ugh—I'm a mother now. I have to be more careful, because when I get in over my head, the boys can get hurt."

"We had an affair that messed us both up," he said. "Since we're still fighting like we used to, maybe we're still not through this. Shouldn't we talk about it? Rationally?"

She looked into his dark brown eyes. He had eyes like Bambi. Eyes you could fall into and drown. Arms by Adonis, face by Prince Charming, temperament by Attila the Hun. She smiled at him. "You have a ponytail."

He had to think for a minute. "Oh, yeah. It's not a bad ponytail, though. Is it?"

"No," she said. Ponytails were in again, but with John it was unclear whether he was being fashionable or lazy. In her memory of him, fashion was low on his list of priorities. Fashion, children and commitment. But he was such a cute renegade. "The Steak House?"

"Yeah. Let's get your keys." He lifted his hand toward her elbow and let it sort of hover there, undecided. Then, with a contrite, helpless look, touched her briefly. She felt a tremor. She knew she was in up to her neck right now. If he touched her again, she would crumble.

Four

Leigh arrived at seven, and John was already there. She wore a silk jumpsuit with a decorative scarf slung over one shoulder, earrings made of shells, and beige flats. She looked fashionably chic according to Jess, who had cheerfully—maybe too cheerfully—checked her over before she went out the door. This time Leigh was not pretending to join the Sierra Club. "You'll be delighted to know that your favorite maintenance man has asked me to meet him for a glass of wine," she had said.

John wore jeans, but decent jeans without holes, and something resembling a polo shirt with a sweater over it. To look at them, no one would know how scared they both were of this meeting. And they were both terrified of the identical things, that their love affair would officially end—and that it would carry on from where they had left it. She had a glass of wine and he a beer. They were on their second round before their words began to work.

"So," he started, "what happened?"

"When?"

"You came back, you said, and found out I was married. I'll tell you what happened to me if you tell me what happened to you. So what happened before that, in Los Altos?"

"Oh, it was dreadful. Max, who was recovering from one heart seizure, almost had another one. He was furious with me."

"Why?" he asked.

She just looked up at him with that blank, bewildered, aren't-you-able-to-keep-up-with-this? look of hers.

"For being pregnant?" he asked.

She nodded. "He said he felt betrayed… That's what he said. I couldn't understand that at all. I mean, it isn't as though I did it on purpose. And there I was… pregnant. Part of me was thrilled beyond my wildest dreams… The other half was amazed at how foolish I'd been. If it hadn't been for my mother, I don't know what I would have done."

"Wait a minute, wait a minute," he said, remembering the way Leigh could get so far ahead of herself, or begin her stories at the end and go backward. He had no doubt she could deliver a dissertation in clear language, but when it came to real life, she meandered. "Slow down, Leigh. He was angry about your pregnancy? Didn't he want to be a father?"

"No," she answered in apparent surprise. "Of course not. I know I told you that."

"I know he didn't think he wanted to, but after you told him you were… " She was shaking her head, looking stunned. "That's a damn shame," John said sincerely. "Even men who think they aren't ready for children usually act civilized when they find out their wife is expecting. I think I would."

Her eyes grew amazingly round, and she looked at him strangely, as if she didn't understand what he was saying. Finally, as though she had shaken herself free of some complex notion, she said, "You said you didn't want to be a father."

"Well, hell, I was being honest at the time. But I think I would have faced the prospect a bit more reasonably than Max did. I don't think I would have accused you of betrayal."

"Wait a minute here," she began. "What do you think you would have done? If you'd discovered your wife, for example, was pregnant?"

"We would have had to work on our marriage." He shrugged. "Harder," he added, in case anyone thought he hadn't tried.

"Oh, dear," she said. "John…have you seen the boys?" she asked.

"No. Just a picture. Jess asked me if I'd take them fishing sometime. They're pretty cute, but they don't look like twins. I guess the dark one looks like his father."

Leigh swallowed and nodded.

"Jess knows I coach Little League, and I still work the ski patrol in winter, part-time, and instruct kids in downhill. She said they're real hellions," he added, smiling. He rested his hand on her forearm.

"John," she said, twirling her wineglass by the stem. "I'm not sure which one of us messed up worse…you or me."

"How about if we just leave it in the past and go from here?"

"I don't know if that will work. The past is following us around. And besides…go where?"

"Take a little drink of that wine, Leigh. Let's get out of here for the rest of this conversation…in case it gets personal."

"I think the rest of this conversation is going to be real easy and involve one little word," she said softly. "No."

"…'No' to what?" John asked.

"I'm not willing to pick this up where we left it, John. It hurt me too much. Even though it was at least as much my fault as yours, it was still very painful."

John caressed her forearm. Boy, did he understand that. He was all through being belligerent and touchy; besides, she was right. All he wanted was to put an arm around her shoulders, maybe hold her hand, and talk about it. He had to resolve things with this woman for whom he'd carried a big, heavy torch for five years. Okay, he did want to see if being close to her caused him to feel the old feeling that he would never get close enough. But he only wanted to know. He wasn't going to go crazy. Right away.

"Let's go for a walk, huh? Alone? Talk a little. And I promise, you won't have to say 'no' again." He held up three fingers. "Scout's honor."

"You were never a Boy Scout, were you?" she asked later.

"No."

"I should have known," she said.

"It was only one kiss," he said. "I just wanted to check and see if it was as good as I remembered."

"And was it?"

"Yep. But what that means, I guess, is that it can be just as bad as it was, too. So we'd better finish that conversation."

They had abandoned their walk because the April night was a bit too brisk and chilled them into the shivers. They were in his truck, parked up on a ridge from which they could see a million miles out into the sky and across the land. If they'd been looking out, that is. With his lips on hers, it was inward that Leigh was looking.

There were things she had learned about herself since the last time they had kissed. She was going to have a lot of startling information for John…but, like a coward, she decided to start slow and sneak up on it.

For example, she explained, her adolescence had been very lonely. She was a woman who had reached her intellectual peak at eighteen and had entered puberty—at least emotionally—at twenty-seven.

John hummed in appreciation, though what he really wanted was to be kissing her neck. He was smart enough to keep that to himself.

Next she went on to explain her marriage, which she knew she had never adequately explained to John before. She and Max had rarely made love. They were a team in the lab; he was her mentor. Since she had never had any friends her own age, since she'd never had a boyfriend in her entire life, she hadn't realized her relationship with Max was peculiar. If she hadn't fallen into a "thing" with John, she might not know even now.

"But you're so gorgeous… "

She shook her head. "I didn't think of myself as attractive. Honest. I thought I was a freak. I never dated anyone. I was twenty before I realized my colleagues were intimidated by me, and women seemed to really dislike me. Well, except older, more matronly intellectual women, and scientists. But maybe the hardest thing about living that kind of life is that if you have a terrifically busy mind, it's fairly easy to avoid looking closely at your personal life. I never bothered to examine my unhappiness closely, because it was easy for me to find something else to think about. It's a dysfunctional behavior."

"Maybe a lot of people would like to have something better to think about than their problems," he suggested.

"No, John, I'm not talking about avoiding self-pity. I'm talking about denying what's going on in your life. The problem with denial is its finite... At some point you run out of it. Usually, by then, whatever you're denying is bigger than you are." She paused briefly and smiled at him. "I almost had what some people call a nervous breakdown when I found myself trying to juggle two tiny little boys," she said quietly. "Two five-pounders...counting on me. I couldn't give them a good life because I had no idea what a good life was. I didn't even know what good was. So Jess came to L.A. to help me, and I went to a counselor—a wonderful counselor who helps kids with abnormally high IQs adapt socially. I was her first twenty-eight-year-old kid."

John was quiet, and she wondered if he was able to understand, fully understand, the significance their relationship had held for her. But apparently he wasn't. "I guess I never thought of your life as hard. I guess I never thought of you as not smart enough to know what to do."

She chewed her lip a little. She should do a scholarly paper on this. She had felt—had been—a misfit. She never learned the eighth-grade boy-girl dynamic, because when other thirteen-year-old girls were finding out how to flirt, she was taking Physics II at the university as part of the gifted program. When other girls were crying because they didn't get asked to the prom, Leigh was crying because she hadn't been admitted to a master's program to which she had applied. One of the neighbor girls flunked her driving test; Leigh lost out on a major grant. When she got her first period her classmate, a twenty-year-old coed who was wearing an IUD, told her to "Stay cool, doll face, and just pin this little puppy in your panties like so, and pretty soon you'll graduate to tampons..."

"Ever have a friend face you with his envy?" she asked John. "With real hot jealousy? Like when you win a medal skiing, and you complain a little because your muscles hurt, your bank account is dried up, your best girl left you because she wasn't getting enough attention while you trained, and you're exhausted. I mean, you worked so hard for it! And the friend says something like, 'Yeah, yeah, cry me a river...didja win or not?'..."

John thought about that for a long time before he replied. He had never been gifted in anything except getting along. He was good at a lot of things, but he wasn't the best at much. He had to remember way back to just before he went into the navy, when he had competed in downhill skiing. He'd gotten into a fistfight with some loudmouth jerk who was taunting him about having some secret "advantage." Hell, John had about killed himself in training and had taken enormous risks. After a while he'd guessed the guy was just jealous. "Yeah. Yeah, I have."

"I never," she said seriously, "had otherwise."

"I was never jealous of you..."

"Oh, John, I know that. But I'd like you to understand why I have never known what to do with a boyfriend… With a lover. I never had one. Never. Max wasn't a boyfriend or a lover. We married in a state of confusion and inertia. He was leaving a project at Columbia to take on a new one at Stanford. He wanted me to go along… It wasn't exactly true love, though I suppose Max loved me as much as he could.

"Then I met you and had no idea what hit me. It was my very first acquaintance with real lovemaking. I think that's why we weren't able to salvage anything. Too complicated. Not enough experience on my part."

"What do you really want, Leigh?"

"Not a lot, actually. I want to be a good mother and have some friends. I just want to be okay like I am. Acceptable. There are a lot of reasons why I was disappointed that we weren't able to work things out. Just one is that I haven't had much fun since we went our separate ways. I know you think I'm a pain, clumsy, forgetful…but I had fun camping and hiking. We used to laugh a lot. I think I might like to learn to ski…"

John frowned as the mental picture of Leigh tripping around the slopes, getting lost and falling down came to mind. Well, there were bunny slopes… How did she imagine she was going to raise two boys?

"I'd at least like my kids to learn to ski and play ball… They already love anything physical and don't read anything that isn't previewed on the Saturday morning cartoons. They're completely normal."

John had discovered, in the years since Leigh had left him, that he actually liked kids. He wouldn't mind taking her boys to a ball game or a ski lesson. Getting them early like this, they might do pretty well.

"You're going to stay here, then?" he asked.

"There's a trust from my father's estate that I could use to live modestly but comfortably, but I plan to work. I've been studying ethics. I'm doing a paper on the ethics of scientific research called 'The Fear of New Knowledge.' It could turn into a book."

"How about the fear of old knowledge?" he asked. And old lovers? "What got you interested in ethics?"

"It's profoundly interesting, both simple and highly complex," she said. "What's your definition of ethics?"

He shrugged. "It isn't too complicated to me. Honesty, fairness, decency, knowing the difference between right and wrong. Treating people nicely, the way you'd want to be treated."

She leaned against the seat, looking out over the vast Colorado terrain, dimly lit by the moon. She was beginning to feel safe. She sighed deeply. She wouldn't bother to tell him that he was right—exactly, absolutely right—and that still she could make a whole profession out of the study. Part of the study would show that the real role models for ethical behavior were people who naturally did the "right thing" without studying the subject. It wasn't as though ethical people were flawless or never made mistakes; they sought rightness and rectified mistakes when they could. Like John.

Which was why she hadn't argued for one second when Jess called and said, "I need you to come home." She was grateful; she had needed a nudge. There were lots of "rights" in there. Of course you came home when your mother, who had been your life raft every time you ever got into trouble, called. And also, Leigh had already been thinking of returning to see if she could tidy things up with John, bury the hatchet and see if there was a way to get along. She'd expected to find him married and had prepared herself to negotiate friendship with him and his wife. And she hadn't made this decision during her preliminary study of ethics, either. Rather, she had known all along it was the right thing to do. However tough it was for her and John to see eye to eye, she knew he was a good and honest man who would naturally do the right thing—and she needed such a man to be a role model for her sons.

For his sons.

"So," John said, "what's next?"

"Do you think it's possible for us to be friends?"

"Well, anything's possible. But what might make it hard is that I remember," said John, "when I held you before. I remembered holding you at the weirdest times. I missed you so much, Leigh. I never told you how much you meant to me. I missed all my good chances to say all the right things, all the smart things. I was absolutely crazy in love with you, and scared to death... You fascinated me. You terrified me. All I can say is thanks...for coming back and making an effort to be friends again, to work things out... I'm such a—hey! Why are you crying?"

"It's nothing."

"Oh, Leigh, it's okay. C'mere. It's okay to come here so I can put an arm around you while you—"

"Easy does it, John. Let's go slowly... Please...?" But she was moving into the protective circle of his arm just the same. She felt so good, so secure, when she curled up against him like this and let herself pretend, for just a second, that there was someone to lean on, someone to care for her.

"Yeah, that's livin' right... Let's pretend everything is okay. Okay?"

"Okay."

Leigh put a hand on Jess's shoulder to rouse her. "I'm home. You didn't have to wait up."

"Hmm? Oh, I didn't mean to wait up. I must have dozed off. Did you have a nice time, dear?"

"Yes, Mom. You feeling okay?"

"Sure," she said, and yawned. "Sure I am. Just dozed off. Did you discuss the landscaping with John?"

"Yes. I think we've covered everything."

"Isn't he a nice young man?" Jess pushed.

"Yes, Mom. I'm going to bed."

"Do you think you'll be seeing him again?"

"I'm sure I'll see a lot of him, since he'll be working on the yard for weeks. G'night."

Jess frowned. "Leigh, have you been crying? Your eyes are all red around the edges."

"Me? I never cry."

Never used to, Jess thought. Only love can really bring on the tears.

"It must have been the cigarette smoke in the Steak House."

"Ah," said Jess. But Leigh didn't smell of smoke. She smelled slightly of woodsy aftershave. Jess hid her smile.

Five

By the first of May, John's crew had cleared away most of the shrubbery that had to be torn out to accommodate the changes and had begun working in the yard. He arrived on site early each day to supervise the work.

Before the work started, he had joined Jess, Leigh and the two rambunctious little boys for dinner one night. The object of the meal was to go over the plans for the way the yard was going to look, review the labor and materials price list and, even though they were friends, sign a contract. It wasn't exactly a simple process, what with Mitch and Ty jumping up and down, spilling and shouting and, before the night was over, just before bed, getting into a fight.

It looked to John as though it was a regular brother thing. He had a brother two years older, and they had done the same kind of wrestling and tumbling that began with a tickle and a poke and escalated into warfare. He was just thinking about how it took him back, watching them, when someone started crying. Twins, he discovered, did everything double. Soon they were both crying.

"Mommy, Mitch poked my eye!"

"Mitch, did you poke Ty's eye?"

"He was tickling me when I told him to stop it, and I didn't poke it, I—"

"Did he ask you to stop, Ty?"

"But, Mom, he told me to tickle, and then I—"

"Mitch, did you ask Ty to tickle?"

John glanced over at Jess and rolled his eyes as if to say, "Listen to the genius," which he had the mental control not to say. "I bet it's bath time," he said instead.

"Nooooo."

"Not yet! Mommmm."

"Yes, it is!" she said, triumphant.

Later, in the blessed quiet of the evening over a little coffee, John advised Leigh, "I don't know much about kids, but I know one thing for sure. You'll never figure out who started it, no matter how far back the questions go. It's a lot easier if you don't get involved. If they can't fight it out, change the activity. Bench 'em."

"Is that how your mother handled things?" Jess asked.

"Wellllll, sort of," John said, somewhat uncomfortable. "Her way was a little more devious. I fought with one brother all the time. He was third, I was fourth. There were two years between us, but we were close to the same size. We both had a hand in starting them. She sent us outside or down to the basement to finish, depending on the weather."

"Oh," Leigh said, "then one of you got to win?"

"No winners," he said, sipping his coffee. "If no one got hurt, it was a draw. If someone did get hurt, the one who didn't got punished. Most of our fights ended with us competing to fake the best injury. My brother once stood on his own hand for so long I had already gone upstairs and to bed by the time he thought he had something good enough to show Mom." He paused as if to think. "Now that I think about it, he's still a little weird."

"But can he type?" Jess asked, chuckling.

"I think his hand made it all right. He's a surgeon. Dr. McElroy… Specializes in good looks. He claims to have helped create half the bodies that come skiing here each winter. When he sees a gorgeous woman, his wife has to threaten him to keep him from asking who her surgeon is."

Leigh realized that she knew very little about John's family. Was it possible she hadn't even asked? And she had accused him of being self-centered…

"So, Jess, we're a go on the yard?" John asked, moving onto safer ground.

They were on one condition, she said. That he take the boys fishing once. They had no uncles or cousins, no one to do that sort of thing with them.

John said he would be glad to.

Sometime between that first dinner and the first couple of weeks of work on the yard, the weather got warm enough for John to choose a Saturday for their fishing trip. And Leigh found an excuse to go along.

"I didn't realize until the first night you came over for dinner that I never asked about your family."

"I'm the youngest of four, and the only one, my mom says, who isn't ambitious. It's a pretty well-known fact that I don't like to work all that much. Well, I like work that feels like play. I found out accidentally that I like to fix things and make things look good. Lucky break, huh?"

"So, what about your family?" she asked. They were

sitting together on the ground right behind the boys, who sat at the edge of the water with long cane poles.

"Bob is the oldest. He's about forty. He has his own tool-and-die business in Denver. He makes a great living and has a terrific wife and three kids. Judy, his wife, wanted ten kids until she had two. Number three, she says, was not her idea.

"Mike, the second one, he's around thirty-seven, I guess. He's a minister… Can you beat that? And not a hokus-pokus type minister, but a real live theological mastermind with his own church in Wyoming, a doctorate in theology. He's married with two kids.

"Ted, my surgeon brother, has three kids and a wife who will never need a bit of work from a plastic surgeon. Chris is a knockout. She's his surgical nurse."

"I wish I'd had brothers and sisters," she said, "but I understand why that wasn't possible. The way my dad had to travel was one thing, and he was kind of up there when he and Mom got married. He was over forty when I was born."

"You didn't know about any of the regular things kids grow up knowing about, did you? About fighting, games, fishing?"

She shook her head.

"How'd you figure you'd know enough to raise them?" he asked, nodding toward the boys.

"Well, first, I knew I wanted children, but I didn't know I'd get them. And second, I didn't know I'd be doing it alone," she said. "And I always had Jess. Do you see your family much?"

"I go to Denver whenever they're all going to be at my mom and dad's. They come here to ski, sometimes in large packs and sometimes in small groups. They're pretty neat people. There's one unique thing about my family. No one has ever had a girl. My mom had four boys, and my brothers had boys."

Now, she thought. Tell him right now.

"Do you think much about what kind of life you want them to have?" he asked her.

"I think about it constantly. I'd like them to have the kind of life you had," she said. Her voice was wistful and dreamy. "And maybe I'd give them just a smattering of what Jess and my dad gave me. I'm working on my own projects less so I can pay more attention to what they're doing. Every day I realize how much of the natural instinct for parenting I lack. Like that business about fighting. I never would have thought of something like that."

"They're pretty good guys," he said. "You must be doing something right. Want more?"

"You don't ask an unmarried woman if she wants children, John. It could get you into trouble. She could think you're discussing the future."

"Okay, okay, unfair question. So, you're working less. That was one of the things you said terrified you."

"When I said that, it was true. I just didn't know the reason. And the reason is simple—whenever I wasn't very busy working on something challenging, I noticed how lonely I was and how everyone else had friends and things to do. Or seemed to. I began to change that before leaving Los Angeles. I was in a women's group, did some volunteer work and generally learned how to make friends. Not the kind of friends you can only find hovering over microscopes and computer terminals, but friends who liked going to ball games, movies and the beach.

"The boys helped me do that. I met some of the other mothers in water-babies classes, tiny-tots gymnastics and finally preschool."

"What would it be like for you to just be a house-wife?" he asked.

She laughed at him. "Just a housewife? This is 1990, buster. Talk like that will get you drawn and quartered."

"Okay, okay… What if you didn't have a full-time job besides being a mother? What would that be like?"

"I'm always going to do some work in addition to raising my family, John," she said. "When I was growing up and advancing past all the kids, sometimes feeling really arrogant and other times feeling really sorry for myself, Jess would always say something to me that maybe a lot of moms say to their kids. 'Your best is good enough, Leigh. But you must always do your best.' I'm exhilarated by work. I'm also exhilarated by my kids. Even though I knew I wanted kids, I wasn't prepared for how great having them would be. But I'm also capable of doing work I love and that can help other people."

"So you'll always work." It sounded a bit like an accusation.

"But maybe not in the same way, John. Maybe if I'm not alone and afraid to be without a huge professional commitment I'll work at a sane pace rather than in the frenzy I used to use to cover up all that was missing from my life. There was another thing my mother said when I was much older and the projects I worked on were enormously important to the world. 'I'd like you to remember one thing—if you have something special, you must respect it, and treat it with wisdom and compassion. It won't do the world any good for you to burn yourself out, but if you have something that will make the world better, give it if you can. If you're a gifted baker, make good bread for the community. If you're a gifted gardener, make the world beautiful. If you're a gifted scientist, make the world safer.'"

He whistled. "It would be pretty hard not to feel guilty about not working with something like that hanging over your head."

"She wasn't saying that to make me feel guilty. She and my dad had a very strong belief that you should use your skills to make every day good and add to rather than subtract from the world." Leigh added pensively, "Now one of my great gifts is Mitch and Ty, and Jess reminded me recently that doing my best with them will include sacrifice. Maybe it includes sacrificing that single-mindedness I gave my work. Jess has been talking a lot about love. You know, dating, men, maybe marrying again."

"I think Jess has it in for us. It hasn't escaped me that she's setting me up."

"I know. I'm sorry. But I am glad to spend a little time getting to know you again. And no matter what Jess does, we'll still just bide our time getting to know each other. Right?"

He just stared at her, then slowly moved his hand to cover hers. "Biding time with you has its high points... and its frustrations." He was just leaning toward her as if to kiss her when Ty yelled. He had a fish.

"Your bid, Jess. Are we playing bridge or what?"

Oooops. The mother of the bride was daydreaming, Jess thought. "Three hearts," Jess said, ignoring her partner's audible gasp. "I can do three hearts alone," Jess said, stubborn in her own defense.

"You're going to do it alone," Peg grumbled.

"She's in never-never land again. Plotting," Abby West observed.

"Any progress? Are we looking at silver patterns yet?" asked Peg, laying down her cards and looking hopefully at Jess.

It was unclear whether Peg was relentlessly curious about the John/Leigh romance being staged by the mother of the bride or whether she wanted a break from bridge. Peg hated bridge and only played to indulge the others.

Jess folded her hand and grinned. She had only been waiting to be asked. Thursday was bridge day for the widows' brigade. Monday—literary discussion group. Tuesday—mah-jongg. Wednesday—garden club. Friday—craft day for seniors. The only thing the women were really serious about was their kids.

Jess's three best friends had been keeping a close watch over the progress of Leigh and John's relationship. While none of the others had this exact problem, they all had the same general problem—grown-up kids who simply weren't as clever or sensible as their mothers. According to the mothers. And the majority of them were still unmarried. Jess at least had grandchildren.

"I think it's going great guns, so far. Since John is working on the yard all the time, I suggested to Leigh that she ask him about activities for the boys. He actually drove them to the community center to sign up for T-ball. Since then, they've spent quite a lot of time together. I wonder how she's keeping him at arm's length." She fanned her face with her hand. "You can almost feel the heat. But there are always two little boys between them."

"If this works, I want my Rebecca married to a doctor by Christmas," Kate, the most cynical in the group, put in.

"It isn't quite that simple," Jess argued. She had explained it all before, and it went like this:

Jess suspected but had not verified that John was the father of Leigh's children. She could be wrong, but it was doubtful. From the moment she learned that Leigh was pregnant and the children hadn't been sired by Leigh's estranged husband, Jess had been scouting for the lover who had somehow broken her daughter's heart.

Okay, okay… At first she was going to find him and kill him. But after she'd spent time helping Leigh cope with the divorce, her job change, moving and multiple pregnancy, she began to understand that it had probably been the other way around. Leigh was such a bungler when it came to romance that she'd probably broken the poor fool's heart. Jess had thought about demanding the name of the responsible man, but then she decided that what Leigh really needed was a specialist who could help her catch up socially with the rest of her age group. Otherwise, Jess's demands for the culprit's name would not have done much good. She might have gotten John as a son-in-law, but it would undoubtedly have been far too temporary.

While Leigh was carrying and birthing the twins—and seeing the therapist—she was also dropping hints about her Durango fling. "He's just a simple, semi-hardworking guy who hates the whole concept of me having a Ph.D. You wouldn't want to have me marry just any old ski bum, now would you?" she'd asked. "Oh, sure, he has a job, but until they form a ski patrol in L.A., he wouldn't budge from Durango. Besides, since this little accident occurred, he's gotten himself married... and he doesn't even know about the babies."

After she had moved back to Durango, Jess called John out to do fix-it jobs at the house and watched him like a hawk. He never asked about her daughter, but she could see him scanning the place for pictures. She kept one old picture in a frame and moved it around the house to satisfy herself that John indeed seemed to look for it and relax around the eyes and mouth when he finally spotted it. She purposely did not mention her grandsons... She was saving that for a time when she needed his reaction. Now she believed she had him cold.

Recently Leigh had herself paved the way for what would eventually become Jess's plan to get her daughter married to the father of her children. It was when Leigh said, "I was always so smart, but so dumb about love. You know, Mom, I might not have picked the right guy, but I sure did love him a lot. And he's not a bad guy. In fact, he's a really down-deep good guy. He just couldn't accept me. I was too much."

"Maybe he just didn't have a chance," Jess had said.

"And now it's too late."

No way, thought the mother of the bride. It was never too late. For one thing, Jess knew that John was divorced, although she'd had to snoop to find out. And all she had to do was look at those little boys to see an obvious resemblance to their father. And knowing that Leigh had truly loved and wanted him and thought he was a good man...well, Jess was ready to have the invitations printed.

In her mind, the marriage was a go. Leigh, however, seemed reticent about returning to live with her mother; she was really dragging her heels. Scared, Jess decided.

Well, who wouldn't be? But the twins were getting big; time had wings. They would start school next fall. So Jess made up a little, tiny, inconsequential heart problem. She didn't want to tell a big lie—just expedite her daughter's return before the boys were drafted into the military.

"It's nothing serious, darling," Jess had said, "and I don't want you to be alarmed. I just want to spend some time with my grandchildren before I die. This could be my last summer…or then again, perhaps I'll somehow drift on through many summers."

Jess had never done anything like it before. It had been Peg's idea, actually, and it had been fun.

Once Leigh was home, Jess had to get her back in close proximity to John, which had proved more difficult to arrange than she imagined. She enlisted the aid of the widows' brigade. It was Peg's idea to tell John about her heart condition, too, as the reason for Leigh's return. Peg really should be closely watched, Jess thought. Deceitful old thing. It was Kate's idea to get Leigh and John working on the same project together— the renovation of the yard. Jess couldn't have cared less about having a stupid gazebo, but there weren't many things she could think of that would take a while to finish. Abby's contribution was that Jess should drop very, very heavy hints that getting married to someone like John would make her old mother happy. "Old women," Abby said, "are expected to play matchmaker. Try to conceal that and they'll know something is up."

Now Leigh was home, working on the yard, watching John while he worked on the yard. And Leigh hadn't said a word. Not a word! But seeing them together—the two of them or the four of them—Jess was convinced they belonged together.

"I thought you said you could do three hearts alone," Peg said, drawing Jess back into the game. "Old liar."

"Don't you call me a liar. You're the one who told me to pretend to have a heart condition."

"I know. You ought to be ashamed of yourself. Do you do everything you're told?"

"I'm sorry, ladies. I cannot concentrate on anything while I'm worrying about that girl. All I want is her happiness. And I'd like her happiness in a hurry, I admit it."

"I'd like to get her married and out of here so we can get things back to normal," Kate said.

"Things have never been normal around here," Abby said.

"But I know that girl. I was married to her father," Jess went on. "She needs a simple, steady, reliable man like John. Believe me, I know. That's what her father needed—a stable, sensible, ordinary person who could keep track of that wonderful, wandering mind. Who would know that better than me?"

"Are we going to play bridge or what?"

Six

Leigh did a couple of weeks' worth of serious reading and writing while the yard continued to develop into Jess's idea of a backyard paradise. She always found a few minutes to spare to chat with John, and he became something of a fixture at their dinner table. Then he asked her to meet him again at their old haunt, the Steak House, and she found herself as giddy as a teenager over the prospect of more hugging and kissing. *So this is why most teenagers couldn't concentrate on their math,* she thought. To Jess she said, "I might be late."

"You like him, then?"

"I like him fine," Leigh replied. *I'm absolutely wacko,* she thought.

He met her at the front door of the restaurant. "I want to show you something," he said. "Do you feel safe enough to come to my house with me?"

"Are you going to behave yourself?" she asked.

"Maybe, maybe not. That's up to you."

She thought about it and decided that when she had first met him she was a fifteen-year-old emotionally, which meant she'd been thinking with her libido. Now

she figured she was at least twenty years old emotionally and could add brains to her already breathless libido. She went.

John had a house in town that he'd been working
on, part-time, for about three years. "I want you to see
it. I want to show you how I think it'll shape up over
the years."

"It's lovely," she said as they pulled up to the curb in
front. It was quintessentially small-town, with its front
porch and white picket fence. A family house, was her
first thought. Her second thought was, *there's no one
here but us, and my brain is going out the window.* But
fear began to run away as John talked about his house.

"It's fifty-five years old. I knocked out the wall that
separated the living room from the dining room to make
more space. I'm working on a new kitchen, but since
I don't do a lot of cooking for myself, it's been slow
going. I'm a good cook, though. Did you know that?"

She hadn't.

He pulled her along. He opened the refrigerator door
and withdrew a bottle of wine. "I plan to replace this
fridge with a subzero one that has matching cabinetry.
And a built-in microwave, new stove and, rather than
this old-fashioned pantry, I'm going to build out into
the back porch, put in a bay window and have a breakfast nook."

He planned more shelves than cupboards, and
showed her a picture of a country French kitchen that
seemed to have a spirit of good food and community.
She began to envision it.

"The attic is unfinished," he went on, digging in a
drawer for a corkscrew. "There are two bedrooms upstairs, and I'm going to open up the staircase, build a

couple of dormer windows and an outdoor staircase to the yard. It's a small yard, but with a covered patio and some landscaping, it'll be beautiful. Come on," he said, abandoning the wine and taking her out the back door.

There was an old two-car garage with a peaked roof. "I'm going to enlarge the garage and build on a workshop. There'll be storage up top, the workshop out back, and separate garage doors." He led her back inside. "I'm going to tile where there's linoleum and refinish the hardwood floors. And the front porch—now it's small." He poured two glasses of wine and handed her one. "Come on," he said, taking her back to the living room. He had a curved sofa that sat before an old-fashioned fireplace. No TV, but a fancy stereo unit. He pointed to the window, outside of which was the front porch. "I'm going to make it larger and screen it, and that will give me more space to enlarge the upstairs."

"It's wonderful," she said, sipping her wine. "How long have you been working on it?"

"A few years," he said. "I've been doing a little here and there, but I haven't done a lot of serious work yet. I can do a lot of the cabinet work myself, but for an addition I'll need a bona fide builder and a permit. I'm just getting serious about it. It has to be a lot larger than it is. I wasn't going to finish the attic, but now I'm going to make sure it will hold two bedrooms with a bathroom in between. I thought about fixing it up to sell it—and now I'm thinking of fixing it up to live in it. It's pretty messy, huh?"

"Just sawdust," she said. "I'm the messy one—I can have a completely finished house and still it's a disaster. I'm getting better, but I never had to do much of that myself while I was growing up. But now Jess is beginning to really get testy about my messiness."

"Look at this," he said, leading her to the upstairs hall. It was a short hall with one bathroom between two bedrooms. Tacked to the wall were pictures torn from magazines of bedrooms, a bathroom, linen closets. The bathroom picture showed an old tub with feet, an antique linen cupboard and baskets holding rolled-up, multi-colored towels. One bedroom picture showed a canopy bed of brushed pine, built-in dressers, and flowered wallpaper with a matching bedspread.

"Try to picture this in there," he said, pointing to the clawfoot tub and then indicating the open bathroom door. The room definitely resembled the picture. And the bedroom had the built-ins done, but the canopied bed was not yet there.

"It's lovely, John. You've already resurfaced these floors."

"That rug was my grandmother's," he said proudly.

"You're really an artist," she said. So much more than a handyman, more than a Mr. Fix-it. There was real skill and imagination in this. The house surprised her. She had never given that much thought to her surroundings. She had always lived well, but she had never put energy into creating her own space.

"The elementary school is in the neighborhood. There's a playground at the end of the block."

"When did you decide to make it larger?" she asked.

"About three weeks ago. Leigh…" he began, struggling with the right words. "We're nothing alike. Nothing. I'm not even sure we want the same things. But…I tried marrying someone just like me. Someone who just wanted to play all the time and wasn't worried about the future, about families. It was awful… We were barely out of the wedding chapel before we were fighting. And what about you? You married yourself a genius who was so wrapped up in work he didn't have time for anything else in his life."

"What are you saying, John?"

"Well, I'm not very good at this." He laughed with some embarrassment. "I don't know how to say it. You've only been back a few weeks. This is hard. I want you in my life. I can't stand it when you're not in my life. I want to know if we can make it work. People put together different kinds of marriages now, different from how they were in the fifties and sixties. It used to be that you had to have the same goals, the same ambitions, or you just couldn't make it. We've talked about how you love your work and how I love to play…I wonder if it's possible, if we try to compromise, for us both to have what we want and each other, too."

"I'm a mother. When I look at the prospect of having a man in my life, I have to know if he's interested in being a father."

"I like your boys," he said.

Now. Tell him now.

"I don't know what kind of a father I'd be, but I know I wouldn't be a terrible one. I get along fine with kids. But I'm not going to lie to you—I wouldn't be hooking up with you just so I can have kids. It's you, Leigh. I never got over you. I might never get over you. I don't get along very well without you. I really regret that we lost each other before."

"We never had a real courtship," she said, but he was leaning toward her, his lips getting closer and closer. They stood just in front of the bedroom door.

"I'll court you till you die…I promise…" His lips touched hers lightly, as if just testing the water. "I could get a lot of work done on the house this summer, and put you and the kids in it… You could vacuum sawdust when you're not saving the world with your ethics paper."

When he put his lips on hers and talked through his kiss, her legs turned to rubber and she felt that fierce longing that she had only known with John.

"John," she said, stalling, but she didn't move away from him, "have there been a lot of women?"

"You mean, do I sleep around?"

"I guess that's what I mean."

"No. After our breakup I did try to find someone who would help me forget you…but I couldn't. And in the tradition of the decade, I played it very safe. It's a whole new ball game—you have to keep a photocopy of your sexual history in your ski jacket, along with a note from your doctor. I'm okay. Soft in the head, but okay."

"You love me," she said, tears beginning to rise to her eyes.

"Uh-huh, I do. And don't think I didn't try to find another way. After you left and my marriage went belly-up, I tried to change everything. I tried to read smart books, but all I got from that was a lot of sleep."

Her laugh bubbled out, but she moved closer into his embrace. He moved into the bedroom and put his wine on the built-in dresser. His arms tightened as he held her, rocking with her. She sat her glass beside his so she could hold him, then kissed him deeply. She didn't want to stop kissing, but he was talking.

"Then I tried to concentrate on business, because if I couldn't be smart, I'd be rich. I kept trying to find a way to deserve you, even if you were gone. But I couldn't stay interested in getting rich. This is all I am, Leigh. I'm Mr. Fix-it. It's what I want to be."

"And I went away to try to learn how to be 'regular.' My lessons were as hard as yours… I had to learn to relax. I had to learn to think of ordinary things. There's nothing like a real ripe diaper pail to help you face reality."

"You love me," he said, burying his face in her neck.

"Uh-huh, I do," she said. "I always have. What are we going to do?"

"We got a second chance, babe. We're gonna try it. That's all we can do. Remember that last fight we had—the one where I said 'Good. Go'? Well, it's gonna take a much bigger fight than that to get me to let go of you again."

Now. Tell him now.

"About the boys… "

"Not now," he said. "They'll be fine if we can work this out. They like me."

"I think they're already nuts about you, John, and… "

But she couldn't keep talking and kissing at the same time. This was what she had dreamed of so many nights—waking up with that gasping, choking feeling that was a prelude to tears. She had truly thought there would never be a way to feel this again. Not with him. Not with anyone.

John covered her with kisses, his lips roving from her neck to her ear, from her chin to her fingertips. The only sound from Leigh was a deep, enormous sigh of recognition, of longing. The only difference between the way she had always wanted him and the way she wanted him now was the proximity. Her body was beginning to respond in that wonderful way; her nipples stood taut, and her insides gathered up in a tight, luscious knot, ready to explode. The warmth of his body against hers, the pressure of his hands on her back, her buttocks, her breasts, brought such intense joy that she forgot where she was, who she was.

"I used to think about kissing you again," he said, cradling her in his arms. "I thought about it at the weirdest times. I'm starting to believe that old myth that there's a perfect mate for every man."

"Are you saying you want to marry me, John?"

"I don't want to be stupid, and I don't want to mess anything up. You've only been back a little while…but does it count as a proposal if I tell you I want to head in that direction?"

"I think so," she said, tasting his ear, his neck. She tugged his shirt out of his pants and ran the palms of her hands up his chest. His skin was hot and dry; his nipples were pointed little knobs.

His hands tugged her shirt out of her pants. His lips demanded of hers, and his breathing became labored. "I want you in the worst way. Can we? Is it okay?"

Details, details. She was going to faint if he didn't undress her right away.

"We can," she said.

"Do you use something? We don't want any accidents."

Damn. "Oh, John… " she sighed. "When I thought about coming back here…I thought you were married."

He chuckled against her neck. "You won't get out of it that easily," he said. "Turn around," he directed. She did; she would have stood on her head right now if that was what he wanted from her. He began undoing her long braid. "I figured you hadn't covered that," he said, digging his fingers into her hair and fanning it wide. "You never did think about the practical aspect of things, so I went to the drugstore."

"Hoping?" she asked.

He sighed from his toes. "I've been hoping since I saw you again. Am I rushing you?" he asked, turning her back to face him. She shook her head as he slowly lifted her shirt over her head and tossed it aside. "I can't get close enough to you. I can't leave you alone. Sue me." He reached around her and unsnapped her bra. "Ahhhh," he said. "You're so perfect."

She closed her eyes and leaned her head back while he touched her breasts with his mouth. At the same time he popped the snap on her jeans, and when he raised his head again he ripped off his shirt in one perfect, fluid motion. And held her. Skin against skin. The soft, hot press of bodies. She shuddered slightly in anticipation and ground her body into his. How she had longed to have this part of her life back.

"This isn't going to last long," he whispered, his voice jagged and raspy. "The next time will last longer."

"I don't care," she said, her own voice strange to her. There was something, she remembered as she ditched her jeans and underwear, about feeling out of control that was so wonderfully alluring. She couldn't stop him any more than she could stop herself. Maybe if she didn't know how finely tuned their bodies were she could have controlled herself. But the feeling that she had no power over her desires made her head spin and her body tremble.

While kissing her, fondling her, touching her in the most delicious ways, he also undressed himself, lowered her to the rug and found the protection he had purchased. She said a tiny, guilty prayer of thanks that he was sensible, because she herself was positively brain dead from lust.

His hand moved down her belly, over her mound of curly yellow hair, and his fingers gently spread her to touch her most delicate, sensitive place.

She shook from within, her legs instinctively tightening over his hand, her hips instinctively arching upward. Her breath came in one giant gasp, which he covered with his mouth and tongue while he pressed his hand harder into her flesh. Slowly, slowly, she came back, her eyes closed, her breath becoming even. He rose above her and looked into her eyes.

"Well, love, I don't have to feel guilty if I can't spend a lot of time inside you. I'm on the edge myself."

She only nodded, flooded with heat and passion. She opened herself up so that he could press himself inside her, and then a new sensation filled her. She loved this; she loved him. He moved, slowly and evenly, picking up speed and moving faster, and she began again, that build and rise. And just as she felt him lunge within, it happened again. Again, she was drenched in pleasure, flooded with heat.

In a half-dazed state, stroking his back and massaging his shoulders, she remembered back…way back… to their first time. She'd had so little experience when John made love to her the first time. And it had been like this before—his touch alone could propel her into ecstasy. She recalled thinking, "Wow, this is great!" like a kid who'd just discovered chocolate.

Now, however, she already knew how great this was.

This time there was something more she had to deal with, think about.

"John?" she began.

"Mmmmm?"

"John, about the boys… "

He kissed her lips. "I'm crazy about the boys, Leigh. I'll adopt them, play with them, be as good a dad as I can…whatever you want."

"But, John, I want to tell you about the boys."

"Not now, Leigh," he said, kissing her ear, her neck, her breast. "We have a lifetime to talk about the boys and their future siblings. Right now is for you and me. We have to be sure, in and out of bed, that we want each other. I learned a couple of things in the past few years. I learned that there's only one way to really deserve you. I'm going to accept you exactly as you are, not try to live up to your brilliance. If you just say that I'm what you want—you'll get just the me you see."

"That's the you I want," she whispered.

Seven

It was lunch break for the crew, and Leigh sat up on the redwood deck with a cup of decaf and a book. The landscaping and building was nearly done; most of the guys had gone to get some fast food, but John had stayed behind to play a little catch with the boys. He had also stayed because Jess had offered him a bowl of her famous vegetable soup and a garden salad. And because he was planning to make a life with Leigh and the boys, if it was possible. At the moment, it looked more than possible.

"Are you playing matchmaker?" Leigh had asked her mother the week before.

"Well, yes, I suppose I am. My grandsons need a man in their lives. Bring me someone you like better and I'll stop working on John."

"Just stop," Leigh had said.

And Jess had replied, "No."

Since Leigh knew there was no one in the universe better than John, she let her mother's interference go. But she didn't dare encourage her. Jess already talked about John more than Leigh did. Leigh was in complete agreement, but she didn't want to scare him away. And they had decided not to rush for one reason only—it was ridiculous to get married after being together for a little under two months. She wasn't entirely sure why it was ridiculous, but it certainly seemed that way.

The boys weren't very good ball players yet, but they sure loved it when John gave them any attention. They had begun climbing all over him whenever they saw him. When his truck pulled up, they ran to him. It took a very stern mother to see to it that he was left alone long enough to get a little work done during the day.

Spring was at its lushest, and Leigh had been home for two months plus a few days. The gazebo was half constructed, the flagstone garden paths coming along nicely, and the barbecue pit would support a few burgers and steaks in another week. Because the lot was huge and abundant with brush, trees and plants, it didn't really appear to be under construction. When the mess was cleared away, it would be stunning. Leigh was so glad to be here; she felt such a sense of renewal. She believed in her future in a way she never had before.

Each moment with John seemed to improve on the one before it. The interest he showed in the boys, seemingly both entertained and fascinated by them, was something she had only dared dream of. Since she hadn't really expected it to go even half so well, she was very pleased with herself.

Leigh remembered when a book had held her interest more than John did. It had frustrated him terribly, back when he didn't understand how she had learned to escape her feelings—and the feelings she had around John were enormous. Now, with her renewed sensitivity to what she felt, the book that could draw her attention away from John for a minute had not yet been written.

He had been so good about re-creating their friendship on her terms. He had taken the boys to sign up for T-ball, gone with them all to get ice cream, and just last Saturday they had attended a movie. Jess invited him to lunch and dinner nearly every day and wasn't fooling him at all.

"Your mother is making me very nervous with this setup. She isn't fooling anyone," he said.

"I know," she replied.

I'm not as dumb about relationships as I claimed, Leigh thought. Years ago she had known she wanted this: a lover, a friend, partner, children. It was one of the critical impulses that had caused her to separate from Max, because he had made it clear that this could never happen with him.

Then there was something else, something frequently covered in paperback novels. Romance. On at least one and sometimes two nights each week Leigh would steal an evening to be alone with John. And while he didn't push her or try to make love to her again, their kissing sessions were simply magnificent, spattered with dialogue, tense with desire, lush with emotion…and they couldn't help themselves. What a lovely thing to not be able to help. She wanted him so badly she ached.

She had made a deal with herself—to be fair, she was going to be sure he knew about his sons before they resumed that part of their relationship. A stronger woman would have kept that deal. She had failed that once, at his house, but she was determined not to fail again. But as much as she longed for honesty between them, as much as she longed to make love to him again, she was still a bit terrified of telling him. She was afraid he would be angry that she hadn't done it sooner. Soon, she thought. Maybe tonight.

She watched as Mitch overthrew Ty with the ball, and John clapped and whooped; they were pretty small to throw so well. He turned to look at Leigh and made the thumbs-up sign; she waved and smiled.

She ached for him, but the last time they had become lovers before they became friends...before they came to terms with what they wanted. It had turned out that they had wanted different things, opposite things. This time she was trying to put first things first, to begin at the beginning and not at the end. This time they were talking, at least. Finding areas of agreement.

"I thought," John had said, "that I actually liked you before I loved you. But knowing that for sure is as important to me as it is to you." He had something that Leigh had never had herself—and hadn't given him credit for the last time around. Wisdom.

Things were good. They were getting reacquainted; they were friendly. They were being sensible, postponing their marriage for a few months, even if they had been unsuccessful in postponing their sexual relationship. They were so hot for each other that they had to watch even kissing, because within seconds they were panting, squirming, nearly dying of longing. Her cheeks grew pink when she thought about him. She wasn't sure she could just sit there on the deck watching him without getting all hot and bothered.

So much for wisdom.

She loved watching him. Whether he was bending his back over bricklaying or playing with the kids, his lithe strength was so appealing.

He stopped playing ball suddenly and straightened his spine. The ball that Ty had thrown his way hit him in the knee, and he didn't move.

"Hey, John!" she heard Ty call.

John looked at Leigh, astonishment written all over his face. He turned back to the boys and said something she couldn't hear, and then the boys began to toss the ball back and forth without him while he turned and slowly walked toward the deck. His brow was furrowed, but his mouth was slightly open. He finally stood before her and simply looked at her for a moment.

"John?"

"Five pounds…each?"

"What?"

"The kids…they were five pounds each. They were early."

"Yes. Well, actually, Ty was four-four…and Mitch was—"

"How early?"

"Almost two months. A little over six weeks."

He winced visibly. He shook his head, then seemed to try to refocus on her eyes. "They're mine," he said.

She felt that old snap of panic in her gut. There it was at last. A little later she was going to be glad this part was over. This wasn't the way she had planned it. She nodded rather lamely.

"Were you going to tell me? Ever?"

She swallowed once and looked over her shoulder to make sure her mother and the brigade couldn't hear. "That's the main reason I wanted to come back…even though I thought you were married… I knew I had to tell you that they—"

"Damn!"

"John," she said pleadingly, "I didn't know you didn't know. Until we met at the Steak House and you couldn't understand why Max felt betrayed… All these years I thought when you heard about them you would instantly know it was you."

"Know? Know and not even care? How could you have thought that?"

"You were adamant! You didn't want a commitment or children. Later, when I came back, you seemed so oblivious to it all. Even when you knew about them, the impact seemed lost on you."

The look of pain that crossed his features was unmistakable. "You thought I was too stupid to figure it out."

"No." She shook her head. "No, I just didn't understand. I mean, sometimes I understood. When I came back here pregnant as a cow and found you were married, I understood that you never knew I was pregnant."

"You didn't tell me!"

"I know…I know…I didn't want to tell you until my divorce was final because, frankly, I didn't think the divorce was going to precede the birth. I had made such a mess of things. Even though I hadn't been with my husband in over a year, I was still legally married and pregnant. My divorce did come through before they were born, and then I was too late. And—"

"Come on, come on… That was then. What about now?"

"Well, after thinking about it, I realized that you probably didn't know all the details of childbirth, of how twins usually come a little early, of—"

"But you didn't hurry to explain, did you?"

"Hey, John!" Mitch yelled.

"Practice, I said!" he shouted back, an angry tone in

his voice. "Why didn't you tell me right away? Right away!"

"I don't know. I was afraid to. And I thought this was better."

"What?"

"Well… " she tried, her voice shaking. Hadn't she made a lot of sense to herself before, when she was figuring this out? "Since you didn't seem to realize they were your children, I thought I'd let you choose them. I tried a couple of times, then chickened out. But I thought we seemed to be headed in the same direction this time, wanting the same things and all. And I thought you might be a little upset at first, but I really thought you'd be happy to find out they're—"

"Good God," he said, shaking his head. "Don't you know there's a huge difference between accepting them because they're part of the deal and wanting them because… And you're going to do a study on ethics. Leigh, it isn't ethical to keep information like that a secret."

"I know, sort of. But that's what makes ethics confusing and complex. Being dishonest is unethical, unless it's the lesser evil. Like, is it more ethical not to name the father of my sons than to name someone who would hurt them?"

"Why would I hurt them?" he asked, aghast. "Haven't I been pretty good with them? Good to them? Without even knowing—"

"But I needed to know you again. What if you didn't want them?" she said, her voice so low he had to strain to hear. "What if you didn't want me? Or me with them?"

He only pursed his lips tighter. "Why couldn't you just tell me the truth? Why didn't you leave me a message that you were about to give birth? If not that, why didn't you write, call, something—to let me know I was a father?"

"I didn't want to bother you. You said you didn't want to be a father. I left because you said that wasn't in your game plan. You said, 'Go. We're just from two different worlds.'"

"Leigh," he said as patiently as he could, "men always say stuff like that. It doesn't mean that much. A guy says something like that, and then his wife gets pregnant and you'd think he invented pregnancy."

"I don't know anything about guys and what they say and what they mean."

He ran a hand through his hair and shook his head. "Leigh, Leigh, stop. Listen to me. What you did to me is really unfair. No matter what happened between us, they were mine. No matter what my marital status was or yours, for that matter—you should have told me I had children. This could have worked out all different. I missed all this time with them because you decided it was better this way. Leigh, I know I hurt your feelings when I said 'Go,' but I didn't take your kids away from you! Is there anything else you should tell me? Anything that you either assume I know, assume I don't know, or…anything?"

"What do you mean?"

"The kids are fine? Normal? No mysterious conditions or anything?"

"Of course not. I would tell you something like that."

"You didn't even tell me that—"

"Soup!" Jess cried from the back door. "Leigh, the girls and I have ours in the kitchen. Why don't you,

John and the boys help yourselves while we go back to our game?"

Leigh and John didn't respond, only looked at each other. "Does she know?" he asked after a long moment.

"Sometimes I think she does, sometimes I'm sure she doesn't. She hounds me about getting married all the time—she decided I should marry someone like you, but I don't know how she could know you're their—" She shrugged. "Maybe you just seem the perfect type to be their stepfather."

"Stepfather," he muttered, the set of his mouth angry. "You really did it this time. I can't believe you didn't tell me. Was it some kind of test…to see if I was good enough?"

"Oh, John, no. Oh, please," she said, tears coming to her eyes.

"Sometimes you have no sense," he said.

"I know, I know, but I thought—"

"Stop it!" He looked away. Were those tears in his eyes? He shook his head again, trying to clear the fog away. "I gotta go, Leigh. Tell Jess thanks anyway, but I need a little time to think. Alone. Let me have that. Okay?"

"Could you just remember one thing?"

"Yeah, what?"

"It's not their fault."

Work on the yard progressed with lightning speed, but without the foreman. John remained conspicuously absent while the roof went on the gazebo and the last brick was laid in the barbecue pit.

"Where is that young man?" Jess asked her daughter. "I haven't seen him in almost a week."

"Six days," Leigh replied morosely.

"I hadn't realized," Jess, who realized each minute, lied. "And here I was getting the impression that he had taken a real interest in you and the boys. Or was it just my cooking?"

Leigh made no response. She gazed off into space, as she had been doing quite a lot lately.

"The boys really miss having him around," Jess said. "The other fellas are just as nice, but don't seem to take the personal interest in them that John did. I mean, signing them up for a T-ball team and everything. What a guy."

"What a guy," Leigh said. What a jerk, she thought. No matter how mad he was at her, he shouldn't let the boys down like this. Of course, the boys didn't know they'd been let down yet, but surely they would notice soon.

"Tell me what you think of this invitation, Leigh," Jess said, handing her a calligraphic page.

You are cordially invited
to the home of Mrs. Jessica Stewart Wainscott
for an outdoor springtime celebration
of food, libation, music and good cheer
on the afternoon of Sunday, June 10. Two o'clock

The address and a request for an R.S.V.P. appeared at the bottom.

"Good heavens," Leigh said. "This is pretty fancy, isn't it? For a backyard barbecue?"

"Well, when you spend thousands revamping the

backyard, you ought to do up the party right. Don't you think?"

"How many people are you inviting?"

"Everyone I've ever met."

"Oh. And are you having it catered, or did you get together a bunch of friends to potluck it?"

"Oh, catered. Naturally. I'm using Berkley's Bakery and Deli. They're fantastic."

"This is going to cost a fortune."

"I only plan to do this once."

"Well," Leigh said, handing the invitation back to her mother, "just so long as you don't wear yourself out and get sick."

"Don't be silly. I'm not even doing any of the work. Shouldn't we get you a new dress for the party?"

"A dress? You're planning on guests wearing dresses?"

"Mom," a small voice said from somewhere below. She looked down to see Ty, the blond, staring up at her. "Wanna play catch some more?"

"Where's Mitchell?" Leigh asked.

"Over there. Waiting for us."

"Okay," she said, moving down to the backyard and holding out her hands. She didn't do this well; another character flaw. Ty fired the first one at her and she missed it, so naturally she had to chase it. "So, Mother," she called, glancing back to the deck where Jess stood, watching them. "It's only three weeks till your party. You think everything will be done?"

"It's almost done now," Jess said, watching as Leigh pitched the ball to Mitch, missing him by miles. Mitch complained loudly and ran after the ball. Two more bad throws followed. "I'm going to have Peg's son, the flo-

rist, bring out a bunch of fresh flower garlands to dec-
orate the gazebo and put arrangements on long buffet
tables," Jess said, wincing as a ball hit Leigh in the leg.
Leigh made a noise of pain and threw the ball—aiming
for Ty, getting closer to Mitch—and both boys whined
their unhappiness.

"Mom," said Ty, "throw it under. Under. Like this."
He moved his hand very patiently, trying to show her
how to do it. It didn't work. Leigh's aim was actually
worse than a four-year-old's. She grouped them closer
together. With them standing just a few feet apart, she
could get the ball to the right person.

"Mom, let's not play," Mitch said. "We'll practice a
while and maybe you can play later. 'Kay?"

"That bad, huh?"

"This is for babies," Ty said. "When's John coming?"

"I don't know, guys. Pretty soon, I suppose."

"Did he say anything to you about being away for a
while, Leigh? If I didn't know better I'd think he was
avoiding us," Jess called.

"I don't know, Mother."

"Why don't you call him for me? Ask him to dinner. I really think that young man has a thing for you.
I know he gets a kick out of the boys. Something must
have happened to—"

"Mother! For Pete's sake!"

"Well, what the heck?" Jess defended herself. "He's
a nice young man. I've known him for years, and I can
tell the two of you like each other. Maybe if you—"

"Mother! Stop it!"

"I am only suggesting," Jess said, in her most patient, long suffering voice, "that I could turn this gar-

den party into a wedding in a snap. Then I could have you and the boys settled and taken care of before I die."

"You know something, Mom? I thought this was humorous for a couple of weeks, but it's quickly losing its appeal. Now, do me a favor, don't bring up John, marriage or death—in a humorous or serious vein—again. Understand?"

"Oh, Leigh," Jess sighed. "You're too young to be so old and crotchety."

"Sometimes I actually think you're serious."

"If you'd get serious, we'd be in business."

"I give up!" Leigh shouted. "I can't take this anymore!"

"Heavens," Jess muttered. "Testy."

It was Wednesday. The brigade was seated in the front room when Leigh came in.

"Mom, Mitch and Ty are in front of the TV in the loft. I want to run to the bookstore, but I won't be gone long. Can you keep an eye on them?"

"Sure," Abby answered for her.

"Yes," Jess said, glaring at her friend. "Buttinsky," she muttered.

"Thanks," Leigh said, fishing in her shoulder bag for her car keys. She went out the back door. When she got to the car, she realized she hadn't remembered her checkbook and went back.

"So I'm stuck with a stupid garden party when what I wanted was a wedding," Jess was saying in the next room.

"Well, at least you tried," Abby consoled. "Do you have any idea what happened?"

"Not a clue. One minute they seemed ready to steam

themselves straight—I've never seen so many passionate glances between two people. The next thing I know—whoosh—John is gone and Leigh is depressed. Kids. They can't even get a simple marriage right."

"The printer can add wedding to the invitations, can't he?" Kate asked.

"I think we're past all that. I'm picking them up tomorrow, and the party's in two weeks. But I could sure get on the phone."

"Well," Peg said, "what if you fake a real heart attack and make Leigh's marriage to John your dying wish?"

"I feel guilty enough just faking a heart condition. Last time I had a physical the doctor asked me if I'd be an organ donor." Jess sighed. "I'm thinking of coming clean about the whole thing."

"That won't be necessary," Leigh said. She stood just inside the kitchen doorway. "Oh, Mom, how could you be so sneaky?"

"Leigh!" Jess had the good grace to slap a palm against her chest as though a coronary might be impending after all—but Leigh was unimpressed.

"Shame on you, Mom. As if my problems aren't tough enough."

"I was trying to help," Jess said.

"She was," said Peg, ever so earnest. "She honestly was!"

"Peg put her up to it," Kate tattled.

"Abby was the one who actually got the idea," Peg confided.

"Oh, stop it," Leigh said. "You're all giving new meaning to the term busybody." She shook her head. "Shame on you all."

"Leigh," Jess said. "I am sorry, darling. I'm ashamed of myself."

"What were you thinking of?"

"I was thinking that you and John are perfect for each other, and I got a little…a little… "

"Carried away," Peg said. "But it's mostly my fault, Leigh. I egged her on."

"Me too," said Abby.

"I warned her from the start," Kate said.

"You should all be grounded," Leigh said, exasperated. "No wonder he ran for his life."

"But why, Leigh?" Jess asked. "What happened?"

"Oh, forget that! I'd be a fool to give you any encouragement at all! I'll be out for a while longer. I want to take a little think-time. Watch the boys?"

"Of course, Leigh," Jess murmured. She just stared at the doorway until she could hear the sound of the car. Then she turned to her friends. "When I figure out which one of you talked me into this… "

Eight

"Fishing," Leigh mumbled, driving along a narrow, mountainous road. It just figured.

She had gone to his nursery to ask where he was. There was no one there except a high-school girl whose only job it was to ring up sales. Then she drove to his house and found a note on the door. "Gone fishin'." She thought that sort of thing had gone out with Tom Sawyer. Then she spotted a truck with John's logo on the door. She followed it, and when it stopped she asked the driver if he had any idea where John usually fished. He gave her three possible locations.

The first two, reasonably close, had proved futile. It just figured that John had to go deep into the woods, down a long unpaved road to a mountain stream. Leigh half remembered a place like this where she had come with John years ago.

She might have remembered some of the details if she hadn't been so busy building up a good head of steam. She was a little tired of this childish behavior. His and hers both. But she was a little tired of feeling guilty about not always doing the right thing. Couldn't people occasionally make allowances for mistakes? When you told a person you were nearsighted they didn't turn around later and point out something far away, then yell at you if you couldn't see it.

And furthermore, how many times was she supposed to say she was sorry? For everything? And how much time did he need before he realized how much courage she'd had to work up to come back here, to the scene of the crime, so to speak, to face him and tell him the truth about his sons, even thinking he was married? He never gave her any credit because he was always finding some fault with her.

She rehearsed all those arguments right up to the point when she saw his truck in the clearing. Yes, this was a place she had come with him. And yes, he was fishing now as he had fished then. And perhaps he had been here for a while, because he had a tent set up and a campfire in front of it. Maybe it was his plan to just become a woodsy recluse until she got frustrated enough to leave.

That was what had happened before when they couldn't communicate, so in one insane moment they threw away all the good things they had shared. Oh, if she had told him then, just told him then, maybe…

It made her cry to think about it. She hardly ever cried normally, but she had done more sniffling since coming back here than she had done in ten years. She jumped out of her car, heedless of the tears streaming down her cheeks, and walked toward him. He had turned and seen her drive in, but he observed her heated approach with apparent calm.

She advanced on him, feeling anything but calm herself.

"I don't know what you want from me," she said to him.

He walked toward her. Very slowly. His lack of emotion only fueled hers.

"Do you want me to beg? Is that it? I'm sorry. I messed everything up from the very beginning because I'm smart in some things and stupid in others. I never thought about protection because my husband and I did not make love. And I never thought about what would happen if I fell in love with someone because I never had fallen in love, even slightly… Not in twenty-seven years! I actually thought some people got love and some people got brains… I didn't know love made people brainless! And I didn't tell you about the babies because you had just gotten married and I thought you loved someone else. And then I didn't tell you because I just plain didn't know how. So what do you want from me, huh, John?"

He stared at her during her tirade. No expression whatsoever.

"Huh, John? What if they weren't yours, but really my dead ex-husband's kids? Wouldn't it be pretty apparent that they're crazy about you just the same? They are, you know. They ask when John's coming, and I don't know how to tell them that John's mad because he just found out he's their real, true daddy and he's upset. But not about being a dad, I don't think. About not being told sooner."

She gave a sniffly kind of gulp and wiped impatiently at her tears. He just watched her face, his arms hanging loose at his sides.

"What more could I have done if I'd wanted to do things perfectly? I just wanted to come back to Durango, where you are, and somehow make it right with you. I never dreamed you would be divorced. I was prepared to find you happily married and the father of a bunch of little, tiny kids. I didn't know if I'd be very good at working things out, but I knew it was right that you know about your sons." Her tone changed. "They're good boys, John. They're sweet, honest, lovable, precious, smart little boys. I thought you'd be so proud of them.

"I was so stunned to find you alone. I was so surprised to find you still had some feelings for me. Honest. I had never given myself credit for being able to have that kind of impact on a man...especially a man I was wildly in love with. And then to see that you couldn't help but have some feelings for them, too... well, I was beside myself with happiness. But I messed up one more thing by not telling you soon enough."

She gulped and hiccuped, then wiped her nose on her sleeve. She hadn't cried like this in a long time. And there he stood, right smack in front of her, watching without saying anything.

"I'm sorry," she nearly shrieked. "Before, when I walked away and got on with my life and had them alone, it was because I didn't know anything. And now I know some things. And if you think I'm going to let you have a temper tantrum and walk away from us just because you're mad, you're wrong! Because I think you love me, and I know I love you! So what do you want from me? Huh, John?"

His movement was so fast that she gasped. He put his arms around her waist and pulled her to him, covering her mouth with his. He kissed her all over her sticky, teary face and held her so tightly that she could hardly breathe. But who needed to breathe?

This isn't likely to solve anything, Leigh thought abstractly. But then her thoughts faded completely, because the sensation of his lips, the taste of his mouth and the hard press of his body against hers made her deliriously, if briefly happy. She held him; he held her. Then it occurred to her. This was what he wanted.

And so did she.

After that long, emotional speech, Leigh could only say, "Oh, John…" Actually, she cried it, but she wouldn't let go of him. She wouldn't let go again. And neither would he, apparently. He lifted her into his arms and carried her to his tent. Inside was an open sleeping bag upon which they were soon tumbling, kissing, hugging, and Leigh was still crying.

"Are we going to be able to figure this out?" She wept. "Ever?"

"I didn't come up here to figure it out, babe," he said, kissing her neck, her wet eyes, her ears. "It only took me about two minutes to remember that I want you… and them. But I had to think about how to tell my folks that I have kids, that I'm going to marry their mother, that it was just a stupid misunderstanding by two stupid people…one of whom just happens to be the genius daughter of a prizewinning scientist."

A laugh bubbled through her tears.

"No one would ever believe this. I may not be as smart as you are, but would you believe one of the reasons I was appointed head of the volunteer ski patrol is that I have this uncanny intuition and great common sense?"

Again a laugh bubbled through. "I love you," she said.

"I know. And I love you. And even though I was pretty mad at first, and even though I wish you'd told me sooner, I'm really glad you brought the boys here. I want to be their dad."

That made her really cry. "I was so afraid you wouldn't. You were pretty adamant about not wanting kids."

"That was just a guy thing. I don't know where it comes from. Men are afraid that if they act like they even condone the idea of having children, they'll be rushed into a Lamaze class. I'm sorry. I was beginning to worry that I might never have kids, to tell the truth."

"Oh!" she said, and slapped his arm.

He kissed her hard.

"You put me through all that and you wanted kids after all?" she asked him.

"We're going to have to adopt a new game plan, Leigh. No way we can make a marriage work if we can't talk to each other. We've been keeping all these things secret. I was jealous of Max before…and afraid you thought I wasn't smart enough to be in love with someone like you."

She smiled lamely. "And I was afraid you thought I was a weirdo. A freak."

He brushed her damp cheek with one knuckle. "You are weird. Are you going to marry me?"

"Yes."

"Are we going to consummate the engagement?"

"If you tell me you just happened to bring along birth control on your fishing trip, I'm going to become suspicious."

"I didn't."

"Well, it's too big a risk, then."

He looked down at her, grinning. "Even though you make some very good accidents, I think I'd like to plan the next batch."

Leigh sighed and embraced him. "I hope I'm not going to keep having them in batches," she said very earnestly.

Although they really couldn't tempt fate and take any more chances, they could lie in John's tent all afternoon, kissing, hugging, touching, telling tender little secrets to each other, and laughing at how close they had come to losing each other again. If they laughed about it, they could keep from crying.

It seemed to Leigh that the only time there was ever any confusion was when they were apart. Together, they did just fine. Apart, they started to rethink everything and realized how little sense it made for them to be wildly in love. She decided they had better get married and move in together before there was time for much more thinking.

And for John, well, he hadn't believed he would ever have a woman like Leigh love him this much. She was not only brilliant, but she was also kind, honest, good and loyal. She didn't think he wasn't living up to his potential. On the contrary, she told him she was proud of everything he did, his commitment to kids, to the community, to the environment.

After a few hours of uninterrupted time to talk and touch and kiss, it was pretty clear that they were headed in the same direction this time. And that there was no point in waiting. So Leigh told him about Jess.

"From what I overheard, she even made up her heart condition. She's been plotting with the widows' brigade to get us married. She was hoping that her garden party would end up being a wedding."

To her relief, John laughed. "It figures. She needs to be taught a lesson. If you're sure her heart's okay."

"I'm sure. Though it may be somewhat weakened if I'm away much longer. Thinking that you've been stuck with four-year-old twins could wreck an otherwise strong heart."

"I'm not sure that's punishment enough. But," he said, grinning, "it's a pretty good start."

John and Leigh took on the widows' brigade. The four women took their tongue-lashing quite well, considering that not one of them would take the blame singularly. They busily blamed each other. And they unanimously swore they had only had everyone's best interests at heart.

"You two make such a wonderful couple," Peg said. "And you seemed to need just a slight push."

"We only want our children settled and happy," said Abby.

"And in a family setting, not this significant-other stuff the young people are doing nowadays," Kate said.

"We're sorry we interfered, but we did think you'd be happy together. Really," Jess added.

"But that's not your place, is it?" John lectured. "It happens that you're very lucky you didn't do some real damage. You're lucky because it turns out that Leigh and I like each other and plan to go on seeing each other. But when and if we decide to marry, it's going to be our decision. Understand?"

The four women nodded with choreographed precision.

"And," added Leigh, "especially since there are children involved, this isn't going to be a snap courtship. John and I have done lots of talking about the kind of family life we have in mind as individuals. We're not going to rush into anything with the boys' futures at stake. We're going to be sure our values are similar and our goals can mesh. We're very different, you know. Understand?"

Four nods.

"From this point on, you are not to involve yourselves in any romantic notions that concern anyone other than yourselves."

Four sets of eyes rolled. As if any of them wanted any kind of romantic notions. Ha.

"And you will not make any plans for anyone else. If you're curious about something, you will kindly ask the question and take the answer, which might be 'none of your business.' Understood?"

"Yes, dear," Jess said. "But before you get yourself all in a lather about this, it was all well meant. And if it had ended in a wedding, we would all have been thrilled. But since it's not—so be it. I wouldn't hurt you for the world."

"But you have to let me live my own life, make my own mistakes, my own plans for the future," Leigh said. "I know I've needed your help before, Mom, but this time you went overboard."

"And now you'll be lucky to get invited to the wedding, if there is one," John warned. "You four are troublemakers. Are you going to behave?"

Oh, they'd behave. They promised.

When John and Leigh left them, he said, "I'd give anything to be a fly on the wall right now."

"They're just going to blame each other," Leigh predicted. "You think our plan is going to work?"

"It's fail-safe. Trust me."

And she did. Completely.

Nine

Jess mailed her garden party invitations without sulking. She and Leigh made up and spoke no more about interference; the widows' brigade got to put in their two-cents' worth about the party, and the yard was finished a week before the event. Leigh suggested having a string quartet play some music and chose the colors of the garlands and buffet table centerpieces. She visited the caterer with her mother and helped Jess pick out a lovely floral dress to wear.

When Leigh was sure her mother had a handle on everything and could spare her, she requested some babysitting. She wanted to fly to Denver for a couple of days; she needed access to the University of Colorado library for some of her research, and Jess said she could keep the boys.

"I'm a nervous wreck," Leigh told John.

"Me too. But it's going to be okay. I don't even think they'll yell. My mother will be relieved, and my dad will be secretly very proud."

"We could have thrown Jess a bone and told her she

was right about that much—that you are the boys' father."

"I'm afraid it might give her the wrong kind of power," John said.

They were standing on the sidewalk in front of a modest, suburban house that belonged to John's parents. Leigh could imagine the activity that must have swelled within the walls of this small, two-story house during the years Mrs. McElroy was raising four boys. Leigh had never been accused of being psychic, but she felt that she would find love and acceptance here, despite her fears.

"Shall we?" he asked.

"Wait. What did you tell them? Exactly?"

"That I want them to meet the girl I'm going to marry."

"And what did your mother say?"

"She said, 'again?'"

"Oh, boy. I don't know if I can walk."

"Come on. Chicken."

"What else did you say?" she demanded.

"I said, 'This is different. I've been in love with this woman for years, and my marriage was on the rebound, but we've got it together now, and it's right.' Well, something like that."

"We do have it together now, don't we, John? It is right."

He kissed her, quick and efficient, and grinned that magnetic grin of his. "Right. Never more right."

Inside the McElroy house was a gathering that Leigh could never have prepared herself for. John couldn't have, either, for that matter. The entire McElroy clan had gathered under one roof to meet and greet the newest addition. They had all hidden their cars down the block and in the garage. There was the aroma of roast beef in the air and a lot of noise in the living room. And right after Jeanette McElroy opened the door and greeted her son, they all yelled, "Surprise."

Minister Mike was the only one who'd had to fly into town for this gathering. He and his wife and kids were staying with Ted and Chris and their clan. Bob had taken time off, and Judy had come over early to help prepare an enormous meal. Leigh was hugged and welcomed by each and every one of them.

"We thought you should have a look at what you're really getting into," Bob said. "This is no quiet little family."

"It probably knocks you out to see this many of us, but don't worry that we'll all converge on Durango at once. We'll give you a couple of weeks of wedded bliss before we do that," Mike said.

"There's a genetic problem in the family that you should know about going in," Chris advised. "This family hasn't produced a girl in generations, and we're counting on you to be the first."

"How did you dare do this?" John wanted to know. "I mean, it's not as though this is my first time around the matrimonial block. Or Leigh's, for that matter."

"Easy," Jeanette said. "I knew in my heart you had finally found your wife. The sound in your voice…I've heard that sound four times now," she said, glancing around at her other sons.

It wasn't until the beef was sliced, the many kids settled in the dining room and the adults gathered in the living room at a long, portable dining table, that someone ventured the hope that John and Leigh planned on having a large family. The conversation slowly ground to a halt as the question hung in the air unanswered. Mouths slowly closed, eyes slowly turned toward John and Leigh.

"Ah," John said, "that's one of the reasons we decided to come out and see you personally. It's...ah... well, we've already gotten a start on that."

Silence was heavy around the table. It was the minister who broke the ice. "That happens. We're delighted you've decided to get married. Double congratulations." The family concurred, slowly coming to terms with this announcement, raising wineglasses one at a time, congratulating, finally laughing and toasting.

"Well... " John began. "Actually, Leigh isn't pregnant. Um, we have a set of twins...who are about... um...four years old."

Again silence reigned. Everyone knew when John had gotten married and divorced. When had there been time to father twins in all that confusion? Even the minister couldn't think of anything to say. Jeanette McElroy's mouth stood open. Leigh's cheeks were on fire. Robert McElroy frowned at his son.

"Four?" someone whispered.

"Twins?"

"That's a start, I'd say."

"Well...as a matter of fact...they're boys," Leigh said, watching the stunned faces turn to regard one another in total shock.

It was Chris who burst into laughter. "You might know. Boys!"

"I can explain..." Leigh began, but they were recovering, laughing and slapping each other on the backs.

"Quadruple congratulations."

"We're mighty pleased you're getting married!"

"No rush, of course, but we do have a minister at the table!"

"Where have you been hiding them?"

"What's the hurry?"

It was Robert Sr. who spoke the only reasonable words. "We'll hear that explanation later. For right now, there are two things we need to take care of. One—when's the wedding? And two—when can we see our kids?"

Our kids. It had a wonderful sound to it. Leigh realized she hadn't known just how smart she really was in choosing the right guy. Not only was John too good to be true, but his family was terrific. One of the things she wanted for her kids was siblings, cousins, grandparents, and a life filled with love and noise and people.

They were a hard group to keep down; the racket went on and on. So did the conversation. Leigh learned a lot about John's family, all their various careers and their children's activities. And they learned about her. Ted was familiar with some of her father's medical research and went on to regale them with tales of his brilliance and breakthroughs. By early evening Leigh was both relieved and exhausted. Most of the children had quieted down, the sun was setting, and those adults not involved in cleaning up were seated in the living room with coffee. There was an afterglow of peace and acceptance.

Leigh offered to get the coffeepot for refills and went through the swinging door into the kitchen. There she found Mike giving his mother a comforting hug while Jeanette seemed to be having a little cry. Leigh was stopped in her tracks. And so were they. They broke apart to regard her, and Jeanette turned away, fishing for a tissue in her pocket.

"Oh, Leigh," Mike said.

"I've made you cry, haven't I? Because of the boys... and because of... "

"No, Leigh," Mike said, moving toward her to give her a hug of support. "You'll find we're not the kind of people who do a lot of looking back. You don't have to worry about that. We keep our eyes cast forward."

"John had a hard time forgiving me for keeping the boys' paternity from him. I was confused... He had just gotten married, and I guess I—"

"No, dearest, no. Whatever your reasons, I don't blame you and I won't ask. I'm happy, Leigh," Jeanette said with a sniff. "I'm delighted to hear I'm a grandmother again, but it's more than that. It's John. I've worried about him having such a hard time finding what he wants—finding the right person to share his life with. I know it's old-fashioned, but all I really ever wanted for my boys was for them to have the kind of family life that would fulfill them."

"It isn't too hard to see that my brother is a new man," Mike said. "We've all hoped he would find the kind of special happiness that we've found. And now he has."

"Thank you," she said. "Thank you for letting me in."

"Leigh, we didn't do you a good turn by 'letting' you into the family. We're honored to have you. And I mean that sincerely."

June tenth was a bright, glorious day. Leigh and Jess got up early; there was a great deal to do. The house had to be straightened, though it had already been thoroughly cleaned. The boys had to get their first bath of the day and their first set of clean clothes.

The first to arrive was the florist, who came at nine in the morning to begin decorating the gazebo and tables. Leigh met his truck, and shook his hand, and he passed her a little bag, which she carried off to her room.

Next the caterers arrived in two vans and began to unload their supplies—food, serving trays, punch bowls, linen and other accessories—into the kitchen. Leigh whispered with the caterers for a moment.

"What is it?" Jess demanded. "What's the matter?"

"Nothing's the matter, Mom." Leigh laughed. "I just asked them to get the tables ready but not to put the food out until the guests start to arrive. We don't want to poison anyone with spoiled potato salad."

"Oh. Of course not."

Next the string quartet arrived to set up their instruments and chairs in the gazebo, though they would leave and come back later to play.

And then John arrived. "John!" Jess said, surprised. "You're early! The party doesn't start until two!"

"I know, I'm sorry. I just wanted to see the backyard all finished, set up and ready to go. Unfortunately I can't come to the party after all."

"Oh, no," Jess said. "I won't hear of it! You're not working, are you?"

"No, but as it happens, some of my family is in town, and I'm going to have to spend the weekend with them."

"Well, bring them!"

"Oh, Jess, I couldn't. It isn't just some of them, it's a lot of them. I have a big family. They do this sort of thing sometimes. My mom and dad decided to drive down, and my brother and his wife decided to come along, and another brother was planning a long weekend with his kids and…this sort of thing happens with my family. They don't necessarily do it on purpose, but they tend to flock. You couldn't ask that many—"

"But I could! Bring them!"

"Are you sure?"

Leigh came into the room. "Oh, Mom, maybe John could just stop by for a few minutes later and—"

"Don't be silly. Bring them all. Half the town's coming. Well, not half, but a grand showing. It would give your family a chance to meet Leigh." They both glared at her. "Oops. Well, if your family happens to be here when my daughter happens to—oh don't scowl. I don't know what came over me."

"Well, can I see the yard anyway?" he asked.

"Sure you can, John." Leigh laughed. And she took him through the kitchen and down the stairs from the deck, and let him get an eyeful.

Next it was time for Mitch and Ty's second bath and second set of clean clothes. Seemed they had been remodeling their fort out in the far back of the yard. The fort had a dirt floor and there was a lot of moss to make grass stains. Leigh welcomed a chance to give them another bath and spend some time with them, sharing a secret or two. During the bath they did a lot of whispering, giggling and splashing.

Finally it was one-thirty. The food was ready to be put out, the flowers decorated the tables and structures, the quartet had arrived, and Jess and Leigh stood together on the deck to look everything over. It was a lovely sight; peach-colored ribbons were woven through the carnation-and-rose garlands. Exotic centerpieces adorned the twelve-foot-long tables. Silver serving dishes shone against the linen tablecloths. And the sun was bright and warm.

"It's beautiful, Mom," Leigh said. "It would have made a good wedding chapel."

Jess turned to her daughter. "Sweetheart, I hope you truly forgive me for being such a busybody. I've never done anything like that before, and I swear I never will again."

Leigh kissed her cheek. "I know. I'm just grateful you don't have a heart condition, and I am glad to be back here. You were right. This is the perfect place to raise the boys."

"I thought I was doing a good thing."

"It was very sneaky of you."

"If I've hampered anything…if I've caused you and John to delay making plans just because I'm such a buttinsky… "

"Now, Mom, didn't we decide you weren't going to have any more to say about that? You have to butt out."

"Yes, yes, but may I ask one question?"

"One."

"Didn't I pick out exactly the right man for you and the boys?"

"Mom… "

"Well…?"

Leigh relented and smiled. "Yes, you did pretty well. And I hope you never try anything like that again. Oh, look, people are coming! And I'm not ready!"

"Well, hurry up. I'll greet them."

Leigh went into the house and sent out the boys. The first to arrive were the coconspirators, Abby, Kate and Peg. Next came Tom Meadows, bringing flowers for each widow and a lovely bunch for Leigh. Next the pastor and his wife, the golf pro, the local librarian, the town council. John arrived with his entire family, who took up three cars. Not surprisingly, the boys ran to him and seemed to be inclined to stick to him like glue. He introduced them to his entire family. Then the butcher, the baker and the owner of a gift shop. Then the Literacy Council and the Friends of the Library. Nearly fifty people were standing around the backyard with cups of punch before Leigh found her way down the redwood steps.

She wore a long peach-colored dress, nothing too fancy, but Jess had no idea where the dress had come from. And Leigh had brushed out her long blond hair and pinned it back with baby's breath. "Look at her," Jess said half to herself.

Tom Meadows cleared his throat. "Are you sure your heart is up to this?"

"Up to what?" Jess asked as Tom began to walk toward Leigh, taking her the bouquet.

John moved quickly toward the gazebo where his brother Mike magically produced a small, black leather book. John said something to the quartet, who stopped playing midsong and began again, a tune that had a very familiar sound.

Jess's and Leigh's eyes met across the yard. Jess's mouth was hanging slightly open, and Leigh's lips curved in a smile. She blew her mother a kiss just before she accepted the bouquet and looped her arm through Tom's. And then, to the melody of "The Wedding March," Tom led Leigh toward the gazebo where John and the two little boys waited. John stooped to say something to them, and they laughed and nodded. Then he stood up to greet Leigh.

An idea began to take shape in Jess's mind. His family had just happened to flock to town. And she had never before seen John in a tie. He wasn't wearing a tux or a suit, of course. But he had on a white-on-white shirt with a peach-colored tie that matched Leigh's dress. It took a moment to sink in. She just couldn't believe what was happening.

"Dearly Beloved," Mike began.

Jess nearly swayed against Peg, and Kate came up on her other side. Abby joined Kate, and the four women stood, not six feet behind Leigh, struck speechless for the first time in all their lives. "He's a minister!" Jess whispered. "I can't believe it!"

Finally, after a few introductory remarks about being gathered in the presence of God in the event of Holy Matrimony, Mike looked over the heads of the bride and groom and said, "Who gives this woman to be wed?"

Peg held hands with Jess, who held hands with Kate, who held hands with Abby. They looked at one another and grinned through the hint of tears. And then all four hands went up in the air, and with a laugh they said, "We do!"

And they did.

When the bride and groom finally sealed their vows with a kiss, a cheer went up through the yard. The hugging that followed was too complex to keep track of, but families were united, children were passed around, glasses were filled with champagne that Jess had not ordered, and confusion of the most lovely sort reigned.

"You sneaks," Jess said.

"We had good teachers," John informed them.

"You're lucky I don't have a bad heart."

"But did you get what you wanted?"

"Well…I did… But I wanted to be in charge."

It turned out that very few people other than Jess were surprised, because Leigh had found a guest list and charged Tom and his receptionist with the duty of informing most of the guests by phone that a surprise wedding would be taking place. Although it was requested that there be no gifts, it seemed that some people just wouldn't be denied the privilege and went to their cars to retrieve presents. There were many toasts to the newlyweds, and finally John proposed one.

"I'd like to propose a toast to my mother-in-law," he said.

"Hear, hear," everyone chanted.

"Jess, I love you, but we'll take it from here."

And she raised her glass and drank.

It was quite late on Saturday night. The caterers had cleaned up, the kitchen sparkled, the music had died, and even the widows had gone home. The house was quiet, and only a few lamps were lit. Jess held her grandsons on her lap; they were heavy and big and smelled of shampoo and fabric softener.

"Gramma, what's a honeymoon?"

"It's when the new husband and wife go away to be alone and get to know each other in private. Quietly. Without any grammas or little boys or anyone."

"Doesn't Mommy already know John?"

"Yes, but they still like to be alone together because they love each other. And then they'll come back home and be with us."

"And John will be our dad?"

"And John will be your dad."

"And take us to T-ball and fishing?"

"Yes, and more things. From now on."

"But what are they doing?" Ty demanded.

"Fishing?" Mitch asked.

She squeezed them tightly and laughed. "Oh, I don't know if they're fishing. I bet they're hugging and kissing, playing lovey-dovey and saying 'I love you' a lot."

"Blllllkkkk," said Mitch.

"For two days?" asked Ty.

"What's the 'moon' part?" asked Mitch.

"I'm glad we didn't have to go," Ty said.

"Why do they have to play lovey-dovey?"

"Just to get in the habit, I guess," Jess said. So they can be friends and lovers for life. Nice habit. *Who says Mother doesn't know best?*

* * * * *

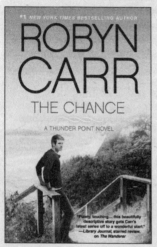

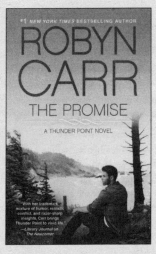

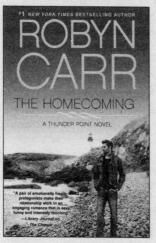

#1 *New York Times* bestselling author

STEPHANIE LAURENS

ushers in a new generation of Cynsters in an enchanting tale of mistletoe, magic and love.

Six Cynster families gather together at snowbound Casphairn Manor to celebrate the season in true Cynster fashion—and where Cynsters gather, love is never far behind.

The festive occasion brings together Daniel Crosbie, tutor to Lucifer Cynster's sons, and Claire Meadows, widow and governess to Gabriel Cynster's daughter. Soon the embers of an unexpected passion smolder between them.

Claire believes a second marriage is not in her stars. But Daniel is determined. Assisted by a bevy of Cynsters—innate matchmakers every one—Daniel strives to persuade Claire that trusting him with her hand and her heart is her path to happiness. Then disaster strikes, and by winter's light, she learns that love— true love—is worth any risk, any price.

Available now, wherever books are sold!

New York Times Bestselling Author

BRENDA NOVAK

**Discover a brand-new *Whiskey Creek*
romance all about heart, hope and
happily-ever-after...just in time for Christmas.**

Eve Harmon has always enjoyed Christmas, but this year it reminds her of everything she *doesn't* have. Most of her friends are married now, and that's what Eve wants, too. Love. A family of her own. But the B and B she manages, and even Whiskey Creek, suddenly seem...confining.

There's simply no one in the area she could even imagine as a husband—until a handsome stranger comes to town. Eve's definitely attracted to him, and he seems to have the same reaction to her. But his mysterious past could ruin Eve's happily-ever-after—just when it finally seems within reach. And just when she's counting on the best Christmas of her life!

Available now, wherever books are sold!

Be sure to connect with us at:

Harlequin.com/Newsletters

Facebook.com/HarlequinBooks

Twitter.com/HarlequinBooks

www.Harlequin.com

MBN1639

REQUEST YOUR
FREE BOOKS!

2 FREE NOVELS
FROM THE ROMANCE COLLECTION
PLUS 2 FREE GIFTS!

YES! Please send me 2 FREE novels from the Romance Collection and my 2 FREE gifts (gifts are worth about $10). After receiving them, if I don't wish to receive any more books, I can return the shipping statement marked "cancel." If I don't cancel, I will receive 4 brand-new novels every month and be billed just $6.24 per book in the U.S. or $6.74 per book in Canada. That's a savings of at least 22% off the cover price. It's quite a bargain! Shipping and handling is just 50¢ per book in the U.S. and 75¢ per book in Canada.* I understand that accepting the 2 free books and gifts places me under no obligation to buy anything. I can always return a shipment and cancel at any time. Even if I never buy another book, the two free books and gifts are mine to keep forever.

194/394 MDN F4XY

Name	(PLEASE PRINT)	
Address		Apt. #
City	State/Prov.	Zip/Postal Code

Signature (if under 18, a parent or guardian must sign)

Mail to the **Harlequin® Reader Service:**
IN U.S.A.: P.O. Box 1867, Buffalo, NY 14240-1867
IN CANADA: P.O. Box 609, Fort Erie, Ontario L2A 5X3

Want to try two free books from another line?
Call 1-800-873-8635 or visit www.ReaderService.com.

* Terms and prices subject to change without notice. Prices do not include applicable taxes. Sales tax applicable in N.Y. Canadian residents will be charged applicable taxes. Offer not valid in Quebec. This offer is limited to one order per household. Not valid for current subscribers to the Romance Collection or the Romance/Suspense Collection. All orders subject to credit approval. Credit or debit balances in a customer's account(s) may be offset by any other outstanding balance owed by or to the customer. Please allow 4 to 6 weeks for delivery. Offer available while quantities last.

Your Privacy—The Harlequin® Reader Service is committed to protecting your privacy. Our Privacy Policy is available online at www.ReaderService.com or upon request from the Harlequin Reader Service.

We make a portion of our mailing list available to reputable third parties that offer products we believe may interest you. If you prefer that we not exchange your name with third parties, or if you wish to clarify or modify your communication preferences, please visit us at www.ReaderService.com/consumerchoice or write to us at Harlequin Reader Service Preference Service, P.O. Box 9062, Buffalo, NY 14269. Include your complete name and address.

ROM13R

ROBYN CARR

32899	JUST OVER THE MOUNTAIN	___ $7.99 U.S.	___ $9.99 CAN.
32898	DOWN BY THE RIVER	___ $7.99 U.S.	___ $9.99 CAN.
32897	DEEP IN THE VALLEY	___ $7.99 U.S.	___ $9.99 CAN.
32868	THE HOUSE ON OLIVE STREET	___ $7.99 U.S.	___ $9.99 CAN.
31728	A SUMMER IN SONOMA	___ $7.99 U.S.	___ $8.99 CAN.
31644	THE HOMECOMING	___ $7.99 U.S.	___ $8.99 CAN.
31620	THE PROMISE	___ $7.99 U.S.	___ $8.99 CAN.
31599	THE CHANCE	___ $7.99 U.S.	___ $8.99 CAN.
31590	PARADISE VALLEY	___ $7.99 U.S.	___ $8.99 CAN.
31582	TEMPTATION RIDGE	___ $7.99 U.S.	___ $8.99 CAN.
31571	SECOND CHANCE PASS	___ $7.99 U.S.	___ $8.99 CAN.
31513	A VIRGIN RIVER CHRISTMAS	___ $7.99 U.S.	___ $8.99 CAN.
31459	THE HERO	___ $7.99 U.S.	___ $8.99 CAN.
31452	THE NEWCOMER	___ $7.99 U.S.	___ $9.99 CAN.
31447	THE WANDERER	___ $7.99 U.S.	___ $9.99 CAN.
31428	WHISPERING ROCK	___ $7.99 U.S.	___ $9.99 CAN.
31419	SHELTER MOUNTAIN	___ $7.99 U.S.	___ $9.99 CAN.
31415	VIRGIN RIVER	___ $7.99 U.S.	___ $9.99 CAN.
31385	MY KIND OF CHRISTMAS	___ $7.99 U.S.	___ $9.99 CAN.
31317	SUNRISE POINT	___ $7.99 U.S.	___ $9.99 CAN.
31310	REDWOOD BEND	___ $7.99 U.S.	___ $9.99 CAN.
31300	HIDDEN SUMMIT	___ $7.99 U.S.	___ $9.99 CAN.
31271	BRING ME HOME FOR CHRISTMAS	___ $7.99 U.S.	___ $9.99 CAN.

(limited quantities available)

TOTAL AMOUNT	$ _____
POSTAGE & HANDLING	$ _____
($1.00 for 1 book, 50¢ for each additional)	
APPLICABLE TAXES*	$ _____
TOTAL PAYABLE	$ _____

(check or money order—please do not send cash)

To order, complete this form and send it, along with a check or money order for the total above, payable to Harlequin MIRA, to: **In the U.S.:** 3010 Walden Avenue, P.O. Box 9077, Buffalo, NY 14269-9077; **In Canada:** P.O. Box 636, Fort Erie, Ontario, L2A 5X3.

Name: _____
Address: _____ City: _____
State/Prov.: _____ Zip/Postal Code: _____
Account Number (if applicable): _____
075 CSAS

*New York residents remit applicable sales taxes.
*Canadian residents remit applicable GST and provincial taxes.

HARLEQUIN® MIRA®
www.Harlequin.com

MRC1114BL